TWENTIETH CENTURY FOX PRESENTS
A MICHAEL DOUGLAS PRODUCTION

MICHAEL DOUGLAS
KATHLEEN TURNER
DANNY DeVITO

The **JEWEL** *of the* *Nile*

MUSIC	—	JACK NITZSCHE
DIRECTOR OF PHOTOGRAPHY	—	JAN DeBONT
CO-PRODUCERS	—	JOEL DOUGLAS JACK BRODSKY
WRITTEN BY	—	MARK ROSENTHAL & LAWRENCE KONNER
BASED ON CHARACTERS CREATED BY	—	DIANE THOMAS
PRODUCED BY	—	MICHAEL DOUGLAS
DIRECTED BY	—	LEWIS TEAGUE

 © 1985 TWENTIETH CENTURY FOX

Other Avon Books by
Joan Wilder

ROMANCING THE STONE

Catherine Lanigan
Writing as

Joan Wilder

Based on the Screenplay Written by
Mark Rosenthal & Lawrence Konner

AVON
PUBLISHERS OF BARD, CAMELOT, DISCUS AND FLARE BOOKS

AVON BOOKS
A division of
The Hearst Corporation
1790 Broadway
New York, New York 10019

First Avon Printing, December 1985

AVON TRADEMARK REG. U. S. PAT. OFF. AND IN
OTHER COUNTRIES, MARCA REGISTRADA, HECHO EN
U. S. A.

Printed in the U. S. A.

WFH   10   9   8   7   6   5   4   3   2   1

For the Jewels in my life:
Rene, Ryan, Nancy, Ed, Bob,
Mom and Dad

Chapter One

1815

RIBBONS OF LAVENDER, PINK AND BLUE DEC-
orated the early-morning sky. A soft breeze rattled
the fronds of the tall palm trees that lined the empty
beach. The tide had washed all markings, both animal
and human, from the sugar-white sands. Huge white-
bellied seagulls swooped down into the gently rolling
waves. They plucked flapping fish from the sea and
then carried their prey into the cove. The seagulls
settled themselves on sun-warmed rocks and began
their feast. They were oblivious to the double-masted
schooner anchored but a few hundred yards away.

It was a handsomely crafted boat of finest teak that
was scrubbed and well maintained. One of the crew
was lowering the foresail, while another sailor and his
assistant tied down the mainsail and the two jibs. The
schooner sat low in the water, as if it carried a great
deal of cargo.

In the captain's cabin, Johanna brushed her long
golden curls away from her face and pinned a white
orchid over her ear. She had no jewelry—at least not
here—not on this, her wedding day. She stepped into
a white Spanish lace gown and fastened it at the waist.

How she wished Matui, her maid, were here. She knew the guests were waiting for her, and it would take her forever to button all these buttons. The air in the cabin was warming as the sun rose. Suddenly, the room seemed to be closing in on Johanna. Her breath caught in her lungs and she could neither let it out nor suck it in. Beads of sweat sprang up on her forehead and her hands trembled. She thought she would faint. Quickly, she opened the porthole and took a deep breath. Then another.

Every time she thought about home, of how life used to be, she was engulfed by these panic attacks. She should be happy today of all days. Instead, she felt as if she would burst into tears at any moment.

She turned around and looked at herself in the cheval mirror. The gown was beautiful, she thought as she pulled the shoulders down a bit farther. She liked low-cut gowns, especially now that she was eighteen and had something to show. She placed a thick lei of multi-colored tropical flowers around her neck. She smiled, thinking they were more beautiful than all her sapphires, rubies and aquamarines. She stepped into a pair of white moroccan slippers and then twirled in front of the mirror again.

She picked up her tiny Bible that she'd draped with orchids and wished with all her heart that her father had been alive to walk with her now. Just as she placed her hand on the door latch, she began to tremble again.

This time she forced herself to be calm. She admonished herself for giving in to this weakness. She had grieved for weeks over her father's and brother Jean's deaths. But there had to be an end. She knew that with her mind, but telling her heart was another matter.

She would never see their white stone house in Port Royal again. Gone were its lush gardens, beautiful paintings, blue silk draperies and imported gilt French furnishings. Matui had run off, if she wasn't dead, and none of the servants had been seen for months. She would no longer be able to visit her mother's grave in the little sanctuary her father had built. That protected world where she had been loved only for herself was gone.

Johanna told herself she was a grown woman—in a few moments, she would be a married woman. But deep inside her, she felt as helpless as a child. Perhaps that was what marriage was all about. Giving strength to each other. She hoped she wouldn't always feel like this. She hoped it would get better.

Johanna squared her shoulders and straightened her back as she opened the door. Sunlight streamed down on her as she peered up at the deck. A sun-bronzed arm encased in a white ruffled silk shirt reached out to help her up the steps. It was Jacques' arm. The man she loved.

Jacques was so handsome he nearly took her breath away every time she looked at him. What a silly fool she'd been to give in to her depression.

Jacques loved her—she could see it shining there in his piercing blue eyes. He took her arm and smiled at her. Together they walked past their few friends and the crew to stand in front of the French missionary priest who was to marry them.

Johanna couldn't stop smiling. The cove at Virgin Marga was where she'd always wanted to be married. It was a dream come true to be here today with him, before his mast, sharing his life.

She remembered the first day she'd ever seen Jacques LeMare. Her father had ordered the open carriage to take them to the harbor. He'd been in an exceptionally good mood that day, with a mischievous glint in his eye.

"Papa," Johanna said as she adjusted her white organdy parasol to block the sun, "why must I go with you to see this ship? I was scheduled for a violin lesson this morning. Now, it'll be two weeks before I can see Monsieur Delaporte again. You know how rusty I get when I have to go that long without proper instruction."

"I should think you would have realized by this time that you have absolutely no musical talent at all," he said with a laugh. Then he chucked her affectionately under the chin. "Admit it, cherie, it's Monsieur Delaporte you'd like to play and not the violin."

"Papa!" Johanna exclaimed, aghast. "If Mama were alive, she'd—"

"She'd know I'm telling the truth. I do, however, apologize for my crudeness." He leaned toward her. "Am I right?"

Johanna looked at the passing warehouses and wooden saloons. "Monsieur Delaporte thinks I'm a child."

"Then he's a fool. But it's just as well. I should think you'd set your sights higher than a music teacher!"

Johanna sighed. "Port Royal has little to choose from," she said as she watched a drunken sailor exit a well-known whorehouse.

"True. It's my fault, I suppose, for bringing you here. But I've always wanted adventure—and riches. Being an importer in Paris offered me neither. Port

Royal, on the other hand, has made it possible for me to acquire a handsome estate. Which will one day be yours."

"And adventure too, Papa?" she asked with a haughty tilt to her head.

"Yes. And that is all we need discuss on the subject," he snapped.

Johanna knew about her father's import business and that he dealt with known pirates and criminals. It was not unusual for him to leave the house after midnight and return shortly before dawn. She never asked him about his "nights," knowing he would never tell her the truth.

That was why she found it quite odd that he wanted her company today. Only once before, when she was twelve, had he allowed her to go with him to the docks. Always, he wanted her to remain at the stone house, surrounded as it was with its iron gates and native guards armed with long sabers. As she looked around her at the dockworkers with their rotten teeth, sallow skins and bloodthirsty gleams in their eyes, she noticed that they stopped their work to leer at her. Suddenly, she was more grateful than ever for those guards at home and the ferocious dogs that accompanied them.

The carriage pulled to a stop and Johanna watched while her father shouted orders to one of the dockhands. The man nodded, doffed his fabric cap to Johanna and then ran out to the end of the pier where a sleek two-masted schooner was anchored. The crew were busily tying down the sails and bringing the cargo onto the top deck. Johanna stood in the carriage to get a better view of the schooner. She squinted her eyes and then put up a hand to shield them from the sun.

Standing on the bow of the ship was a blond man staring back at her with equal intensity.

Johanna felt her heart lurch and she almost fell back into the seat. He was the most handsome man she'd ever seen. She watched as he scrambled down into the dinghy and was rowed to the pier. He greeted her father as if they were family! Johanna was not only puzzled, but shocked by her father's behavior. Quickly, she looked around to see if anyone saw them. Should any of the Crown's spies witness her father conversing with, let alone embracing, a pirate—for that was surely what this man was—they could all be in terrible danger.

She watched as they approached her. They were laughing and smiling. Johanna became increasingly tense. When her father reached the carriage, she bent down to him and whispered.

"Papa! Be careful! There are many in Port Royal who would like to be rid of you."

He pecked her cheek affectionately. "You flatter me. I'm not all that important. And besides, Jacques is simply a merchant. Much like myself."

Johanna looked at him. He didn't look like a pirate. He had clear golden skin and the bluest eyes in the Caribbean. His lips were full and sensual, and when he smiled, his teeth were white and even. There was no guile in his expression, and she found herself mesmerized by the sound of his voice as he finished his conversation with her father.

"Would you like that, Johanna?"

"I'm sorry. I wasn't listening."

"Would you like to come aboard my ship and inspect the cargo before we unload it?"

"I don't understand."

Her father's smile was wide and proud. "For your eighteenth birthday, I wanted you to have something special. Jacques is the son of a dear friend of mine in Paris—an antique dealer. I told him I wanted something for 'my princess.' What Jacques has brought are items from Marie Antoinette's boudoir. I want you to go with him and choose your most favorite. The others Jacques can sell in the United States."

"Papa! This is . . . well, more than I deserve." She bent again to kiss him, and this time she noticed that Jacques was staring at her breasts. She straightened immediately, but she felt curiously triumphant.

"Nonsense. Now you two go ahead. I have some papers to sign at my lawyers'." He checked his watch. "I'm late already, I see." He helped Johanna down and then climbed into the carriage. "I'll be back at two o'clock. Take good care of her," he said to Jacques.

"Yes, sir," Jacques replied.

As the carriage rode away, Jacques walked Johanna down the pier to the little dinghy and then they rowed out to the schooner.

Johanna couldn't decide which she liked better, the powder-blue petit-point fauteuil chair or the pink hand-painted lingerie chest. She had decided against the canopy bed, for it was too massive and her own bed was more delicate and to her liking.

Johanna sat in the chair and spread out her white linen skirt with the lavender sprigs embroidered on the hem. It was a sturdy chair, and she even felt like a princess sitting in it.

"I like this best." She smiled when she looked up at him.

He was watching her intently and she felt a warmth rise inside her. He wasn't smiling, and in response she felt her own smile fade. His eyes were searing her, delving into her. She felt instantly vulnerable, and yet oddly strong. She didn't feel invaded, which should have been her reaction. She should have been indignant and walked out of this cabin immediately.

Instead, she sat riveted to the chair as he walked toward her. His shirt was open halfway to his waist, revealing a powerfully built chest. His tan breeches were cut tightly across his flanks, so that every time he moved she would have to be blind not to see his muscles flex. Johanna felt her mouth go dry and her hands become clammy. She wished it were the other way around so that she could say something. Anything to break the tension between them. She noticed that twice he opened his mouth to speak, but instead he licked his lips. It was so sensual a gesture; Johanna thought her pulse had trebled.

Johanna couldn't understand what was happening. Even with Monsieur Delaporte, she'd never felt anything but a smattering of butterflies in her stomach. Now, as she watched him lean over to her, his eyes capturing her, she felt as if she would explode from within.

Tenderly, he kissed her and then pulled away. She guessed he was checking her reaction. It was all Johanna could do not to throw herself into his arms. His lips were cool, when all the rest of her was hot. Then, as if he'd read her mind, he put his arms around her and pulled her out of the chair. Holding her gently, he kissed her ears, her cheeks and her throat.

Johanna thought she'd go insane with desire. At

once she felt chills course through her body and that fire from inside her leap to the surface and warm her again. She felt weak in the knees and so she leaned further into him. When his lips finally claimed her mouth, she wanted to shout for joy.

She felt his hand plunge into the scooped neckline of her gown. Her breast filled his hand and her nipples hardened against his skin. She felt totally possessed. She could no longer think on her own; her body was in command.

His kisses overwhelmed her. She could hear him moaning as they sank to the floor. She put her hands on his chest and allowed them to wander at will. She was curiously calm, thinking that somehow she knew him from somewhere, some other life. That was why she was unafraid. She wanted him to make love to her. She wanted to be a part of him.

They knelt on the floor facing each other as he unfastened her gown and lifted it over her head. Slowly, he peeled off her chemise and pantaloons.

He gasped when he looked at her. "I've never seen skin so white." He stroked her hip. "And smooth— like the petals of a white rose."

He kissed her again and then discarded his own clothes.

He looked at her as he caressed her. She thought it was as if he were studying some new species, he was so intent. She felt his muscles and nerves tense, but still he held himself back. Finally, he kissed her again, this time probing her mouth with his tongue. Johanna thought she'd never felt pleasure this exquisite. He kissed her breasts and explored the regions of her belly, hips and thighs with his tongue. Every time he kissed her, each time she felt his darting tongue, Johanna thought she could stand no more.

As he rubbed himself against her leg, she felt him become hard. He moved onto his elbows, and suddenly all she could see were his eyes. When he entered her she let out a painful cry, but he covered her mouth with his. Slowly, he moved back and forth, and what was once pain became pleasure again.

Johanna opened her eyes and he was there, assuring her without words that he would always be there. She closed her eyes and this time she felt everything spinning as if she were riding a pinwheel against the wind.

She felt tiny and the world seemed so big. She tilted her hips up to meet him. It seemed she could not have him deep enough inside her. She wanted more of him. She wanted all of him.

Johanna felt as if she were spinning so fast that surely she would be pitched off the face of the earth. Suddenly, her climactic cry filled the room, and before she could catch her breath, Jacques covered her mouth with his lips once again.

As she slowly opened her eyes, she realized that it was his cry he was trying to stifle. She held him closer if that were possible and stroked his sweat-slick back.

"Johanna, I'm glad I was your first man. I've always dreamed I would be the first for you—and the last."

She peered at him. "What? What are you talking about?"

"You don't remember me? I thought surely that was why you let me make love to you."

"No, I don't remember."

His smile was wide and he did not appear upset with her answer. "Perhaps you were too young to remember. I was only eight years old myself when I first saw you in Paris. You were riding in your father's coach, much the same as you were today. And you were dressed"—he looked over at the linen dress with lavender flowers—"in a dress almost like that. It was at my father's shop and I had just broken an expensive Ming vase. My father was ready to beat me, but then you interceded for me. He always respected your father, and you were so thoughtful, so caring. And I had never seen a more beautiful little girl."

"That was you? Why, I could only have been four or five at the time. I don't remember ever seeing you after that."

"We moved to London, and it wasn't until six years ago that my father moved back to Paris."

Johanna threw her arms around him once again. She peered into his eyes. "It's your eyes I see in my dreams at night. I never understood those dreams about a handsome man who would come to me one day and tell me he loved me."

He gathered her into his arms. "I do love you, Johanna. I always have and always will. I'll never allow anyone to take you away from me."

Jacques had been right about that, she thought as she looked at the priest. He'd stayed in Port Royal and made that his base so they could be married. She had planned a lavish wedding, with all her father's friends and her brother, Jean. That was only one of Johanna's dreams that had been shattered. . . .

Suddenly, Johanna realized that the priest was saying something to Jacques. The ceremony had begun.

"Do you Jacques take this woman to be your lawfully wedded wife and do you promise to cherish her and keep her so long as you both shall live?"

"I do," Jacques said with a smile and squeezed Johanna's arm.

Johanna felt chills race down her spine. She always felt like that when she was near him—as if this moment were pitched on the edge of time.

The priest turned to her. "Do you Johanna take this man to be your lawfully wedded husband and do you promise to honor and obey him so long as you both shall live?"

She inhaled deeply. "Oh, yes!" She stammered. "I mean . . . I do."

The priest turned to Jacques. "The ring, please."

"Huh?" Jacques was so entranced with Johanna he was puzzled by the question. Just then he was nudged by Phillipe, the best man and Jacques' first mate.

Phillipe handed the ring to Jacques with a wink.

The priest took the ring and blessed it with the sign of the cross. Then he sprinkled it with holy water. He smiled as he handed it back to Jacques.

Just as Jacques was about to place the ring on Johanna's finger, from out of nowhere a fencing foil spun through the air straight toward Jacques' hand. The ring went flying. The fencing foil slammed three inches deep into the mainmast. Johanna was wild-eyed as she watched the sun glint off her wedding ring as it spun around the shaft of the weapon.

Hearing excited, menacing shouts, Johanna spun around and saw a band of pirates scrambling over the side of the boat. Quickly, she scanned the sea around them, but saw no mother ship. They must have been waiting on shore, she thought.

Their steel swords, diamond earrings and gold teeth reflected the sun's light. Pirates were a terrifying breed of man. Nothing was sacred to them. They respected no man, defended no woman and feared nothing. They displayed eye patches, wooden legs and hand hooks like medals of honor. Despite all the treasures they stole and hoarded on Tortuga, to a man they were dressed nearly in rags and were disease-riddled. Johanna thought that the stealing was only an excuse for these men to pursue their real goal: killing and maiming.

The largest and ugliest pirate swooped down on deck and grabbed Angelique, one of the Jamaican locals, Johanna's best friend. Angelique shrieked with horror as the man grabbed her around the middle, his left hand painfully wrenching her breast. Emile, Angelique's husband, lunged at the pirate, trying to save his wife. The pirate coolly raised his sword and plunged it straight through Emile's heart. Angelique screamed again and tried to wrestle out of the pirate's grasp. The pirate was too strong for dainty Angelique, but she kept kicking and jabbing at him.

Suddenly, Johanna heard a familiar, swarthy laugh. Instantly, her spine stiffened. Braced, Johanna turned to face Levasseur.

He was a giant of a man standing over six and a half feet tall. As always, his dark, handsome face struck her at once as being dangerous and unnervingly sensual. He had hair blacker than a raven's wing. His eyes were like the black pearls only the most skilled divers could uncover from perilous briny waters. His nose was straight and his jawline square. His lips were full, and though his teeth were perfect, there was a crink, a twist to his smile that revealed him as the devil he was. He was the most massively built man Johanna had ever seen. The slightest movement of his arm caused a ripple in his muscles she could see through his open-necked shirt. To Johanna, Levasseur was the embodiment of all that was evil.

She thought they had been rid of him when he sailed away from Port Royal with all the treasure her father had amassed over the past ten years. Fool! she thought. Levasseur had come today, as he had then, to claim her. He had always wanted her.

Johanna's mind flashed with the scene of the first time she'd ever seen Levasseur. It couldn't have been over a year ago, she thought, but it was. It was Jean's twenty-first birthday, and the family had gathered for an elaborate dinner. Jean was overjoyed that day, for he'd just been made a full partner in their father's business.

Johanna remembered how handsome Jean had looked, his golden hair gleaming in the candlelight. He was a gentle man, a bit immature for his age but with a heart full of kindness for anyone he met. She thought that sometimes he reminded her more of the saints the nuns taught her about in school. Johanna knew that Jean would be an asset to the business, with his schooling in accounting and bookkeeping. She prayed, however, that her father did not involve him in the more unseemly side of "importing." Johanna hoped neither she nor Jean would ever have to meet one of their father's "business associates."

They had retired to the salon only fifteen minutes when Johanna found that hope shattered.

He came barging into the room before the butler

had an opportunity to announce him. He'd filled the doorway, his shoulders were that wide.

"Moreau! I will not be kept waiting by you or anyone else!" His voice boomed to the rafters.

Johanna clutched the arms of her chair and looked at the crystal chandelier overhead. She was certain it was rattling.

Jean was instantly on the defensive. "Who are you? And how dare you storm in here—upsetting our family!" His indignation sputtered from his lips.

"Captain Levasseur I am, as well your father knows."

"Lavasseur, I sent a message to your ship to change our meeting to tomorrow night. My daughter planned a special evening for my son's birthday."

Levasseur's black eyes roamed from Jean to Johanna. She was certain it was the first time he'd realized she was there. He gazed at her a long moment and then took inventory. As his eyes traveled from the tips of her crimson leather slippers to the soft folds of her silk gown and finally to the fashionably low-cut neckline, Johanna could feel a heat emanating from him. It was as if he were undressing her—peeling off each layer of clothing until she was totally nude. He lingered at her breasts, eyeing their creamy skin. Johanna could almost feel his hands upon her, his gaze was so intent.

When he explored her face, he actually licked his lips. Johanna clutched her stomach she was so repulsed.

Levasseur recoiled from her rejection. His eyes narrowed to evil slits and his smile looked demented. "Your excuses mean nothing to me. We had a bargain. You have broken your word to Levasseur. No man does that and lives!"

"See here," her father protested as Levasseur turned and started for the door. "It's only a day—"

Johanna and Jean followed their father as he continued to plead with the pirate. Johanna hated watching her father crawl to this man. She had never seen him like this—powerless.

Levasseur yanked the door open, and on the other side were four of his most dangerous-looking crew.

"We could have discussed our business here—in your house."

"Never!"

"You made a mistake, Moreau, thinking you were better than I." When he spoke, his eyes were riveted on Johanna. She had the distinct impression that Levasseur was speaking to her.

"Please, let me make amends—" her father was saying, but Levasseur only stormed out into the darkness.

Now, as she stood aboard Jacques' ship, she knew Levasseur was going to make good his threat. The money had been incidental to him, although he'd stolen everything they owned and laid the rest to waste. Levasseur was here for one thing only—her.

But this was her wedding day. Jacques was not weak like her father. He loved her. And this time, Jacques would defend her and rid the islands of this evil man. Yes, she thought, it was a shame that Captain Levasseur picked that moment to visit the island.

Jacques pulled Johanna behind him to shield her from Levasseur. Just then, Jacques gave one of his crew the high sign. The man tossed him a sword, which Jacques plucked out of the air. Johanna smiled.

"It's just like him to show up without a gift," Jacques quipped.

"I'll have what I came for this day!" Levasseur snarled, looking straight at Johanna.

Johanna clutched Jacques' shoulders. She wanted Levasseur dead. He was such scum—Levasseur, who burned Port Royal, who tortured her brother and drew and quartered her father, now meant to spoil her wedding. But she knew Jacques would put an end to him.

The screams of the guests and the hollers of the pirate crew created an inhuman sound. Johanna wanted to throw her hands over her ears, but she knew it would do no good. Pirates swarmed over the deck like deadly black spiders. Their swords brandished in the air like whirling guillotines. Johanna could feel death all around her.

The guests crowded behind Jacques, knowing as Johanna did that he was their savior. He scanned their faces, reading desperation and hope in their eyes. With a deep breath he readied his sword for combat. He couldn't, he wouldn't disappoint them.

"Beware the scorpion, mon ami," Levasseur sneered at Jacques as he leveled his sword.

Johanna could see that the thought of Jacques' blood on Levasseur's sword made the pirate drool with anticipation. She felt bile lurch in her throat, but she fought to gain control. She had to trust Jacques. She had to believe.

"Kiss steel, you son of a bitch," Jacques retorted.

Johanna looked in front of her and saw even more pirates boarding the ship. They seemed to materialize out of thin air. She opened her mouth to scream, but no sound escaped.

Jacques grabbed the boom and swung at a group of four pirates who were bearing down on him from the left. Johanna heard a loud "whack" as the force of the boom hit the four pirates across the chest and sent them sailing over the side of the ship. A huge splash drowned out their pitiful screams.

Johanna turned to see Jacques swallowed in a clash of blades.

It looked like lightning, she thought, as Jacques' sword clanged and twisted around his opponents' lances like metal snakes.

The guests cowered, covered their faces in terror and then finally fled to the bow of the ship. Johanna felt her blood run cold, knowing Jacques could not hold out forever.

Suddenly, Johanna froze. She could feel Levasseur's eyes on her back. She turned to face him and saw again the lust in his eyes. She had been right. Levasseur *had* only wanted her. This had all been a game to him. Killing her father and brother was nothing more than sport. Fury rose inside her until she trembled. Her jaw tensed and her jade-green eyes narrowed. He would never have her! She would rather die than be raped by him.

Levasseur held out his hand, beckoning to her. She felt bile rise in her throat at the idea of that hand touching her. His smile was sinister and, worse, it was confident.

She was frozen with fear. Jacques was still dueling with the pirates. He couldn't save her. In desperation, she clutched the missionary's shoulders. He was a man of God. Surely he could save her from this devil.

As if he'd read Johanna's thoughts, the priest pulled

out his rosary and held the cross high into Levasseur's face. But the evil man did not perish. He merely snorted at the priest's foolishness. Panicked, the missionary fled, leaving Johanna to face Levasseur alone.

Johanna swore under her breath. If she was going to die, she would take him with her. Quickly, she grabbed a flaming tiki torch from its niche in a mast and rammed it at Levasseur's face. He yelled and backed away. His anger was inflamed as he made another lunge for her. Johanna thrust the flame at him again, this time singeing his beard. She glanced around. Where was Jacques?

Retrieving his sword from the belly of the last of his opponents, Jacques spied Johanna. She had fended off Levasseur, but she needed his help.

"Hold tight, I'm coming!" he cried to her as he ducked quickly, in time to miss the dagger slinging through the air. It hit the mast and sank a full four inches deep, splitting the wood. Suddenly, a pirate's boot appeared out of nowhere and kicked Jacques' sword from his hand. Jacques spun around and grabbed onto the dagger, but it was too deeply wedged. Again he forced it, but it was no good. Jacques skirted behind a group of crates, put his foot on an overturned barrel and sent it rolling toward the uglier of the two pirates. He raced toward the other man, meeting him head-on in hand-to-hand combat.

While Jacques fought for his life, the barrel picked up speed and slammed into the wall, pinning its prey against the wall. The pirate screamed with the impact. The barrel sprang open and spilled a thick layer of oil onto the deck.

Finally, Jacques jammed his fist into the pirate's face, knocking him cold.

Johanna thrust her torch at Levasseur again, but this time he kept advancing. The flame had nearly died.

Seeing her predicament, Jacques raced to her side, but skidded on the oil slick.

Johanna's torch crackled. Levasseur's laugh was diabolical as he tarried with her, relishing her fear.

Jacques picked up speed as he skidded across the deck. He aimed his body toward the hulking pirate captain. Coming off the upper deck, Jacques somersaulted in midair and cocked his feet toward Levasseur's head. He slammed his heavy boots into Levasseur and knocked him unconscious.

Johanna held her arms open for Jacques as he crumbled, exhausted, against her. Her one true love had fought bravely. . . .

But it wasn't enough, she saw, as she peered at the side of the ship. Coming over the side were nearly a dozen more pirates; more menacing, more cruel-looking than the first group.

Jacques was physically spent. He grabbed Johanna's faintly flickering torch and threw it astern as he pulled Johanna toward the bow. Suddenly, the oil slick burst into flames.

She looked down into the shark-infested waters as the missionary untied the lifeboat. It was crammed with their wedding guests. There was only room for one more person. It was her love or herself.

"You go, my darling," she said.

"No, I won't let that maggot get his hands on you."

"He won't have me long. I have consumption and will be dead within a year."

"What? Why didn't you tell me?"

"I didn't want to spoil things."

"You were going to marry me with consumption?"

"Go now. Live to fight another day," she said, clutching his arm, pulling him toward her in a gesture that negated her words.

Jacques looked down at Johanna, her gold hair blowing in the wind creating a halo around her face. Her eyes were filled with love and earnestness. She was his dream—one he'd waited for all his life. He loved her with all his heart.

His eyes darted back to the pirates who were bearing down on him through the flames. They had only seconds until death visited them. His options were horrifying. If he stayed with her, they would both die. If he fled, he would have to live with the fact that he'd abandoned her. He knew he'd never live through the nightmares of knowing Levasseur had raped Johanna. En masse, the pirates let out a bloodthirsty cry as they raised their swords to kill Jacques.

Jacques pulled Johanna into his arms.

"Well, if it will make you happy." He kissed her hard, the pressure of his lips stinging her mouth. And then he jumped over the side into the safety of the lifeboat.

She looked down into his mournful face and then she heard Levasseur's steps behind her.

She turned as he rose from the flames. He wanted her now for revenge as much as for lust. He loomed over her. Suddenly she knew she would never be rescued. This was the end of her freedom, her salvation. . . .

* * *

"Hey gorgeous, how's it going?" It was Jack's voice that interrupted Joan's concentration on her new manuscript.

Joan looked up from her typewriter into blazing Mediterranean sun. Swaying sheets of golden heat and haze rose from the deck of the *Angelina* like the flames that had engulfed Jacques and Levasseur. Again she heard Jack's voice call to her.

He was bombing behind a roaring speedboat on a slalom ski. Had it only been a week ago that he'd tried the single ski for the first time? He was having the time of his life. To Joan he looked like all the rest of the jet-set crowd that swarmed over Monte Carlo this time of year. Except for his obnoxious Hawaiian baggies, she thought. He was sun-bronzed a deep golden color; his blond hair was wet and slicked back off his smiling face. He waved and executed a perfect spin on his ski. Never, Joan thought, had she seen such a physically beautiful man. His muscles were taut as he held the towrope and conquered the speedboat's wake. He jumped wave after wave and "pulled out" alongside the sleek black cigarette boat and signaled with a thumb's-up for the driver to increase the speed. As he circled back past the *Angelina*, he saluted to Joan and then blew her a kiss.

Even from here, Joan could feel his blue eyes spark that electricity inside her. She actually felt chills blanket her skin. She wondered if the day would ever come when she could control these adolescent sexual binges her body went on.

Suddenly, Jack hit choppy water and went somersaulting into the air. It was a perfect flip, just like that of Jacques' somersault in her story. As she watched

Jack land in the blue-green water, she wondered if her writing had become prophetic.

Jack emerged from the water and waved again to her, signaling that he was all right.

Relieved, Joan adjusted her thick terry-cloth robe over her legs. She reached over to the deck table and grabbed her jar of zinc oxide. With tense movements she applied it to her very tender nose. She smeared another layer under her eyes. She wiped her hands on a towel and pulled her extra-wide-brimmed sun hat down over her face. How she'd grown to hate the sun. In the past six months that she'd been cruising the oceans of the world with Jack, she was certain she burned away five layers of epidermis. Already she had freckles and sunspots on her shoulders and arms. Two weeks ago, she'd noticed those ugly brown blotches showing up on her shins. At this rate, she'd need plastic surgery before she was thirty. If they even took her.

Joan's body was not conditioned for such torture. In the yearly eighteen and a half days of sunshine that blessed Akron, Ohio, Joan had never had so much as a tinge of pink when she was growing up. Once she'd moved to New York to live with Elaine, she virtually lived at the typewriter. Joan was more in danger of growing blind from working too late at night on one of her books than she was of getting sunburned.

Joan looked over at the yacht docked next to them at the pier. Music was blasting from every porthole, and as usual there must have been twenty partygoers on deck.

"Yoo-hoo. Could you maybe keep it down?" she

called out to the young, reed-thin girl lying in the sun. She was some princess, she'd heard. "I'm writing."

The girl was oblivious to Joan's plight. Joan glared at her. She was the kind she could really learn to hate. She was wearing a designer swimsuit cut high over the thighs, uncovering her hip bones, and cut so low in front that Joan thought only her nipples were covered with the black fabric. Joan already knew there was *no* back. The girl slathered on yet another light film of Italian sun oil. That kind with carotene in it. The princess' skin was devoid of freckles and blemishes. Joan guessed it was probably the most beautiful skin she'd ever seen. It was smooth like porcelain—and most disgusting of all, it tanned perfectly.

Joan looked across the bow of the *Angelina* to the Monte Carlo harbor. It was like a scene from a movie. Voluminous clouds scampered across a robin's-egg-blue sky. A light breeze flitted through the lush palm trees and on to the fabulous Exotic Gardens where thousands of tropical plants were laid out on terraces on the rocky cliffs. From her vantage she could see the flower-filled parks, glittering hotels and posh cliff-side condominiums. It was the home of the Grand Prix, the famous casino and a prince who made a princess of an American girl. The harbor was filled with pleasure yachts, sailboats and motorboats. Farther on to the shore, the sands and terraces of hotels were overflowing with bikinied men and women, all soaking up the sun. It was like a crown jewel set between Italy and France. The only bad thing Joan had to say about Monte Carlo was that, out of a given year, it boasted three hundred days of sunshine.

Joan looked down at her typewriter and rolled the sheet up.

"Was this the end of my freedom, my salvation . . ." she read aloud. "My career?"

Joan sat back with a worried frown. She had worked harder on this book than on any of the others. But something was wrong, and damned if she knew what it was. She spent hours reading and rereading. Writing and rewriting. But suddenly, she, Joan Wilder, famous for getting her hero and heroines into trouble, couldn't seem to get them out again. Joan had racked her brain, trying to understand her dilemma.

Joan closed her eyes and tried to think. Music blared from the next boat—except that she considered "Twisted Sister" to be insanity, not music. It just wasn't like it was in New York. Perhaps that was the problem. She had always been able to write in her apartment. She'd been disciplined, organized and able to concentrate. She missed those familiar surroundings.

Joan rubbed her forehead. She didn't know what was wrong with her or her writing. Only that there had to be a reason why she felt this—incompleteness. She wasn't happy, at least not as she thought she should be at this point in her life. Every time she tried to place the blame on her relationship with Jack, she realized she was guilty of shifting the burden. She had waited for Jack all those years. She had dreamed of him, written about him and planned a life around him before they'd even met. Was it only a little over a year ago she'd sat in that bar in New York explaining to Gloria that she "knew there was somebody out there waiting for her"?

Gloria had thought her crazy then. Joan thought she

was crazy now. Perhaps she'd discovered some new kind of senile dementia. She was almost positive she'd lost her mind. Jack loved her. It showed every time he looked at her, made love to her. No, there couldn't be anything wrong with Jack. And if that were the case, simple logic told her that her depression—if that was what this was—had to be with her writing.

Just then Joan realized the partygoers had switched to "Prince." She could tolerate that—almost. Joan looked up to see two cigarette boats drag-race past her. Their engines gave off a tremendous roar, like war machines. The second boat rooster-tailed to the right and spewed water in a dazzling rainbow-colored wave all over Joan.

Stunned, Joan watched as seawater dripped off her face and onto the typewriter. Her writing was ruined! She was about to yank the paper when suddenly she heard the ear-splitting roar of a helicopter. She looked up to see an ominous black helicopter hovering directly above her.

The force from the whirling chopper blades created a whirlpool in the sea. In an instant, skiiers were downed, swimmers fought their way to the pier and boats of all sizes were pitched to and fro. Joan held onto the rail of the *Angelina* for support as she peered up at the menacing 'copter.

It bore strange markings—in Arabic, she thought, though she wasn't sure. Joan covered her ears, chiding herself for complaining about her neighbor's music. She wondered what the chopper wanted, for there was no landing pad located in the harbor. She looked up again, wishing it and its deafening sound would go away. Suddenly, it did just that and disappeared into the hills.

Joan looked down at her soaking-wet typewriter. Everything and everybody on this planet was against her. With frustration exploding with megaton force inside her, Joan picked up her Smith-Corona and pitched it over the side of the *Angelina*.

It was the end of Jacques and Johanna. No one would rescue them now. Not even Joan Wilder.

Chapter Two

A LONG STRING OF BUBBLES FOLLOWED THE typewriter to the sandy bottom of the Mediterranean. Its descent was slow and strained, as if it knew it should have stayed aboard the *Angelina*.

Just below the hull of the *Angelina,* a diver dressed in complete wet suit, fins, and face mask stopped his work to watch the typewriter sink past him. He was wearing double tanks, the kind divers wear when planning extra-deep dives or lengthy stays beneath the water. He adjusted his mask and resumed his steady, even breathing. His air bubbles mingled with those of the typewriter.

He turned again to the hull of the *Angelina*. He withdrew underwater putty from a long cylindrical container and replaced it in his supply belt. He pulled out three wires, one red, one green, one white. He tied three sticks of explosive to the small square box that controlled the wires. He pulled a tiny antenna out of the box and then flipped a silver switch. A tiny red light blinked on and off. Had the diver been on land and not under the water, he would have smiled. He had completed his task in half the time he'd allotted.

He was just about to swim away when overhead he saw the churning water created by a motorboat. It was cruising exceptionally fast. The diver held onto the hull of the boat until the wake passed. Then, swiftly and silently, like the angel of death that he was, he disappeared into the lapis-lazuli-colored water.

"Joanie, watch out!" Jack screamed at her from a distance.

Joan looked into the distance wide-eyed. Coming straight at her at nearly eighty miles an hour was Jack. The speedboat driver had a devilish glint in his eyes Joan could see from the deck. Jack must be crazy, she thought. Just at the point where Joan thought the driver should have turned away from the *Angelina* for safety's sake, he didn't. Instead, he continued to bear down on the *Angelina*.

Jack was going to be killed.

Stunned as the speedboat raced straight for her, Joan covered her face and ducked, knowing Jack would crash.

Jack held the towrope super-tight and counted the seconds. He negotiated over to the far side of the wake. Eight. . . . He balanced himself. Nine. . . . He bent his knees at the perfect angle. Ten. He shouted and lifted off the edge of the wake and cleared the aft deck of the *Angelina*, boom and all.

Joan shook her head. Six months ago she would have put a stunt like that in a novel. Now she could only wonder if that was what she and her hero were all about—skiing acrobatics. Was that all there was to life? Thrills and chills, like the circus? Somehow, she thought she should be doing something more with her life. Something serious. She couldn't blame Jack and his skiing exploits. He was only trying to entertain her. And wasn't that what she did every time she sat down to the typewriter? Entertain? She certainly wasn't trying for the Pulitzer Prize.

Joan threw her head back in frustration. What was wrong with her lately? Why couldn't she be happy like Jack? He was thrilled to pieces with everything.

She picked up the stack of papers. No, she thought, this was no Pulitzer winner. And neither was her life.

He did it! He was out of breath, and his bones and muscles would never be the same, not to mention his nerves, but he'd done it! His smile was at least a mile wide as he circled around. He signaled to the driver to tow him back to the *Angelina*.

Jack dropped the towrope and swam to the rope ladder extended over the side of his boat. He hoisted his ski onto the deck and then came aboard.

He looked at Joan. He could tell she was impressed. Hell, who wouldn't be? Shouldn't she be applauding or something? Where was his trophy? Where was his kiss?

She just stood there with a forlorn look on her face, staring at her book—her unfinished book. He grabbed a towel from the storage compartment. He wiped his face and walked over to her. He wanted to cheer her up. She'd been taking everything too seriously lately. He had nearly killed himself out there on skis trying to make her laugh. "The princess who couldn't laugh." That's what he'd called her about two weeks out of Lisbon. He'd teased her mercilessly; he'd taken her shopping, swimming, to the Casino de Monte Carlo—

anything to cheer her up. But he'd failed. Jack had never been a quitter and he wasn't about to start now.

"Hey, gorgeous."

Her eyes narrowed as she looked at his arm. "You're cut."

He glanced down to the gash that stung like hell, but he kept it light. "I'll live. Honey, did you by any chance get time to—"

"No," she said exasperatedly, "I did not get time to ransack Monte Carlo in search of a Heineken." She had more important things to do than cater to his whims, she thought as she stole a glance overboard. Like tossing her typewriter in the drink.

Jack put his arms around her waist. "I guess you can only get that in America."

He looked over at the stack of pages sitting on her desk. It didn't look any deeper than it had earlier that day . . . or the day before . . . or last week.

He didn't know much about writing or writers, but he was learning fast. He knew they were difficult to live with. He thought of the many times she'd left him at night to jot down an idea or two. Or when he would be trying to talk to her about something and she would be a million miles away. "Plotting," she'd said. Jack had found for the first time that one could be extremely jealous of an inanimate object. Jack knew he'd probably never have to worry about another man in Joan's life—only a few dozen affairs with typewriters. He almost wished it would be a man. At least he could count on a fair fight.

"How's it goin'?" He nodded toward the book.

"It's not."

"No wonder. What'd you get 'em married for?"

"What's wrong with marriage?" Joan asked, looking up at him with puzzled green eyes.

Those damn green eyes, he thought. She could melt him with those eyes. He wished she wouldn't look at him like that. He turned to putty when she did that.

"It's old-fashioned," he stuttered.

"It's 1815," she countered in that sultry, sexy voice of hers.

"It cramps their style," Jack replied, losing his earlier conviction. He picked up the edge of her terry robe and carefully wiped the zinc oxide off her face. He peeled the robe off her shoulders and gazed a long minute. She was still pink and white like a newborn baby. He liked that. He was glad she wasn't like all those leathery brown women on shore. He liked Joan with her delicate, sweet-smelling skin. He leaned down and kissed her smooth shoulder. Instantly, he felt himself get hard. It was always like that for him.

He wanted to laugh at himself for thinking a typewriter could steal his Joan from him. Maybe he was feeling insecure about the way he'd treated her lately. He knew he wasn't easy to live with, either. He shouldn't give her such a hard time about her writing. He could do a lot better by her. He should read more, be more like her New York friends.

"Okay," Joan was saying, "they don't get married. That's an idea. It's not one I like, but I don't like anything at this point. Oh, Jack..." she moaned.

He felt her tongue flicking against his neck. She drove him nuts when she did that. He pulled her into him and felt her breasts crush against his chest.

Maybe he shouldn't worry so much about what he should or shouldn't be doing and just do it.

"Jack . . ." she moaned again.

She kissed him hungrily with a passion that always stunned him. Despite her fame, Joan had never given into affection. There was no artificiality or snobbery in her character. Joan was just as easily at home in the jungles of Colombia as the palaces of Monaco. Of all the things he was discovering about Joan Wilder, that ability to take all people just as they were gave her the same zest for life that he had. In some ways, he thought her very much a child, for she always blurted the truth without much forethought. It never occurred to her that her desire for him should or could be tamed. She never held herself back, taking from him all she wanted and giving back all she could.

There were times in the middle of the day while working on the boat, puttering with the engine or seeing to the sails when a momentary mental picture of her would flash across his mind. Within seconds he would find his body responding. He would drop what he was doing and rush to her. Just this afternoon, he knew he could have skied much longer, but knowing Joan was watching him and, yes, worrying about his safety . . . well, he just had to be with her.

Sometimes, he thought he was the one who acted like a child. He didn't think he would ever be able to live the kind of life most people did where he would have to leave Joan for eight, maybe ten, hours a day. He had to hold her at least a dozen times a day. Feel her next to him—reassure himself that she loved him.

Jack unbuttoned the red cotton blouse she wore and slowly ran his hands down her back. She was wearing those cute shorts he liked that showed her legs. Damn! And she had great legs, too. He put his hands on her hips and slowly let them travel over and down to the backs of her thighs where her buttocks met her legs. He squeezed that soft, firm flesh. He heard her moan again and sink further into him for support.

This time when he kissed her, his mouth was everywhere. He couldn't get enough. He liked her needing him, wanting him like this. It made him feel secure—safe.

"I know, I know," he said as he looked at her. He hadn't the slightest idea how to resolve her dilemma for her. "Joan, look out there . . ." he said, nodding to the horizon. "Do you know what's out there?"

Joan's green eyes were hopeful. "What?" Something deep inside the recesses of her heart told her he held the key. Jack could unlock her strength somehow. She needed the answers, the end of her confusion.

"Greece," he said.

Joan recoiled out of his arms. "Greece?" Was he nuts? What kind of a metaphysical answer was that? Her shoulders slumped. She'd forgotten. Jack only knew practicality.

"Yeah, you know. Mykonos, Rhodes, the Parthenon. . . ." Surely that would make her happy. Imagine, he thought, seeing all those ancient places. Places that would inspire her; give her thought processes a turbo boost. He wanted to see her eyes dance with that fire again. It killed him to see her like this.

"I thought you said we could go back to New York for a while."

"Right . . . right after summer. Isn't that what we agreed on?" Now what was she thinking? New York? Was she homesick? Maybe she wanted to see her sister. He hoped it was something simple like that.

Joan peeled away from him. She picked up a bottle of sun block—#18, the high-potency stuff. It'd be like the second eruption of Pompeii if she went to Greece, she thought. She wanted to get off this boat, out of this sun. She wanted—

"I don't want to wait. I don't want Greece or Rhodes or any more ruins right now. Jack, time is flying by. I mean, shouldn't we be doing something more?"

"What more? Sailing the Greek Isles on the *Angelina*, seeing the Parthenon... the Parthenon! Who knows how much longer it'll be there?"

Why couldn't she feel as he did? It would be so simple to take his simplistic view toward life. He was content to be with her, seeing all the wondrous sights of the world. But for Joan, it wasn't enough. She felt she was spinning on a carousel and couldn't get off. She was living her life through him and she was losing herself... her values.

"Great, but I need shore leave or something. *Extended* shore leave. I mean, I was supposed to finish this book, but I—I can't! I don't know what happens next!"

Surely he could understand that. She had committed herself to her publisher. She had millions of readers out there waiting for the next Joan Wilder novel. They depended on her, counted on her, and she was letting them all down. Maybe Jack didn't know about responsibility the way she did. He seemed to carry his life around in a kit bag, and whenever the mood struck him, he sailed off into bluer seas. Maybe that was the part she couldn't abide.

Jack knew he should understand her, but he didn't. He couldn't quite put his finger on it, but something had changed between them ever since ... since when? What? He racked his brain trying to remember what had happened to change Joan. She'd been so happy the first leg of their trip, going places she'd only read about. He'd felt like a king showing them to her, too. It was a dream of dreams. It was their dream, wasn't it?

"I thought you wanted to see the world with me."

"I do. But not all of it this week. Everything's become a blur of exotic ports, great parties and spectacular sunsets."

Jack couldn't believe his ears! She certainly didn't feel like this in Lisbon. He could never forget the way they made love the night they sailed out of Lisbon. He thought they'd gone to the moon and back. Obviously, they were not on the same wavelength. Jack felt his insides land on the floor. He felt as if she'd just pulled out a gun and shot him. He almost wished she had. Surely it couldn't be any more painful than this. He wanted to shake her, pound some sense into her. Why wasn't she happy with him anymore? She used to be. He *knew* this for a fact because she'd told him so many times. Come to think of it, she hadn't said she was happy since Lisbon. What had happened there to change her mind?

Jack searched his memory for the one incident that would give him a clue. They'd eaten seafood at native beach cafes, and wound their way up those steep hilly streets—streets so narrow not even a car could pass. They had danced in that plaza near the Palacio de Belem where that young couple had been married. Joan was beautiful that day. He'd bought her a lace mantilla—a white one. He'd even told her it reminded him of a wedding veil. He remembered looking at her and wondering why she looked so . . . sad.

Yes! That was it. She had *not* been happy in Lisbon; she'd been sad. But he never pressed her about it and she'd never said anything more. As he thought about it now, he realized that Joan *had* changed once they'd sailed from Lisbon.

In fact, there were a lot of "things" Joan hadn't said anything about. One of them was marriage. She avoided it like the plague. But then, so did he. He had good reasons, though. In the past, whenever he got serious about a girl she either split for the hills or started changing him. He didn't want that to happen with him and Joan. He wanted them to last forever. Jack didn't believe in rocking the boat. They were having a great time, or so he thought. She always wanted to do what he wanted. If he wanted to hoist anchor, so did she. She never argued. He thought she had wanted it that way. He thought he had been pleasing *her*.

Today, when she'd been talking about that wedding scene in her book, was the first time Joan had ever spoken the word in his presence. He'd been stunned by his own answers to her. At that moment he'd felt trapped and scared. He had reacted defensively. Now as he looked at her, listened to her, he felt his protective walls rise again. Shit! She was scaring the hell out of him.

"Yeah, rough duty," he replied, trying to hide the crack in his voice.

"Jack, it's . . . it's both too much and not enough. It's . . ." She couldn't believe she was saying this— feeling this. Something was drastically wrong and she didn't know what it was. She needed something and she wasn't getting it. She needed direction. She couldn't go on as they had, aimlessly sailing from port to port, with not even a Triptik to schedule their time.

She couldn't believe she was telling him she'd had enough of all this exotica. She could set and plot stories for the next three lifetimes on all they had seen and done. But Joan felt she needed to explore the world through her writing, not from the bow of a ship. Wasn't that what life was all about? Growing and extending one's self. She needed a challenge to her talent—a commitment.

"Not enough?" His words bristled in the still air. What was she telling him? Why wasn't he enough for her? Jack thought maybe he'd been living with a crazy woman. He'd done everything for her. He damn near got killed for her in Colombia. He took her wherever she wanted to go. Maybe all writers were nuts like her. Maybe what she wanted didn't exist.

She turned away from him. A bad sign, he thought. He couldn't let this go on. He had to bring her back to him somehow.

"It's . . . it's . . ." Joan mumbled, feeling tears well in her eyes. How could she explain it to him without him thinking it was something he'd done? It wasn't Jack that was wrong—it was Joan. She was the one in a career crisis, not Jack. Damn! This was such a mess. She felt her insides tumble.

"It's what?" Jack demanded, his voice rising with his fears. "Isn't this the way you always wanted it? You said it was."

Jack stepped around to face her. He motioned to

the bay, the *Angelina* and finally to himself. She couldn't reject all of them, could she?

"You got what you wanted and now you don't want what you got?" Jack gulped—maybe he was forcing her hand too soon. Maybe he shouldn't have said it quite that way. That was his problem, always letting his anger blow instead of letting it simmer and then go away. But he had to know if she loved him.

"I've got work to do is what, serious writing I should be doing instead of more—I mean, how much romance can a woman take?" A life filled with imaginary heroes and heroines just wasn't enough anymore. She wanted to write about real people—real heroes.

Joan leaned over the railing and looked down at the spot where she'd pitched her typewriter. Maybe she should give up writing altogether....

Just then a bouquet of the largest and most nearly perfect white roses she'd ever seen were thrust in her face.

"Miss Wilder?" she heard a thickly accented voice ask.

Standing in a shiny blue and white fiberglass Evinrude motorboat was an enormous, hulking Arab complete with tunic and turban. His mahogany skin gleamed in the sunset. There was a wide scar on his face running from his temple to his jaw. Joan noticed that his shoes, clothes and jewels were quite expensive. She wondered why he hadn't had plastic surgery—everyone else in Monte Carlo had, and for a lot less reason, she thought.

"White roses from the sacred garden," the Arab said.

Jack's voice was terse when he asked, "Sacred garden? Whose?"

The Arab motioned toward shore. He said nothing more, and without a word or signal, the driver suddenly gunned the engine. The Arab was still standing and still watching Jack and Joan as he sped away.

Joan looked up into the seaside cliffs. There, amid green trees, lush flowering vines and strategically planted annuals, was a majestic white stone condominium. Its bronze glass reflected the setting sun, making it look as if the hillside were on fire. Atop the building, standing on an elaborately railed penthouse balcony, was a lone figure. Joan shielded her eyes, but she could only see that he was wearing a turban and long, flowing robes. He too was an Arab. She glanced down at the roses and again at the man who had now disappeared inside. This was all very strange, she thought, and quite romantic.

Chiding herself for thinking she'd had too much romance, she quickly opened the card.

Jack read over her shoulder. "'Tonight we meet . . . awaiting the moment.' Tonight?" Quickly he looked at Joan, who seemed in a trance. She hadn't even met this guy, and already she was intrigued. Jack felt the ground slipping away from under his feet. Naw, he thought. That was just the movement of the boat. Joan loved him. He didn't have anything to fear from some— he looked up into the cliffs—oil sheik?

"Must be someone who's coming to my party," Joan said, thinking that was all this could be.

"That's not till next Tuesday," Jack said, thinking the worst.

"This *is* next Tuesday!" she said and walked away. She *knew* they should have had a Triptik.

Chapter Three

IN THE MID-1800'S THE THEN RULER OF THE
tiny principality of Monaco, King Charles III, was
faced with a dilemma. A treaty with France to protect
his country's independence had lost Monaco most of
her territory and, alas, most of her source of income.
Charles III had little acreage left, but what remained
was dramatically beautiful. In order to get outsiders
to come to his country and, he hoped, spend their
money, he decided to build the most lavish and palatial
casino the world had ever seen. He took his plan even
further and surrounded the Casino de Monte Carlo with
formal gardens and spectacular and extremely expensive hotels. He wanted to ensure that all the guests to
Monte Carlo were entertained in the grandest of style.

From November to Easter, the casino's Salle Garnier, named after Charles Garnier, the architect hired
by Charles III to design the casino, is the setting for
glittering operas, ballets and concerts. Only the finest
troupes and composers have been chosen to play in
Monte Carlo.

Monte Carlo boasted the best of the best.

Because Joan knew of the city's history and reputation, she was aware of the honor being paid her by her publisher, Avon Books, to have an autograph party in the ballroom of the Hotel de Paris. She also knew she had nothing appropriate to wear.

When Joan received word from Gloria Horne's office in New York that she would be having this party in her honor, she instantly began flipping through her dresses. She had a two-year-old winter cocktail dress she'd purchased at Loehman's. There was a black crepe that bunched at her hips—she couldn't wear that— and a frilly chiffon print Elaine had made her buy.

Joan stuffed a wad of francs in her purse, wondering how much a couture gown would cost, and set out.

She found nothing in several native-run boutiques, and little at the dress shop in Lowe's Monte Carlo Hotel. But in the boutique at the Palace Hotel, Joan gaped at the vision in the mirror, thinking it must be someone else.

"It's a St. Laurent," the saleswoman said.

"Of course," Joan replied with knowledgeable aplomb. She didn't care who the designer was, it was beautiful. The woman called it a "bustier," this kind of bodice that was strapless and tapered down to a tight-fitting waist. Joan wondered how they'd taken so much lavender silk and crushed it into these tiny folds and ripples that made up the skirt.

Joan bought the dress—had it *really* cost that much?—and the Ferragamo shoes, and the Dior earrings, bracelet and necklace. They were costume jewelry, but they looked perfect with the dress.

while the saleswoman tallied her purchases and wrapped them, Joan wandered to the jewelry counter again. She peered into the glass case containing fabulous rubies and emeralds. She wondered what the pinched-mouth little man behind the counter would do if she were to show him the size emerald she had once held. She chuckled to herself, which drew his attention.

He inspected her from head to toe and must have decided she was not a bona fide buyer and went about his duties. Joan shrugged her shoulders and moved over to the next counter. Here were lovely diamond solitaire rings. There were oval cuts, square-shaped, round, marquise and pear-shaped stones.

As she gazed at the rings, Joan was suddenly overcome with an inexplicable sadness. She looked at her left hand and wondered what a diamond ring would look like on her third finger. She glanced up and noticed the little salesman was also staring at her hand. He shook his head despondently and then quickly looked away.

Suddenly, Joan couldn't wait to get away from that counter and those rings. She scurried back to the dress department, took her things, paid the bill and rushed outside. It wasn't until she walked onto the *Angelina* that she felt relieved. She wanted to recapture that excitement she'd had about her dress and the party. She was being silly. Her costume jewelry would look great. She didn't need a diamond ring.

As Joan went belowdecks to dress for the party, she remembered that she hadn't told Jack about the incident. After all, what was there to tell?

Jack watched her descend the steps. He glanced at the last crescent of the setting sun. Tonight was her party. Maybe seeing Gloria would cheer her up.

Jack started down the steps and nearly bumped into

Joan. She'd been looking at the wall of snapshots he'd taken during their cruise. Politely, she smiled at him as if he were just another passenger on a cruise ship. He plastered his back against the wall, allowing her to pass.

What had gotten into her lately? He remembered when they used to laugh about this narrow passageway. He remembered using it as an excuse to hold her to his chest. He looked at the snapshot of them standing at the fishing village south of Marseilles. He remembered a lot of things. . . .

Diving naked off moon-glazed rocks near Majorca; Joan learning to scuba dive; Joan teaching him to make bisquits; his falling more in love with her every day. Now she said she wanted something different—she wanted change. Jack didn't want things to change. He liked his Joanie just the way she was—with him. Sometimes he felt as if the walls were tumbling down around him. Things *had* changed—without his consent.

He looked at Joan picking her way across the messy cabin. Jack glanced once more at the snapshots. He had to find a way to make her smile like that again. He had to.

As Jack went to the head to shower and shave, Joan climbed over Jack's surfboard. It was an antique, he'd told her. "The last piece of salvage from my high school days in California." It was wedged across the cabin, and Joan wished it had stayed in California where it belonged. Just as she'd maneuvered over the surfboard, she nearly tripped on his basketball. Why the hell this had to travel with them she didn't know. They hadn't seen the inside of a YMCA since New

York. There were scuba tanks, wet suits, dirty clothes, wet mildewed towels—she took a whiff of one and tossed it back on the floor—and two unplugged speakers for his non-working stereo. And everywhere, hanging from the ceiling, plastered to the walls and on top of the furniture, were travel souvenirs. Jack couldn't go anywhere without buying his memories. She often wondered why the memory wasn't enough for him.

In Spain he'd had a special clock made to resemble the *Angelina*. Now that was a worthwhile purchase, she thought, glancing over at it.

"Jack," she called into the bathroom, "we'd better hurry!"

Joan went to the chest of drawers and pulled out one crammed drawer after another. She started cursing under her breath. Every time she cleaned these drawers out, he messed them up again. She found her bathing suits in the drawer with his T-shirts. She also found a can of sardines, a package of muffin mix, a pair of broken sunglasses and half a sandwich. It was a wonder they hadn't been eaten alive by cockroaches!

Still not finding her new pantyhose and beige slip, Joan continued her search. She tried another drawer, but it was jammed. She pulled harder, placing her foot against the bottom of the cabinet. Finally she yanked it open, and out popped a bug-eyed alligator. Clutching her heart and repeating her own name so she wouldn't curse, Joan picked up the small stuffed reptile. She stroked its head, thinking of when she and Jack had met in Colombia.

Somehow, that time seemed as if it had happened to another Joan. She had been happier then. She and Jack had been—well, more solid then. They had needed each other, depended on each other. What was she thinking? Didn't they still need each other?

Just then Jack emerged from the head. Quickly, she gathered her things and passed by him in the narrow corridor. In Colombia they seemed to communicate more without words than they did now with thousands of words. Something was missing between them, but she wasn't sure what it was. She knew she was confused about her career and perhaps she'd been preoccupied. Jack smiled politely. He acted as though she were a stranger! She glanced at the wall with snapshots so he wouldn't see the tears that were threatening her eyes.

She dashed into the bathroom.

Jack walked over to the chest of drawers and gently pulled out a drawer containing his socks, belt and a pair of rolled white pants. He shook them out, and a funnel of dust spun around him. He coughed, and as he turned around he noticed a tie hanging directly in front of him. He would have to be blind not to see it. He took the tie and glanced in the direction of the head.

Joan had put that tie out for him. He hadn't worn a tie since his Wall Street days. But for Joan, he'd do anything. Including wearing a tie. This was a special night for her. He'd show her he could handle the hoity-toity crowd just as easily as he did the skis this afternoon.

Jack finished dressing and went on deck for a quick smoke before they left.

Joan emerged from the tiny head completely dressed. She even amazed herself that she could cram a full set of steam rollers, a blow-drier, all her makeup, fake-nail kit and clothes into that minuscule space. She wondered absentmindedly if *that* qualified her for a Pulitzer.

Joan was daintily climbing over the surfboard trying not to run her stockings when Jack came down the stairs. She looked up.

"The tie!" she said, surprised and pleased. She'd never seen him with a tie, and she knew he'd made the gesture just for her.

"For you . . ." he said, smiling.

He looked more like one of her heroes every time she looked at him. But especially tonight. He put out his arm for her and she took it. He paused for a moment and pulled her a bit closer.

He couldn't tear his eyes off her. She was still the most beautiful woman he'd ever seen. Ever since he'd met Joan, he hadn't been able to look at anyone else. He felt excited every time he thought about her. And when she stood this close to him . . . he wondered if they could be "fashionably late" this time. Naw, he thought. He'd better not ask. Joan wanted this night to be something wonderful and he wanted to be the one to give it to her.

They turned to walk on deck when,—WHAM!—Jack struck his head on a hanging scuba tank. He rubbed his head, thinking Joan looked a bit fuzzy to him. She was smiling at him, that beautiful dimpled smile of hers that always turned him to jelly. She touched his head. He could see concern in her eyes. This time Jack couldn't stand it anymore. He pulled her into his arms and kissed her deeply.

* * *

Joan leaned into Jack. There was still a passion between them she could never deny. Suddenly, she wished they didn't have a schedule to meet. She who had been complaining for days that they needed one. She wanted to feel his hands on her body, she wanted him to make love to her. She wondered if he had any idea what his kisses did to her.

Joan buried her head in his shoulder for a moment, reveling in the protectiveness of his arms. Then they went on deck. They walked out to the end of the pier, and there sat one lone vehicle—a motorcycle.

Joan looked down at her St. Laurent gown and then at Jack.

"I thought you were going to get a car."

"Sorry, sweetheart. Slipped my mind."

Joan sighed with resignation. Jack would never change. "It's okay."

Jack climbed on. "It's like a car, just not as much room."

Somehow this was not the picture she'd envisioned for her arrival at the hotel tonight. Gamely, she got on—side saddle—so as not to ruin her costly dress.

"I said okay."

Jack started the bike, no small effort since it took three choke adjustments before revving up. With a loud roar, the motorcycle zoomed down the street.

On the dock only twenty-five feet from the anchored *Angelina* sat three stacks of storage boxes. The first stack was small crates filled with Jack's essential provisions—beer and snacks. The second stack contained new hemp, motor oil and parts of machinery for the

Angelina. At the end of the two stacks was one large wooden crate with no markings.

Just as Jack and Joan disappeared on the motorcycle, there came a low-throated growl from the area by the wooden crates. No animals were allowed in the area and few were known to stray near the piers. A cough then marked the intruder as clearly human.

The *Angelina* bobbed contentedly in the water, her tall mast skimming the night sky. As the minutes passed, she witnessed no more strange nocturnal noises.

Chapter Four

INDIGO SKIES STUDDED WITH TWINKLING
flecks of light were suspended above Monte Carlo.
The evening air was warm and brushed with a whisper
of fragrance from the multitudes of blooming flowers.
The sea was calm, and every street in the city was
filled with expensive sports cars, sedans and limousines headed for the casinos and hotels. Spotlights lit
trees, flowers, parks, hotels and restaurants.

As Jack and Joan rode past the Casino de Monte
Carlo, Joan thought it looked as if it were fashioned
of solid gold. Like a dowager queen, the casino ruled
over her subjects, for nothing in the city was quite so
grand. The two ornate domes on the roof above the
second floor were centered with an intricately carved
clock. The three sets of glass doors were open and a
lush red carpet extended all the way to the curb.

Located nearby, the Hotel de Paris was an equally
awe-inspiring sight. Its Belle Epoque architecture made
Joan feel as if she were traveling back in time. It was
almost overwhelming it was so beautiful, she thought,
staring at the gilt mirrors, crystal chandeliers and richly
covered walls. And everywhere, outside in the gardens

and in the gaming rooms, were fabulously dressed women on the arms of wealthy Americans, diplomats, foreign dignitaries and French military men in full dress.

Joan had never seen so many designer gowns and jewels in her life. More than ever she was glad she had bought this gown. She was supposed to be the star. Already she felt engulfed in a sea of chiffon, crepe de chine, organza and silk in every color in the rainbow. From the bright jewel-toned satiniques on the arms of elder statesmen and ambassadors to the young parfait-tinted fabrics on their daughters—those were their daughters?—Joan now recognized a few of the designers. She saw a ruffled lemon silk Oscar de la Renta. The sleek black-and-white flowing print was a Valentino and the wide-shouldered crimson gown was definitely a Nolan Miller.

Her shopping expedition had been more educational than she'd thought.

While Joan greeted Gloria with a hug and put on her "public face," Jack wandered around through the crowd feeling very much out of place. There were dukes, lords and ladies, a marquise and a maharajah with his maharanee. Everyone was dressed to the nines. Jack stuck his finger in his tight collar, hoping for relief. He'd worn a tie all right, but everyone else was in tuxes. He glanced over at Gloria who was watching him. She seemed to gain some perverse pleasure seeing his discomfort.

Jack wanted to scowl back at her, but the only reason he put up with Gloria and all this was because it was important to Joan.

He looked at her. She was radiant and smashing in

that dress. She was being bombarded by her public. She smiled at them all, signed their books and answered their questions.

Waiters appeared bearing trays filled with glasses of champagne. Jack took one, downed it and then promptly had it filled by another waiter carrying a bottle. Just then, Jack noticed a silver-haired baron quieting the crowd and holding his glass high.

"A toast—to the woman who keeps the romance in our lives, my dreary little life in particular. May Joan Wilder write a *thousand* more!"

Joan gulped. "A thousand..." she mumbled under her breath. She certainly hoped not. "Thank you all very much."

Jack raised his glass and drank to her, too. He was proud of her. It had been a long time since he'd told her that. Maybe Joan felt he didn't appreciate her work. He could do a lot better about supporting her. Come to think of it, he'd only finished one of her novels. He should have read them all by now. Instead, he'd spent too much time attending the *Angelina,* or focusing on having a good time—this kind of good time.

He should make it up to her, he thought, starting toward Joan. Suddenly, a new group of people rushed into the room and surrounded Joan. To Jack it looked as if she'd been swallowed up. Jack knew with his mind that this was not the kind of crowd Joan went with in New York. In fact, she'd always been a loner. But he also knew she fit in more with these people than he did. She had an air about her, a sophistication, he would never learn. She'd been born with it. "Background shows," his mother had always said. Jack had laughed at her at the time. He wasn't laughing now.

Jack felt dreadfully out of place at a time when he wanted to be a part of all this—for Joan's sake. A waiter walked up and refilled his glass—again.

Over an hour later Joan thought her smile must surely have cracked and fallen on the floor by now. Gloria told her she had greeted over three hundred people. She was exhausted.

"Many kudos, Joanie, all deserved." Gloria hugged her.

"You gave 'em hell, angel," Jack said with a distinct slur to his voice.

Joan looked at him. His tie was askew. She wished they'd eaten something before coming here.

On Joan's left side was an Italian viscount who told Joan he read her books only while traveling between his six villas scattered the world over. On Joan's right was a New York matron here on holiday visiting her daughter, a marchesa. Joan could tell they were waiting to be introduced to Gloria and Jack.

"This is my publisher, Gloria Horne . . . and this is Jack Colton."

"A publisher, how nice . . ." The viscount turned to Jack and shook his hand. "And you're a—What is it you do?"

"Casino work." Jack didn't like the way that guy kept ogling Joan's chest. He was tired of these plastic people. He stuck his hand in his jacket pocket where he'd placed a small stack of chips he'd bought earlier.

"I'm gonna go punch in," he said to Joan. No sense in spoiling her good time if he was in a bad mood.

"Jack—" Joan tried to grab his arm, but it was too late. She watched as he left the ballroom and headed toward the gambling rooms.

Just then the matron turned to the viscount. "What is it he does?"

"Gambles, I believe," he replied pompously.

"Oh."

Joan felt mortified and in need of some fresh air. She hurried toward the terrace doors. She passed the violinist, the elaborate buffet table, thinking the doors kept getting farther away. What was the matter with her these days? Things were changing between her and Jack, and she didn't know why. She blamed herself. Her emotions had been anything but stable lately. She seemed forever tossed between highs and lows. There had been that inexplicable sadness when she'd looked at those diamond rings. Now that she thought about it, perhaps she was simply more prone to depression. And worst of all, it showed in her writing.

She rushed to the balcony railing and took a deep breath.

It was beautiful out here. The lights of Monte Carlo were a luminous spectacle. Why wasn't Jack on *her* side anymore? He knew how important this night was for her. A lot of people had gone to a lot of trouble just for her. Why couldn't he be civil, just tonight. She wanted to cry; she wanted to brain him.

Gloria, fast on Joan's heels, arrived on the terrace out of breath.

"Don't panic, Joan. You can't blame him. These literary crowds . . . I mean, Jack's favorite author is the man who wrote 'pull to open.'"

Joan's voice was strained. "Gloria, I'm his favorite author, as it happens." At least she used to be.

"Still?" Gloria asked, noting the ashen look to Joan's skin and the less than convincing tone in her voice.

Even Gloria could tell she was losing Jack. She didn't want to explain anything to Gloria, mainly because she didn't understand it herself.

Just then a waiter approached Joan and Gloria.

"Drinks, ma'am?"

Joan looked at him quizzically. She hadn't expected to see an Arab waiter. He looked uncomfortable and out of place in his uniform. Almost comical, but she appreciated his bow to her.

"A vodka gimlet," Gloria said.

"Tequila," Joan answered.

Gloria looked stunned at Joan's order as the waiter bowed and left.

"Tequila? Two-fisted."

"No, just a taste I acquired in Colombia. Now those were the days," Joan said, thinking of when she and Jack first met. Had the magic faded? Was that it?

"If you look back on near-death-by-crocodile with nostalgia, I hate to imagine what you've been doing lately." Gloria paused for a moment, thinking of the exchange between Jack and the viscount. Clearly, things were not peaches and cream in paradise.

She went on. "Actually, what *have* you been doing? I didn't come three thousand miles to break croissants with you. I'm here because your book's three months late."

Joan hated Gloria's "editor voice." It had such a condemning tone.

"I'm on the last chapter." Joan tried to smile.

Gloria shook her head. "Your smile's wearing a little thin. What gives? Too much time with Peter Pan on the Good Ship Lollipop?"

Joan bit her lip but didn't say anything. Just then

the Arab waiter appeared, bearing their drinks. He handed the straight tequila to Gloria. Joan noticed his eyes darting about the terrace. His mind was on anything and everything but his work, Joan thought.

"No," Gloria said. "I had the gimlet."

"Oh, so sorry." He apologized. He then took the drink back from Gloria, placed it on the silver tray; then, in one motion flipped the tray completely upside down and then right side up again.

Joan blinked twice, thinking what she had seen wasn't real. But now the drinks had switched sides. She wondered if he were a genie. Politely, she took the drink he handed her.

Suddenly, the waiter became nervous, his eyes again darting from face to face.

"Thank you very much," he said and then backed away and suddenly disappeared. Logic told Joan that he was there in the crowd somewhere, but her eyes told her the man had vanished—into thin air. Like a magician.

Joan and Gloria clinked their glasses. They did not notice the five Arab bodyguards weaving their way through the crowd. Joan did not see that the largest man wore a thick red scar down the side of his face.

"Well, here's to the last chapter," Gloria said with a smile.

"Gloria..." Joan bolstered her courage. "...I'm not going to finish it."

Gloria's eyes were saucers. Startled, she stammered, "Wh—what? Why ever not?"

"Because for one thing, after seventeen books, I suddenly don't know how it ends anymore."

Joan was about to go on with her explanations when a white rose was thrust in her face.

"Then permit me to tell you."

Joan looked up to see the most handsome Arab she'd ever laid eyes on. He was tall, wearing a turban and a beautiful silk tunic. He was surrounded by an entourage, including the scar-faced messenger of this afternoon. He was like a fantasy out of the *Arabian Nights*. Joan easily envisioned him riding a strong black stallion across the Sahara brandishing a long scimitar as he rode into battle.

His voice was melodic and compelling. "It doesn't end . . . only begins anew with your journey down the Nile . . ." He paused, his dark sensual eyes roaming her face. ". . . with me."

Joan was transfixed as he handed her the rose.

"Omar Khalifa, as I live and scarcely breathe," Gloria sighed.

Joan looked over at Gloria who had instantly become moony-eyed staring at the exceptionally good-looking Omar. Joan couldn't believe it. Gloria never acted like this. Gloria, the cool, intelligent businesswoman who always figured a person's angle and slapped a label on him in less than three seconds (she was trying to get it down to two)—Gloria, Joan's best friend, was starstruck!

"You're the one who sent the flowers."

"They pale by your beauty."

"I like this guy," Gloria leaned over to whisper in Joan's ear.

"I've read all about you," Joan said, thinking that no one had ever correctly described the charisma this man had. There was an overwhelming aura about him.

He'd knocked Gloria out of her seat in no time. Joan could feel herself succumbing to him. It was like being sucked in by a powerful whirlpool.

"Yes," he answered her. "But rarely the truth. I have a story to tell unlike any ever seen or heard. And you, Joan Wilder, must join me and write it."

"Do you 'know' my books, my work?"

"I know everything," he said in that velvet voice that convinced Joan he knew the size of her underwear. She wouldn't dare dispute a thing he said. He held her hand. He caressed her finger with his thumb. There was no mistaking the smoldering look in his eyes. Joan wondered if all Arab men looked at women like that. Maybe it was second nature with them. All she knew was that if Jack looked at her like that, they were in bed in less than ten seconds!

With the subject once again on publishing, Gloria's tactical mind snapped out of its reverie. "Then you must know that Joan isn't—no offense," she said to Joan. ". . . exactly an investigative journalist."

Joan rushed to her own defense. "I don't want to be an investigative journalist—exactly."

Omar smiled. "Exactly. Miss Wilder understands."

"I do?"

"Who is more perfect? In your gifted storytelling, it becomes clear that you actually *like* men. That you see in them their finest qualities. I have been misinterpreted all too often and simply seek your clarity."

Gloria's business brain told her there was something amok with all this.

Omar instantly picked up on the skeptical look in her eyes.

"My life has involved great risk and daring, all for

a wondrous cause. And I am offering your widely read author a chance to record history."

His words were like music to Joan's ears. Finally, a chance to grow and extend her talent. She could really do something with her talent. Joan was certain now that all her misgivings about her life, her trouble with her writing, even her doubts about Jack had been there for a purpose. They had led her to this meeting with Omar who was about to make a pivotal change in her career. She couldn't pass it up. "We make our own luck," she'd once heard her agent say. And wasn't luck simply "preparedness meeting opportunity"? Benjamin Franklin had said that, she thought: he'd said everything else worth remembering.

Joan took the arm Omar offered her. He turned to Gloria.

"Do you mind?"

"Maybe. Joan, what about my book?" Gloria's voice was strained and Joan could see that tense set in Gloria's jaw.

Joan was too excited about this new turn her career was taking to think about anything else. Surely, once Gloria had a chance to think about it, she too would agree Joan had made the best decision.

Joan looked over her shoulder. "I'll call you."

Chapter Five

THE CHAMPAGNE CORK EASED OUT OF THE bottle labeled proudly with Dom Perignon's name. Jack knew the casino was buzzing about his prowess at the roulette wheel tonight. It had taken him just over an hour to win sixty thousand francs. He hoped Joan hadn't heard that it took less than ten minutes to lose it. His luck had split faster than an AMEX stock. For the life of him, he couldn't understand why he still played this game. Maybe he wanted to see if he would get any "thrill" out of it. He found he didn't. After that last pass of the wheel, he was glad he hadn't started out with more than a hundred bucks. After he counted his money and tipped the croupier, he was only down twenty-five bucks. No more than the price of a good bottle of wine in the Village in New York. He could handle that.

After he'd left the gaming table, he wove his way through the casino patrons, smelling designer perfume, brushing against designer couture gowns and being blinded by designer jewels.

He was getting sick of this place and all these haughty

people. Maybe Joan felt the same way. He wished they were back on the *Angelina* setting sail. . . .

Just then Jack spied Joan. As he approached her table, he found she was sitting with an excruciatingly handsome Arab.

It's the oil sheik, he thought. He had enough turbaned bodyguards around him. Jack didn't see any obvious jewelry on the man. That was a bit unusual. He'd heard most of these guys flaunted their millions any chance they got; especially in front of Americans. The French didn't much care. They were unimpressible.

Jack looked at Joan. She was utterly enraptured by what this guy was saying. The hairs on the back of Jack's neck stood on end. He remembered when Joan looked at him like that. Every bone, muscle and fiber of Jack's body was instantly on the defensive.

With a coolly sophisticated smile, Jack leaned down and placed the cork in front of Joan.

"And just what is it we're celebrating now?"

Joan rose and grabbed his hand.

"The Nile!" she exclaimed.

The Arab rose slowly, his eyes scrutinizing every inch of Jack. Jack assessed his opponent in the same manner.

"The Nile?" Jack didn't know *exactly* what was happening here. Maybe he did, and didn't want to know.

"We're invited to North Africa," Joan bubbled. "Jack Colton, Omar Khalifa," she introduced them.

Jack shook his hand, feigning geniality.

"He's asked me . . . ME . . . to chronicle his story!" Joan gushed.

Jack was skeptical. He'd never seen Joan act like this—about someone else. "Oh, and what story might that be?"

Omar's smile was friendly. Jack didn't trust him. "That of a man chosen to unite the tribes of the Nile and end the internal strife that has bloodied our land since our beloved Redeemer."

"Chosen, huh? By who?"

"By the people, and by the Unseen. I was visited by a spirit, a holy spirit who has given me guidance. I am sure a man of your religious convictions can appreciate that."

Jack wasn't buying any of this. He took Joan's arm.

"Pardon us a moment."

"Certainly," Omar said most politely; and then with more emphasis he said: "Mr. Wilder."

Now Jack knew Omar was after Joan for a lot more than a story. This guy was a bullshit artist if ever he saw one. But that wasn't the point. The point was, Joan kept looking at this guy as if he were her dream come true. He guided her to an area secluded by some ferns. He wanted to make sure Omar couldn't see them. He wouldn't be at all surprised if Omar read lips.

"The Nile? I thought you wanted to go back to New York."

"That's all changed."

"That fast." How could she have changed so quickly? He suddenly felt as if his whole life were spinning around like that black roulette ball. And this wasn't a winning pass, either.

"Jack, to write a biography, something real, that's the kind of thing I've been looking for." How could she explain it to him without hurting his feelings? It wasn't enough for her to live a nomad's life like his. This was her career they were talking about, not just one of his little pleasure jaunts. She'd never pressed him before about *anything*. They always went wherever *he* wanted to go, whenever *he* wanted. Why couldn't he indulge her just this once? Make her happy.

"C'mon, Joan. Spirits? Visitations? This guy's been in the sun without his turban."

"But it's what I've been wanting." She said that with so much conviction, she'd almost convinced herself. She *thought* she was doing the right thing. These days, Joan had more questions than she had answers. She hoped she would find some answers, if not through Omar and his story, then through the growth her work would take.

"So you're gonna just barge down the Nile with Sabu?"

"This is a big chance for me, and you're invited too. It might be fun, adventure. Africa, the Nile."

Jack blinked hard. They'd been having a little communication problem the past weeks; Joan had been a little depressed, he thought; but to suddenly strike out with someone else steering her mast . . . Now he knew why he'd been so defensive about this guy sending roses. *Joan wasn't his!* He'd duped himself into thinking she was. Maybe she was only with him for the ride and now Omar was offering a better one. Jack had been testing Joan for weeks, trying to get her to commit to him, but she wouldn't do it. He wanted to push her even further. He believed, maybe foolishly, that she would choose him.

"Got your heart set on it, then."

She nodded, thinking he wanted to go too.

"Well, mine's set on Greece."

She was stunned. Not once had she thought of going anywhere without him. What good was extending her talent if Jack wasn't there to share her triumphs with her, or help her pick up the pieces when she fell. She wasn't at all sure she could do this work. She only hoped she could. But she had to *try*. Didn't she?

Jack delved deeper into Joan's eyes. "So, you're going then. When?"

"Well . . . tonight. He's got this private jet, and . . ." Joan's voice trailed off.

"Aah, private jet . . ." Jack looked at her, took off his tie and draped it around her neck. He forced a smile and hoped she wouldn't hear the crack in his voice.

"Looks better on you."

Joan was speechless. How could he let her go alone? Jack loved her! Or did he? She told herself he did. And he had told her he did. But what had he done lately to prove it to her? Real proof. Was that what she was after? Was that why she felt so—empty sometimes, even lonely, when she was with him? What had happened to them? She had based all her dreams on Jack. She had lived his dream with him just to be near him. Didn't he know that?

Well, if he didn't want her anymore, that's the way it would be. She wasn't going to grovel at his feet. She wouldn't beg him . . . not because she had too much pride, but because she would never recover from the pain if he turned her away again. Joan wanted to throw up. She wanted to run away from him and cry her eyes out.

"Hey, we had a good run." He was baiting her, but he didn't care. He wanted her to come with him.

"Jack, this is only gonna be four or five weeks of research." Was this begging?

"Right. Maybe that's what we need. A little break."

"I know it's been a little tough lately."

"For you." It had been heaven for him. He didn't remember having half these problems before she met this Arab. Jack's eyes narrowed as he glanced at Omar, whose eyes shone with triumph. How could this guy have gotten so far so fast with this girl? She must have been more willing than Jack figured.

"Maybe I can meet you in Greece." Joan was fishing for a commitment. She had to know it all couldn't just end right here. Why wasn't he fighting for her? Why did she mean so little to him? Maybe she'd been excess baggage all along.

Jack could barely speak. Joan's intentions stung him like daggers, but Jack remained calm on the outside. He shrugged his shoulders nonchalantly. He felt dead inside, but he couldn't just let her go.

"Sure, yeah. Or maybe I'll come down the Nile . . ."

"Yeah," Joan said wanly, knowing the truth now. What a fool she'd been to press him for a commitment like that. Jack didn't want her. Everything they were, everything they had, turned to ashes before her eyes. What did he want from her? She'd gone through the tortures of hell with him in Colombia, waited for him to come back to her in New York, and she'd sailed halfway around the world with him. She should have known which key to turn inside him to make him see what he was throwing away. But she didn't. She just stood there, her eyes burning, knowing she would always love him—even if he didn't want her.

"Right," he said coolly. "Either way."

"I'll write you."

"Yeah," he said. "Where?"

Joan thought they sounded like two kids at the end of summer camp, making assurances they would stay friends, knowing they wouldn't.

"Yeah, right. Where?"

Feigning a casual grin, then clearing the emotional frog from his throat, Jack smiled at her one last time. He couldn't help thinking of that first day they'd met in Colombia. She'd been soaked to the skin by the torrential rains, her blond hair skimming her face— her beautiful, dimpled face. He'd laughed at her at the time; she'd nearly killed herself trying to keep up with him, carrying that giant American Tourister. Callously, he'd pitched it over the side of the mountain. But he'd made up for it. He'd brought her new things in Paris, hadn't he? Idly, he wondered if she would take any of them with her.

"Y'know. I think I'll go give that roulette wheel one last chance."

Jack leaned over and kissed Joan quickly, stinging her lips with his. He didn't want to make a scene, but he wanted her to remember—as he would . . .

"Jack, you'll take care, won't you?" She felt the earth quaking beneath her, as if her whole world were slipping away.

"Don't I always? Stay out of trouble, huh?"

Jack could feel Joan's eyes on his back as he walked past Omar. Jack looked at him for a long moment. Why would Joan give up his love for this guy? She wasn't a gold digger. It couldn't be money. Power? He peered into Omar's black eyes. They were completely opaque—the kind he didn't trust.

Omar's black eyes sparkled when he spoke. "Why do I think I should not say 'Welcome Aboard,' but instead, 'Bon Voyage'?"

Jack felt he'd done all he could. He walked away still hoping she would come after him. He kept hoping until he hoped his way right out of the hotel and into the street. He hailed a cab.

As he looked out the taxi window one last time at the ornate hotel, Jack realized he'd lost more at the gaming tables than money. He'd lost his heart.

Chapter Six

FERRARIS, MERCEDES, AND ROLLS SEDANS all made room for the jet-black stretch limousine in front of the Hotel de Paris. Incandescent light reflected off the glittering sequined gowns of the guests as they ogled Omar and Joan coming out of the hotel. Joan thought it looked like Academy Awards night. She wished she felt that gay. Instead, her insides had turned to stone. Gallantly, Omar waited for her as she slid into the limo.

Joan looked back at him just in time to see a brilliant shaft of light. Suddenly, she realized that it was a knife! And it was headed straight for Omar's heart. With a heavy thud, Omar fell into the limousine. Joan saw a dark man's shadow dash through the crowd. She tried to get a better view, but the bodyguards slammed the door shut and took off running after the man.

Joan heard a tremendous commotion as others joined in the chase. Then, she heard the sound of a gun being fired. Reflexively, Joan ducked down in her seat. The driver started the engine and quickly pulled away from the curb, throwing Joan about the backseat.

Joan was scrambling for the door handle for support

and did not see that the bodyguards had accomplished their mission.

Clutching a bleeding shoulder, the Arab waiter who had served Joan and Gloria their drinks barged through the elegantly dressed crowd. Women screamed and men gasped in horror at the sight. The waiter raced for the terrace railing with three of Omar's bodyguards still in pursuit. He dove over the railing and in midair achieved a perfect somersault. He landed on his feet two stories below and then vanished into the night like the genie he was.

Joan was wide-eyed, watching Omar grasp his tunic where the knife had slit the delicate silk. He pulled and tore the fabric, rending it from his chest. The sound of the ripping silk filled the limousine.

Joan gasped when she realized that beneath the tunic he wore a steel mesh vest that encircled his chest, back and rib cage. She looked up at him.

"Don't be frightened," he said. "A man of vision has many enemies, so, you see, this kind of thing at times will occur."

He smiled and patted her arm reassuringly.

Though she smiled and nodded, Joan wondered what kind of holy man this was. She had never heard of the Pope wearing a bulletproof vest, or Ghandi. Omar was fascinating, she thought . . . and frightening.

Jack watched the limousine pull away. The dull thud of his heart hammering against his chest drowned out the sound of the automobile's engine as it rushed away from the dock.

He looked around him at the Monte Carlo harbor, the lights on shore, the dark night. It was different now—not as shining. It was lifeless.

"Well, Angelina, it's just you and me now, baby."
He took a deep breath. "Hell, I was carrying your
picture around a long time before hers."

He stood up. He wove back and forth on very
unsteady legs. Maybe he'd been wrong about being
sober . . . . He walked up the gangplank onto the dock.
He went up to the second stack of wooden boxes. He
rooted around in the box holding provisions. He withdrew a bag of pretzels, Cheez-its, some Fritos and a
bag of caramel corn. Farther down he found some
squeeze-on cheese spread. He looked at the case of
beer. Naw. He needed sustenance. As he looked at his
choices for the entree he hoped he wouldn't get heartburn.

He had enough heartburn.

"There's still gonna be the same ports of call, same
sunsets to sail off into, same fun to be had . . . only
problem is—"

Jack rammed his foot into the empty wooden box
and sent it flying into the air.

"—you can't sleep with a boat." His father had
raised a damned fool!

"Dummy!" he chided himself. "You just let her go!"

Jack turned around slump-shouldered and headed
onto the boat again. Who was he kidding? Nothing
would ever be the same without Joan. Why couldn't
she love him? He wasn't such a bad guy. He wasn't
any hero out of one of her books. He was just a guy.
But he loved her. God, he did love her.

Just as Jack reached the deck, the lid of the largest
wooden crate slowly opened. A pair of eyes blinked
and then—Blam! Out jumped Ralph! His familiar white

suit was now in tatters and he was waving a big revolver at Jack.

"Don't cry, scumbag. I'll keep you company."

Jack knew it must be the champagne, for he was seeing things. This couldn't be real. That gun was real, though, and it was Jack's bet that it was loaded. Jack raised his hands in the air.

"Colombia! Cartegena!" Jack said—almost delighted to know Ralph had gotten out of there, too.

"Didya miss me? I missed you. You're all I've thought about for the last six months. All the time I was hiding with the rats in that pisshole country I was thinking of you. When one of 'em bit me and I had ten weeks of rabies shots like this"—he demonstrated by holding his hands two feet apart—"I was thinking of you. Even when they threw me in that stinkin' Spico jail and everyone was trying to hire on as my proctologist, I was thinkin' of you. Only you."

"Hey, I'm flattered, but I'm pullin' out tonight. I'd be glad to give ya a C-note."

"A C-note? I'll give you a one-way ticket to harp land!"

Ralph tried to step out of the wooden crate, but his feet got tangled in the hemp rope inside. He lifted his right leg and shook it but only succeeded in wrapping it tighter around his ankle. Rather than losing sight of Jack to unwrap his leg, he decided to step out with the other foot instead. As soon as he did, Ralph tripped and fell onto the dock. The gun went off with a loud bang. Fortunately, he'd been aiming straight into the air. Ralph's luck must be running a little better this week—he was glad he hadn't shot his own foot. Still lying on his back, Ralph kept his wits about him and pointed the gun at Jack. Priorities, he thought.

"Hey, I'm not playing games here! What'd you do with it?"

"What?"

"The stone, moron! Come on down." Ralph motioned with the gun for Jack to come back onto the dock. Ralph wanted Jack close where he could see him more clearly.

"It's gone," Jack said as he walked down the gang-plank again.

"I'm cocked here!" Ralph looked pointedly at his gun.

"I sold it. I bought the boat, been sailin' around, eatin' good, doin' a little gambling. Nothing left ... just the boat."

"What about the twenty thousand in cash you had sittin' under the bulkhead in the galley?"

Jack instantly panicked. This little turd couldn't have ... Jack turned toward the boat. He had to check ... that was his stake money. Money he was gonna use for a house, maybe—if Joan wanted one—or a bigger boat if she wanted to sail around. It was money to keep her ...

"Don't bother. I've taken the liberty of puttin' it in a safe place."

"You asshole." Jack's fury jumped to the surface. He wanted to wring this little weasel's throat. How could he ever compete with some powerful Arab without his stake?

"Fine way to plead for your life," Ralph snickered. He waved the gun at Jack again. This creep was gonna have to realize that Ralph was not a man to be trifled with. When he meant business—it was all the way.

"Where's the rest of it?"

"That's it. I swear."

Ralph didn't believe him. He remembered the last time somebody—a Zolo somebody—asked him to hand over his fortune and he'd damn near let his blond girl friend's hand be chomped off by a crocodile before he gave up. Ralph might have to use more persuasive measures with Mr. Jack T. Colton.

"Did I tell you I got malaria in that jail? I still get the shakes . . . in my trigger finger."

Jack started backing away. Maybe he'd underestimated Ralph. There was a determined look in his eyes, one born of cruelty he hadn't seen before. Maybe Ralph had been through more than Jack imagined. Ralph's finger was very slowly squeezing the trigger.

"Hey, come on," Jack tried to plead with him.

"Your good times are about to end."

Jack took another step back, but this time there was no escape. Ralph almost looked demented. Ralph was going to kill him.

Ralph had thought of nothing but that giant emerald and of killing Jack all those months in that rotten jail. Seeing real fear in Jack's eyes had kept Ralph alive; wanting to live for his revenge. He'd dreamed of this moment for so long, Ralph wanted to milk it for all he could. He liked this kind of power that came with knowing you could end somebody's life. Especially when that somebody had fenced the biggest emerald in history.

Ralph started to pull the trigger when, out of nowhere, seven Arabian daggers whizzed through the air in quick succession, pinning Ralph's coat up against the storage box. Ralph had jerked his hand, and the revolver went flying onto the dock.

Jack was stunned. "What the hey . . . ?"

From behind another storage bin leaped the Arab waiter from the Casino de Monte Carlo. He was bleeding at his shoulder and his beady black eyes were wild. Jack couldn't tell if the Arab wanted Ralph dead or if he was a bad throw.

The Arab turned to Ralph. "Next time you will not be as fortunate, little man."

"Holy shit!" Ralph exclaimed in shock, looking at the array of knives over his head and around his arms. "Holy shit!"

The Arab turned to Jack. His voice was level and deadly serious.

"I am Tarak. I saw you and your woman at the casino with Omar Khalifa. Tonight I tried to kill Omar Khalifa, but I failed. So I call upon you! You must come with me, now!"

"I don't think so, buddy."

"But you must! Omar has stolen our Jewel!"

Suddenly, Ralph was all ears and smiles. "Jewel?" Perhaps his luck had really turned. Lose one emerald—find another. He was proud of himself for being the stalwart person he was. For seeking out Jack Colton—for traveling all these miles; for living for revenge. Perhaps revenge was sweet, after all.

"You were invited with the woman; you can get inside the palace, my people cannot. But you, you can!" The Arab was speaking frantically.

"Wait, wait. Just hold on."

"We must find the Jewel!" he screamed wildly.

"What jewel?" Ralph asked. Shit! He wished this Arab would cut the hearts and flowers about Jack's girl friend and get to the meat of the matter.

"The Jewel of the Nile. Our most holy Jewel."

"Oh," Ralph said with a knowledgeable smirk. "*That* jewel. Sure, I heard of that jewel. And it's been stolen?" Ralph looked at Tarak. There was no way Ralph was going to let Jack slip through his fingers this time. If Jack was going up the Nile, then so was he. One way or the other, Ralph did not intend to come up empty-handed. He'd done that once, and Ira had pissed all over him. But not again. He'd come too far, lived through too much to be anybody's second banana.

Jack shook his head in amazement. He was surrounded by weirdos! First this midget gangster jumps out at him from his Fritos box, and then Ali Baba materializes out of thin air doing a knife-throwing act. Jack's head was pounding from all the booze he'd consumed, and to top it all off he'd lost his lady. It had been a rotten day.

He turned to Tarak. "Look, I don't know where you're from and I sure as hell don't know what you're on, but I'm sailing. Tonight."

Tarak was insistent, and grabbed Jack's arm. His voice was steely when he spoke. "Your friend is in danger, as are my countrymen. Omar is a false prophet who trades lives for power—and with the Jewel in his hands, nothing can stop him."

"That scum," Ralph said. "I spit on him. You show us where to go, we'll get your jewel back." Ralph wasn't about to lose this chance—this golden chance at a treasure. Jack or no Jack.

Jack waved them both away. He didn't want any

more to do with Arabs or jewels. He'd had enough treasure hunts for a lifetime. He was nursing a battered heart. He just wanted oblivion.

"Look, ah, Tarak, love to help. Maybe next month. Call me."

Jack turned to leave, but Tarak grabbed his shoulders. He was stronger than Jack had thought.

"No, now! His proclamation is in three days!"

Jack threw him off. "Come on, Angelina, we're leaving."

Jack started toward his boat. Suddenly, there was a tremendous explosion. Flames shot into the air, licking the night sky with crimson tongues. Jack, Ralph and Tarak dove for cover behind the crates.

Teak boards, splinters, flaming sails and debris shot into the air as another explosion occurred. There was fire everywhere.

Jack was stunned as he watched a board with a gold-painted "ANG" go skimming across the sea. His dream was shattered and raining down around him in ashes and flame. This was a nightmare! His Angelina! It was as if Joan had turned the hands of fate against him. When she left she'd taken everything. Now he didn't even have his Angelina.

"No . . . Angelina . . ." he whimpered.

How could this be happening? Jack hadn't been careless with anything on board that could cause this disaster. He had always been scrupulous when it came to the *Angelina*. Joan had done the same. It made no sense. He looked into the air, now filled with billowing black smoke. He could hear excited voices on shore and other boaters scrambling to their decks to see the spectacle. She was gone.

Ralph was stunned. "The boat blew up. THE BOAT BLEW UP!" Ralph grabbed Jack's lapels. "I coulda been killed!"

Jack threw him off and stood. He stared at the ruins, devastated. "Who . . . Who would do this?"

"Omar would do this. In case you interfered. In case you didn't. It would make no matter to him. And if the writer woman had refused him, he would not have wanted her to live."

Jack stepped to the end of the dock and watched the remainder of his destroyed yacht sink into the harbor. He should have trusted his instincts. He had been right about Omar. But Omar was more than a "bullshit artist"—a whole lot more. If Omar was capable of this kind of destruction without real motive, Jack wondered what he would do if he were angered. Jack hoped he wouldn't be too late to save Joan.

"I will take you to Omar," Tarak said.

"I'm comin' too," Ralph piped up.

"The hell you are!"

"Colton, ain't you forgettin' somethin'? I got everything you own . . . partner. Wherever you go, I go. So, where're we goin'?"

"Africa."

Chapter Seven

JOAN LOOKED DOWN FROM THE HELICOPTER at the long line of African women wearing traditional gabbis, those long swaths of cotton material forming cape and turban. They carried huge bundles of twigs on their heads. There were no cars or trucks on the dusty narrow path, no evidence they desired a modern alternative to their ancient ways. They moved slowly, and Joan thought they looked like a serpent slithering out from the underbrush. They were oblivious to the helicopter's roar as it swooped past them and headed into the sun.

Circling over the city, Joan saw a few scattered trees, red clay ground and tiny huts with thatched roofs huddled in small clusters. She wasn't impressed until the helicopter turned to the left. There, like huge flat slabs of marble, the walls of the city rose to the sun. The tops of the walls were carved and decorated with ancient markings. On the centermost area, two domes made of shiny brass reflected the sunlight. Wind, rain, sandstorms and time had worn away much of the painted decoration around the city gates, but even from her vantage point, Joan could see that the artwork was extraordinary.

As the helicopter floated over the city, bells tolled and strange-sounding clappers announced their arrival. She saw tunic-garbed men dash out of cafes and buildings into the streets and point to the sky. She was surprised when they flew over the city to the northernmost outskirts to land.

The pilot received signals from the ground crew and began his descent.

A long airstrip, newly paved and lined with enough lights to rival La Guardia came into view. On either side of the airstrip were huge fields filled with rows of military equipment. There were Jeeps, Chevy trucks, fire engines, Ford vans, armored vehicles and desert half-tracks. Joan saw Soviet-made T-62 main battle tanks—the same kind she'd seen on *60 Minutes*. Omar's loyalties could easily be bought, she thought.

Joan checked her camera and put it around her neck and then held onto her seat during the bumpy landing. Sand and dust whirled around them, blinding her vision as they darted for the Mercedes roadster convertible that was waiting for them. She thought an air-conditioned sedan would have been more suitable. She choked on the dust as the helicopter shut down.

"Is this all yours?"

"Yes," Omar replied.

Joan looked to the end of the runway where an F-16 was parked. It was shiny, sleek and brand-new. She could almost bet money it had just been delivered. She held up her camera to snap a picture of it, but Rashid, the bodyguard with the scarred face, stepped in front of her. She lowered the camera and smiled sheepishly. Rashid's icy glare continued.

Omar put his arm on Joan's shoulder. "Why point out the negative? There'll be no need for this in a few days." Gently, but quite firmly, he ushered her to the car. "Come, let me show you to the real village."

Joan climbed into the car and sat in the back next to Omar, but all the while she was acutely aware of Rashid's glaring eyes.

They rode through a stone archway into the main Suq of the village. The marketplace was filled with merchants and villagers. At first Joan thought it was like a scene out of *Casablanca* with the natives bartering for goods. She saw filigreed brass and copper trays, ornamental bowls and urns. There were beautiful hand-painted tiles and pottery. Dresses, tunics and shawls dyed every color in the spectrum hung from wooden pegs on sunbaked clay walls. Children sat in the sun, their knees pulled up under their chins.

But as the "advance car" honked its horn announcing Omar's procession, she noticed the natives began to line the streets, making room for them to pass. They chanted Omar's name in low, lethargic tones. As the roadster drove farther, she noticed the smiles were gone from their faces and their eyes were dull. Looking farther into the crowds, Joan saw fierce-looking soldiers in desert camouflage fatigues bearing rifles. Straining a bit, Joan noticed the bodyguard in the "advance car" shouting orders to the soldiers. Suddenly, the villagers' chant became louder.

Plastered on the clay walls above straw-roofed stalls, Joan saw Omar's picture. The farther they drove, the more abundant were the posters and pictures of Omar.

Omar waved to his subjects, an egotistical smile on his face. "My people love me. I am blessed."

Joan looked again at one of the soldiers as he rammed a rifle butt into an old man's back.

"Yeah, they all seem so . . . enthusiastic."

Just then Omar pointed to a small boy dressed almost in rags. His brown eyes were vacant and seemed to fill his face, he was so thin. His mother had shoved Omar's poster into his hands.

"There. There I have a good shot for you. A little boy holding up my picture."

"Yes. That's wonderful." Joan hoped he couldn't feel her tension. She was starting to shake so much she didn't think the picture would turn out.

"The best day to come to the Suq is on Thursday," Omar said.

BANG! Joan heard what she thought was an engine backfiring. Instantly, Omar dove for cover. Joan looked down at him, scrunched in a ball on the floorboards of the car. Joan glanced around and saw what looked like a wave of soldiers step out from the crowd inspecting the people for a possible assassin. She was amazed at their number. She couldn't help wondering why it took so many to safeguard just one.

The roadster was instantly surrounded by camouflage-shirted men. Joan peered between them to watch the crowd become silent and still. There was a long pause when she would have sworn no one, including her, even breathed.

Just then the driver of the last vehicle in the motorcade shouted something in his native tongue. She saw the backs of the soldiers relax and heard them mumble to one another. It was just as she'd thought, only a backfiring motor. There was no danger.

Omar quickly sat up as if nothing had happened and resumed his conversation right where he left off. Joan's mouth gaped as he continued waving to the crowd who also took up their dull chant.

". . . Thursday the people come from miles around to sell their wares. It's very colorful." Omar pointed ahead of them. "Ah, my home."

Joan squinted her eyes trying to see the palace. She had envisioned something made of white-painted lattice, stucco towers and lush gardens. Instead she faced an unimpressive, almost formless structure. It was framed with two long walls, one of which had an old tower attached to it. Though the structure appeared to be new, the tower was in need of repair. It was possible he was not finished with it yet, she thought. It looked like a glop of clay, unfashioned and ready for the artisans. As they drove up and through the crude gate, Joan wondered if the village children had constructed this place. Omar certainly had not used union labor.

"I can only assume what a writer of your stature is used to, but we will try to make you comfortable." Omar put great emphasis on the last word.

The Mercedes roadster pulled to a stop at the front door, a simple flat piece of wood with a cast-iron handle. Omar helped Joan out of the car, and as he held her hand, Joan distinctly thought he'd squeezed it just the way he had at the hotel. His soldiers snapped to attention in his presence. He saluted them, but his manner was easygoing. He continued to keep his hand on the small of her back, guiding her through the door.

Joan almost felt as if that hand were burning a hole

in her. And, there was something about the way he looked at her. It was more than desire as she'd initially thought. He wanted her, not only sexually but as one of his possessions.

The moment Joan stepped through the door, she felt as if she had entered another world. Outside she'd found neglect, hunger and poverty. Here were glittering gold and pink marble tiled floors, delicately frescoed walls and priceless antique furniture. Italianate cornices, molding and columns framed the doorways off the main hall. With every turn, Joan saw reflections of the past, from the days when Africa had been ruled by the French, Italian and British Empires. She recognized an eleventh-century tapestry on a long wall as being one that had disappeared from Narga Selassie Church at Lake Tana, an Ethiopian Orthodox church. There were Austrian rococo mirrors and mahogany cabinets filled with delicate Venetian crystal. Three matching brass chandeliers containing thousands of tear-shaped prisms dangled above the main hall. Carved marble statues from the thirteenth and fourteenth centuries lined the hall, and she noticed that each was turned to the right just slightly, so as to pay homage to the one who reigned in this room.

Joan looked straight ahead and saw black marble steps rise to a platform where an enormous oil portrait of Omar was lit by two rows of track lights. Joan was astounded at the luxury and frightened by the man.

She looked at Omar. His black eyes gleamed with anticipation. He wanted her to be impressed. She thought him even more strange then. She was only a novelist. It made no sense to her why he should consider her opinion of his home as important. But as she looked deeper into his eyes, she knew she was not mistaken. Her reaction was important to him. She felt it imperative she give him what he wanted.

"I have a genuine Degas horse in the library. When you freshen up, you must come and see it. Are you familiar with the Impressionists?"

"The Impressionists . . . Yes, they're wonderful." If he'd read any of her books he would have known she loved the Impressionists. Omar was clearly baiting her, but she didn't know why.

"It's one of my ambitions to have the largest collection of Impressionist work outside of Europe."

Joan's eyebrows shot up. She wondered if he would buy them, or simply steal them as he had the tapestry.

"Where is the sacred garden?" she asked.

"The sacred garden? In my imagination."

Joan noted the sultry look in his eyes. Brother! She'd sure been stupid to fall for that one. He walked toward her, taking her hand again and leading her to the fabulous curving staircase. It reminded her of the one they'd seen at the Ritz Hotel. She'd better check right away and make sure this wasn't stolen, too.

Just as she placed her foot on the first step, a blood-curdling scream filled the hall. It came from inside the palace.

"What was that?" Joan felt her nerves prick.

Omar paused for a second, not answering her directly. He cocked his head, waiting to hear it again. "I don't know," he finally said.

Joan glared at him. He better not say it was the wind, as her father used to when she'd wake up in the middle of the night complaining of strange noises.

"Come," Omar said, going up the staircase. "You like the carpeting? It's new."

They went down a wide hall papered in damask and newly painted. He stopped at the third door on the right.

"I hope this is satisfactory." Omar opened the door.

Good Lord! she thought, gazing around at the splendor. If this was a room at the Plaza Hotel, it would go for a thousand a night. The king-size canopy bed was draped in easily a hundred yards of cotton—no, she touched the material: it was silk! The bedspread, the ruffled shams, the dust ruffle, the curtains were all white silk. Even the Plaza didn't—that couldn't be a *real* Chippendale chaise, but it was. And the nightstands, the pullaway steps to the bed and the dresser were all Honduran mahogany. It was her guess they were circa late 1700's and probably came from the Bahamas. She'd read enough *Antiques World* magazines to know that much. This was incredible. This was a room she'd dreamed of all her life. She looked at Omar—how had he known?

At the other end of the room was a Queen Anne library table which completely dwarfed the IBM Selectric sitting atop it. From her desk she could look out the window onto a beautifully planted courtyard below. In pots, planters and flower beds were blooming pink geraniums, azaleas, jasmine and white camelias. Who could ask for more?

"Yes, this will be . . . okay, fine."

Omar crossed to the desk.

"This is where you will write your masterpiece."

"I . . . I have some questions."

"The writer is already at work. Good. Explore your

new world. Feel free to go anywhere, see anything, talk to anyone. I'm glad you're here, Joan. Together we will make history."

Omar turned and left the room, leaving her alone.

Joan looked around her at the opulent room. It was the most fashionable cell a woman could want. But that was just how she felt. It was his last words that frightened her the most. Omar wanted more from her than just her body. He *had* wanted someone to chronicle his story for him, but not the truth. She knew now she would never be able to write the truth. He wanted her to fictionalize him; make him into a hero, a god.

Joan dashed to the door and opened it. Five of Omar's uniformed guards snapped to attention. Their rifles gleamed brightly, looking bigger and more lethal somehow. Joan closed the door, thinking it was only her imagination.

She went over to her desk, and for the first time noticed the dozen or so framed pictures on the wall. They were all of Omar at different stages of his life. He was an uninteresting baby, she thought; but as he grew, he reminded her of the little boy she'd seen in the Suq today. He'd been thin and his clothes were not much better than rags. It was the third picture that haunted her. He must have been about five then. It was the first picture where his startling good looks were apparent, though his nose had been much broader then and in the subsequent pictures taken during his teen years. Rhinoplasty? she wondered. Michael Jackson had his nose thinned. But it wasn't his nose that caught her attention. It was the eyes. There was a desire, a determination that was apparent even on film. It was the same kind of fire she'd seen in pictures of Cornelius Vanderbilt, a young Howard Hughes and J. Paul Getty. As she looked at the photos, she could see that Omar had been a poor boy wanting to be rich. Except that Omar had chosen a very dangerous route to win his money and power.

Just then a sweet, haunting melody being played on an old Arabic flute wafted into the room. It was a mournful sound, and it drew Joan to the window. She peered out into the courtyard, hoping to see the musician. There was no one save a gardener picking the brown leaves off the geraniums. He straightened and looked at her. He didn't smile, only walked over to a far wall where a hose was hooked up and began spraying the plants.

The music continued. Joan leaned out the window, supporting her face in her hands. She realized that the music was coming from the tower across the way. In the highest level on the back side, Joan could now see a small square window with vertical bars. There was no glass to block the music.

The sad tune only depressed her more. She glanced at the IBM, wondering how she could write Omar's story. He was more clever than she'd thought. He'd played on her vanity and vulnerability, hoping he could get her to write another piece of fiction, not a journalistic work. If she told the truth, she would never get out of here alive. She wondered about her fate if she did as he wanted.

Joan couldn't help thinking about Jack and the *Angelina*. Thank God he hadn't come with her. It was bad enough she'd gotten herself in this fix. She would never have forgiven herself if she'd dragged Jack into this danger.

She wondered if he'd left Monte Carlo. She supposed he was headed for Greece by now. She should have listened to him and stayed with him, but in the end it would have all turned out the same, anyway. Jack had made it clear he didn't want her. He must have had a good laugh every time he saw her practically swoon when he walked into view. He had exercised a lot of power over her—the power of love. She'd given it to him willingly, but he'd never done anything with it. Never wanted anything more than to sail from port to port. He'd never wanted anything permanent with her. Not a future. She'd seen him hang onto a Heineken longer than he hung onto her. Joan couldn't fight her tears anymore. She slammed her fist on the windowsill and wished this sinking pain inside her would go away. But she knew it would be around for a long, long time.

"Damn Jack Colton."

Chapter Eight

A SILVER PAN AM 727 NOSED DOWN ONTO THE runway at the Sudan International Airport. A member of the ground crew directed the huge jet to the assigned parking spot near the one-story terminal. A man wearing a blue windbreaker, orange cap and earphones drove a cart with a trailer attached. On the trailer were the portable steps for the passengers. The door to the plane popped open and the passengers began disembarking. Jack was the last off the plane following Ralph and Tarak.

The terminal was crowded with dark-skinned African men and women wearing traditional garb and carrying ... designer luggage. Jack looked around at the fairly modern facility. It couldn't be more than eight years old. It was probably thrown up in less than a week by some American oil company for their employees and executives. The walls were plastered with lighted Hertz and Avis posters. There were advertisements for Host International and McDonald's. Jack saw American candy bar and cigarette machines and a stand-up hot dog place. It looked more like Arizona than Africa.

Jack walked outside where taxis, buses and limousines were parked waiting for their fares. Jack saw little children begging travelers for money or candy. There were dark old men in fezzes watching natives and tourists filter through the terminal. A Sudanese bus driver wearing a red fez held a sign bearing the name of "Mr. Tortelli." As the passengers passed by him, his face wore a worried look. It looked to Jack as if Mr. Tortelli didn't make the flight.

Jack, Tarak and Ralph made their way through the noisy crowd.

Ralph unbuttoned his top shirt button. "Hot. Why do these Third World stinkholes always gotta be so hot?"

Just then the bus driver raced up to them. "Mr. Tortelli?" he inquired of Ralph.

Ralph swatted the sign away. "Get the hell outta here, conehead."

Jack turned to Tarak. "Where are your brothers?"

"They'll be here," Tarak assured him.

Tarak stopped dead-still, threw his head back and sounded the high-pitched dervish cry. Jack threw his hands over his ears before his eardrums were split. Tarak's cry was returned by several voices.

A band of desert dervishes dressed in traditional caftans rushed to Tarak. Their faces were filled with joy as they embraced one another. They whirled each other around, their colorful capes slapping Ralph in the face.

"Oh, Colton," Ralph sneered, "I can see we've hitched our wagon to a star."

"We go to Omar!" Tarak announced suddenly, full of energy and not mindful of his shoulder wound.

The dervishes rushed off.

Ralph looked at Jack. "This jewel better be worth a friggin' fortune."

As passengers climbed into the buses and taxis filled with luggage and affluent Africans pulled away, Jack noticed the Sudanese bus driver had found his Mr. Tortelli. Late-model American cars parked under the roofed parking area nearest the terminal pulled away as American businessmen basked in their air-conditioned comfort.

"I can imagine how these psychos drive," Ralph said, wondering where Tarak had parked their car.

The dervishes moved away from the last bus. Jack stepped out of the way as the bus cranked up its rickety engine, sputtered, and then with a grinding noise drove away.

Jack had a clear sight of the dervishes as they crossed the parking lot to a pack of awaiting camels. Jack put his arm around Ralph.

"Hold on to what you've got. It's gonna be a rough ride."

The sun riddled the Suq with heat as Joan picked her way from stall to stall. She inspected a China-blue piece of silk banded with a gold-worked border. Elaine would love this, she thought. It would be perfect with her eyes. She tried to barter with the native, but she didn't speak the language. She paid him and knew from the expression on his face she could have bought it for less. In the next stall were beautiful green, teal and jade beads. The woman vendor explained through sign language that Joan could design her own necklace by chosing the stones she liked. The woman would then string the beads and attach the clasp. Joan spent painstaking moments choosing just the right ones. For the clasp she chose a gemstone that reminded her very much of an emerald. When she handed it to the woman, she thought of Jack.

She wished he were standing here with her. He would have loved this. This Suq was his kind of exotica. She couldn't believe it. Here she was, buying souvenirs, just the thing he'd always done and she'd thought it so trite, so . . . sentimental. And so like Jack.

The cafes in the Suq were flat-walled and windowless buildings sporting only a front door and painted hieroglyphics over the entry. Early in the morning the proprietor placed two or three small round tables and chairs outside. Old men dressed in bright caftans would then be seated for their coffee. It was a strong thick drink that the waiter poured from a long-necked copper pot—and from nearly four feet away. It was like watching a floor show, Joan thought.

As she walked along, she saw a snake charmer, a basket weaver, a glass etcher, and everywhere were wary, mysterious faces. She was unsure if their distrust of her was because she was American, or because they'd seen her with Omar. Unless she approached a vendor with intentions to buy, nearly all these people shied away from her. Some had even turned their backs so as not to speak to her at all. She'd never felt so ostracized in her life.

There were no other Americans, or even Caucasians, in the crowd. But Joan knew her nationality had nothing to do with it. She turned around. The natives feared the five guards who followed her.

She hadn't been able to make a single move without these men. She'd gotten up in the middle of the night, thinking surely there was a kitchen someplace in the palace where she could get something to eat. When she went to the door, the first guard had said he would bring her what she wanted.

She told him she wanted to raid the icebox, but he didn't understand. He also didn't understand that she had no idea what she was hungry *for,* only that she was hungry. What she wouldn't have given just to stand in front of a refrigerator and stare at the interior. It was her favorite pastime. Finally, she'd gone back to bed. Hungry and frustrated.

In the morning, she'd gone for a stroll in the courtyard. They had followed her there . . . and to the breakfast room where she'd eaten alone and in silence.

She turned around and looked at them. Why did they all have to follow her? Wasn't one enough?

"Would you mind if I walked through the marketplace alone for a little while?"

One of the guards waved her ahead. He smiled cordially.

"Thank you," Joan said, smiling and relieved she wouldn't have her pack of basset hounds on her trail anymore.

She went to the brass vendor's tent. She'd been eyeing these goodies all afternoon. She picked up an unusually shaped oil lamp. It was like Aladdin's lamp, she thought as she held it up to the sunlight. Just then she realized that the guards hadn't left her at all. She put the lamp down and started walking away.

The guards continued to follow her as she turned a corner. Just ahead was a young boy of about twelve years spray-painting something in neon-yellow letters on the clay wall. Joan couldn't read what it was. Arabic graffiti had never been one of her strong points.

Suddenly, Joan heard one of the guards yell something at the boy. The boy spun and saw the menacing uniforms and shiny rifles. Instantly, he dropped his spray paint can and took off running.

The guards did not take up the chase as Joan had expected, but instead dropped to their knees, raised their rifles, aimed them and opened fire on the graffiti-covered wall.

Bullets and hunks of clay wall flew through the air. Joan nearly jumped out of her skin. She tried to scream, but nothing came out. She shut her eyes while the crack and ping of automatic weapons assaulted her ears. She heard the villagers screaming in terror. Suddenly, everyone was running for cover, ducking behind tables, crates and ox carts.

Joan was practically in the middle of the gunfire and had no place to go. She was certain she would be hit by a ricocheting bullet. Joan thought soon the wall would simply explode.

Joan slammed her hands over her ears. "Stop!" she screamed at the guards. "What are you doing? Stop!" But they couldn't or wouldn't listen to her. Pieces of clay wall flew into her face. Joan touched her cheek. It was bleeding.

Finally, the guards ceased fire as a huge cloud of smoke settled over the area. Slowly, the villagers rose from their hiding places and resumed their work as if nothing had happened. Joan was incredulous. This was their town. How could they let these men bully them this way?

Joan rushed over to the head soldier. She put her face next to his. She was not intimidated in the least.

"Why did you shoot that? What was he doing? What did that say?"

The soldier's face was implacable. He said nothing and walked away.

Joan grabbed a villager, the old woman who was selling mangoes. "Why did they shoot that? What did that say?"

But the old woman only shook her head and slinked away. She pretended she didn't understand Joan. But Joan had seen the look in the old woman's eyes. She may not have known Sudanese, but Joan knew fear when she saw it.

Joan still would not give up. She grabbed another villager. He was a young man about thirty. The kind with family and responsibilities.

"What was he writing?" Joan demanded. "What was he writing?"

The man peeled her arm off his and moved away. There was a ferocity in his eyes coupled with shame. Joan felt she was getting close. Maybe he would tell her later, when the guards were not around.

From the midst of the crowd behind her came a voice.

"Return the Jewel."

Joan spun around in time to see an old man's head pop back into the crowd. She couldn't see him now.

"Return the jewel? What jewel?" she asked of the crowd. Suddenly, she realized there was not as much language barrier here as she'd thought.

The guards went over to Joan and picked her up by

her elbows. They lifted her off the ground and moved off with her.

"Hey! What are you doing? Le me go! Let me go! I'm a guest here!"

With one guard in front of her elbowing the villagers out of the way with his rifle, the guards moved through the crowd with Joan. The more she seemed to struggle, the more they tightened their grip until she thought they would crush her joints. She started kicking and demanding they put her down, but they would not relinquish their hold.

Omar gazed at his reflection in the lighted mirror. He watched as the makeup man carefully applied dark contour powder beneath his high cheekbones and then, with a fatter camel's-hair brush, applied a bronze tint to his entire face. Omar scrupulously analyzed the effect. His skin glowed but looked natural. It was very important the makeup not show. His people could not understand or accept the idea of a man wearing makeup. But he was wiser than they. He smiled at his reflection. And, he thought, he was more beautiful.

The makeup man plucked a few stray eyebrows over the bridge of Omar's nose. Then he applied black kohl around Omar's huge round eyes. The makeup man used a Q-tip to correct his mistakes. It was difficult to work around Omar's thick black lashes.

Omar opened his eyes. "No more eyeliner. I'm not Valentino."

The makeup man bowed and removed the large plastic cape he'd placed over Omar to protect his uniform. It was an elaborate and costly uniform. There was none like it in the rest of the world. Omar had expressly hired Yves St. Laurent to design it for him. The material of the pants and jacket were a deep royal blue blend of cotton and silk. It was an unusual blue, the blue of the dark Sahara night just as the sun sets, Omar thought. Each of his buttons was solid gold, and in the center was a blue sapphire. He wore a red-orange sash around his waist and gold epaulettes on his shoulders. Though he'd never been in formal military service, Omar believed he'd waged enough wars in the streets during his younger years to warrant the ribbons and decorations he wore on his chest. To this day, it surprised him that no one asked where they'd come from or what they meant. If they did, he would have them—the inquirer, not the ribbons—"removed."

Adjusting the towel around Omar's neck, the makeup man inspected his work. He said "tsk-tsk" and spun around and dabbed a tiny brush into a pot of brown eye shadow. With light flecks he applied the shadow, which made Omar's eyes seem even more penetrating. Omar analyzed the effect. He liked it, but was it too much for the cameras?

Just then there was a knock on the door. Omar turned to see Joan.

She was dressed in a loose-fitting white cotton jumpsuit that was belted with a deep raspberry sash. She had a smaller waist than he'd thought, and he liked the way the folds of the material fell over her hips and derriere. Her blond hair was loose and flowing down her back. He loved the way Western women dressed, but it would be dangerous to see a great trend toward Westernization in his country. He needed the men and women to remain as they were—his chattel.

She looked agitated as she walked toward him with

long, confident strides. Her eyes were determined. Omar sensed something was wrong.

"Joan, come in, sit down. I'm just being made up for my daily television broadcast. There is this hunger among my people for what I do, what I think. Do my eyes look too dark to you?"

"No . . ." she said, looking at him. She hadn't realized before that he wore makeup. "They're fine."

"Good, good. Are you enjoying yourself?" he asked politely. His eyes gleamed at her, filled with concern that she be comfortable, her needs cared for.

Joan thought he sounded more like a hotel manager than Omar, the chosen one. She hoped he could not tell she was upset. She hoped he couldn't see the fear in her eyes. She'd made a lot of mistakes in her lifetime, but she'd never been this foolish before. She'd placed herself in a great deal of danger by falling prey to Omar's charm. He'd played her like an instrument, using her confusion over her writing to get her to come here. None of this was like her. Joan didn't make decisions quickly. She'd been known to take days deciding what movie to see on a weekend, and she'd accepted Omar's proposal in less than two hours.

The incident this afternoon confirmed her feelings from last night. She'd gotten in way over her head. Maybe Shana Alexander could get her kicks out of this kind of work, but Joan realized now that she was best off in the land of make-believe.

She only hoped she *could* get out of this.

"Oh, yes, everything is just . . . just fine. In fact, it makes what I have to say that much harder. I suddenly realized that I have to be in New York by Thursday night. You know, with travel and making connections and everything...I guess I got my dates mixed up, but on the twenty-third I'm contracted to be at a book fair. It's a once-a-year event; my circulation depends on it; and as much as I'd love to stay for your proclamation, I'm afraid I'm going to have to go."

She hoped she sounded earnest and not frightened. She had tried to keep it light.

"You can't leave," he said flatly.

"I have to. But if you send me all the information, I'll still be happy to write the book." She sensed his ego needed assuaging. After all, this man just asked her if he wore too much eyeliner.

"This is most distressing."

"Imagine how I feel," she laughed. Quickly, her smile faded. He wasn't buying it.

"You have to stay."

"If Mailer and Bellow and Updike have to show up, I certainly have to." She was reaching, but she felt this was life and death.

Omar rose and took Joan's hand. He was the charming Omar now. Cool, smiling and sultry.

"Joan, I am not a man as you know them. I have been chosen by heaven to be the redeemer. In two nights you will see."

"I can't. I'd love to, but..."

Suddenly, his eyes narrowed, almost looking red. Joan had gone too far.

"I think if you will ask around you will find that I have never taken no for an answer."

Joan was speechless. Was this the "deal she couldn't refuse"? Just what *was* he going to do with her? she wondered.

Omar took off his towel and tossed it—a bit too

forcefully, she thought—onto the chair. His voice was tight when he spoke. His anger was clearly directed at Joan.

"Now, if you will excuse me . . . my people."

He turned and headed for the door.

"What is the jewel?" Joan blurted. She was surprised she'd even said it aloud. But she had to know. He was already angry with her, she might as well go all the way.

He stopped and cocked his head toward her. His eyes were deadly serious and there was no smile on his lips.

"The Jewel. Yes, I thought you might ask. The Jewel is a legend. I am real."

In Mexico this time of day, when the afternoon sun beat down on the marketplace, the custom was for the villagers and vendors to take a siesta. In Omar's village, when the Suq was shut down completely . . . it was time for *Dynasty*. In one bazaar after another, American and Japanese-made television sets were tuned in to a dubbed Alexis Carrington battling it out with Krystal. Munching on native fruits, Hershey bars and barbeque-flavored Fritos, Omar's subjects were engrossed in the story. The women pointed to Krystal's silver lamé Nolan Miller gown, approving of the wide, padded shoulders. The younger woman villager adjusted her veil, trying to get more comfortable. The older woman next to her made a comment about the freedom American women had in their clothing.

Just as Alexis lunged toward Krystal in what was meant to be hand-to-hand combat, the screen went black for a moment. Instead of resuming with the fight between Krystal and Alexis—a moment the villagers had been awaiting for two weeks—they now viewed Omar's smiling face.

From every bazaar, every tent and every stall in the Suq went out loud groans, moans and angry catcalls. Omar's people were not as hungry for his word as he believed.

Oceans of sand rose in peaks and waves to form magnificent golden mountains in the Sahara. The chameleon desert was blazed with fiery reds, oranges and russet from a setting sun so huge it seemed to swallow the earth. Through swaying ripples of heat rising from the dunes marched a caravan of camels. They were over a dozen in number, their dress, mode of travel and habits all descended from an ancient civilization.

Suddenly, the lead camel stopped, his golden tassels and bridle swaying about his solemn face. The rider threw his head back and sounded the piercing dervish cry. The stillness of the Sahara shattered around them, but none in the caravan reacted save the two riders on the last—and smallest—camel.

Jack kneed the camel, hoping it would pick up the pace, but nothing seemed to work. He should have brought spurs, Jack thought. They had been riding through the desert for hours with only one stop at an oasis around noon. Jack had never thought much about an oasis before. Even in Colombia, he was never really too far from a village where he could get a beer. When they'd finally reached the small grassy area surrounded by palm trees, he thought he'd found paradise. Never had water tasted that good. They had rested for almost two hours. The heat of the noon sun would be too much, Tarak had said. Jack touched his nose. It was burned to a crisp, even with wearing a hat. He couldn't help thinking of Joan's nosekote. And of Joan.

He kneed the camel again. He thought about the nights they'd made love under the stars, the way she laughed at the trinkets he bought in one fishing village after another. He thought of her in Paris, trying on couture gowns and sharing croissants in a tiny café on the Left Bank. He remembered the way she would watch him shave in the morning and the way she tickled his feet. Mostly, he remembered holding her, feeling her heart beat against his chest, reaffirming that she was alive and very much with him. And through every leg of this journey, he could hear her voice in his head telling him she loved him. Maybe he could escape the visions of her, but always, always her voice would haunt him.

It was well after sunset when they arrived at the dervish camp. It was a large camp with over a half-dozen multicolored tents erected in the middle of the desert. The largest tent was decorated with red, gold and black tassels hanging from a scalloped awning. Jack assumed this tent belonged to Tarak and his brothers, since they were the leaders of the tribe. Giant bonfires roared with long tongues of fire licking the dark sky. Crackling sparks rose into the air and spun around the camp looking like fireflies.

As they dismounted the camels, Jack noticed that the women and children racing toward them were all colorfully dressed in sheer silks and printed veils and tunics. The women wore a great deal of gold jewelry, even dangling medallions from their veils and head scarves.

He heard the sound of flutes, tambourines, drums and woodwinds. Dancers appeared from everywhere as well as jugglers and saber dancers. Whirling long, shiny swords in the air, young men dressed in harem pants, no shirt and turbans began a centuries-old ritual dance. Everyone, including the children, participated.

Jack noticed that everyone bowed and waved to Tarak as he made his way from his camel to the camp. One of the brothers leaped off his camel and was met by a beautiful woman and young boy. The brother reached into his knapsack and produced a ghetto blaster, complete with tape-to-tape recorder. The young boy squealed with delight and motioned to his friends. Half a dozen children came running over to the brother. They embraced their father, and then with his signal, they took the ghetto blaster and raced away again. The brother looked down at the beautiful woman, peeled off her sheer veil and kissed her deeply.

Jack had to look away.

Just then Tarak walked up to Jack and Ralph.

"Come. We have food, we have drink."

"Do you have a toilet?" Ralph asked.

Tarak ignored him and turned to the tribe. "These are our friends from America. They are going to help us bring back the Jewel."

At Tarak's words, a loud cheer rose from the crowd. They rushed over to the camel and helped Jack and Ralph to the ground.

Several veiled girls took Jack's hand.

"All right. Rough trip, but now it's Miller time,"

he quipped as he rubbed his behind. He hoped they would have a long rest before the next camel ride.

The girls reached up to help Ralph off the camel, but he slapped them away.

"Get away. Don't touch me. The last thing I need is more shots."

Ralph started to follow the crowd and then realized, with every step, that his backside was not only sore, it was chafed. It would take an entire week of rest and salve to heal it. And Ralph didn't have a week, not if he wanted that stone. Just then the camel snorted at Ralph. Ralph looked around to see that no one was looking and went back and kicked the camel in the shins.

"That's for you, Mr. Ed."

Ralph turned to walk away when, suddenly, the camel spit Ralph right in the face! Growling, Ralph took out his handkerchief and wiped his face. This jewel better be worth everything he was going through.

The camp was alive with music, both that of the ritualistic tribal melody and the rhythm of Chaka Kahn's sultry voice coming from the ghetto blaster.

The children sprang to their feet and began break-dancing—nomad style. Several of Tarak's brothers took up their brightly colored balls and bats and began juggling to the tune.

Under the protection of Tarak, Jack and Ralph were invited to join him in his tent. The walls were festooned with long, colorful silks and gold chains. It was cool at night, and Tarak had given Jack a striped woolen tunic to wear. Around a portable brass-looking hibachi sat the elder leaders of the tribe. Though Jack had been introduced, he couldn't remember any of their names. He found that "sir" was accepted by all of them.

Tarak clapped his hands, and suddenly beautiful women clad in bright harem pants appeared bearing huge brass trays of food. There were dates stuffed with pecans, and cheese, fruits, melons, berries and nuts. There were fabulously spiced meats Jack could not discern were pork or lamb. Some had been roasted; others coated with flour, he thought, and fried. There were strange sausage patties, goat's cheese, and lots of wine.

Suddenly, the air was filled with flying knives, skewers, fruits and meat chunks. For a moment Jack was unsure if he was in danger or if this was a food fight. Then he realized that these people didn't pass food, they sort of juggled it to one another. He joined in the fun, grabbing fruits, meats and vegetables to create his own shish kebab. He placed his skewer on the hibachi. He waited while a girl filled his gold goblet with wine.

Tarak was chatting with the women and men. Dancing girls came into the room playing tambourines and flutes. Jack's eyes were wide, watching utensils fly in front of him and dancing girls begin shedding one veil after another.

Tarak was half-drunk when he leaned over to Jack.

"We dance, we sing, we celebrate our oneness with heaven. This is the dervish path."

Ralph elbowed Jack. "Will you look at these guys? No sheep is safe tonight."

Tarak took a long gulp of wine. Suddenly, he seemed instantly sober. "In the desert there are many different tribes with many different ways, and yet, before Omar's men took away our Jewel, we all managed to live together. Now there is only suspicion and injustice."

Jack only nodded, absorbing everything Tarak said. Tarak continued.

"My brothers and I will take you to the outskirts of the village. We cannot go any farther. We are recognized as enemies and would be shot on sight. Help us find the Jewel and we will give you everything we own."

·Whispering, Ralph said to Jack, "Hear that Colton? What a deal. We spot their rock, and we get a set of steak knives."

"You better watch yourself. These guys catch you with their jewel, they're gonna cut you in half now and still come after you for six afterlives."

Ralph guffawed and waved Jack away. Who'd this Colton think he was scaring with all that bullshit? Ralph could remember days in Colombia with Zolo that were a whole lot worse than a bunch of Arab ignoramuses. As he thought about it, he was glad Colton was afraid. That meant he'd have a better chance at getting away with the stone and Colton's twenty grand.

Ralph took out a cigarette. "You let me worry about that," he said to Jack.

Ralph looked around for his Bic lighter, but his pockets were empty. Damn! Had he left it at the oasis? He checked his jacket pockets one more time.

The dervish seated next to him turned to Ralph and blew on the cigarette. A giant flame burst from the dervish's mouth, igniting Ralph's cigarette.

* * *

Three, four, five perfect smoke rings circled in the night air above Jack's head. He drew heavily on his cigarette and blew another. He looked up at the moon. He knew they were close to the equator, which was the reason why the moon looked like another planet zooming toward him. He'd heard about the desert moon, but always chalked up the stories about its size to exaggeration.

Jack looked over at the camp as everyone retired under the striped canopies. The fires dwindled to twinkling embers. All was quiet now, with only the low snorting camel sounds to break the stillness.

Jack had never been the hero type, but these people were looking to him to save their jewel. He shook his head. How had he gotten to this point?

He'd been mercenary in Colombia, always and only after the treasure, till he fell in love with Joan. Now, he was after a treasure again, but this time he *knew* he wouldn't be keeping the stone. There was no money in it for him this time. He'd meant what he'd said to Ralph about trying to make off with the dervishes' jewel. They would rip him to pieces. Jack didn't want anything to happen to Ralph. What a funny guy Ralph was. Jack almost felt protective toward him, too.

Jack wondered what had gotten into him lately. Two days ago he'd shunned even the idea of *talking* about the responsibility of marriage to Joan. And now here he was, trying to be a big brother to Ralph, a savior to a band of nomads whom he barely knew, *and* trying to save his Joan.

If she was his to save. Jack took out a snapshot of Joan he'd kept in his wallet. The only thing to survive from the *Angelina*. The moonlight illuminated the picture so that Joan's face stood out in relief. He'd been crazy to let her go. He should have confronted her right in front of Omar, Gloria and all those book snobs. Did she only want the adventure they'd found in Colombia? Is that what she'd needed so much? He should have asked her why she was rejecting him.

He didn't want to be a hero to these dervishes or to Joan. He wanted to be just a guy. Perhaps that had been the problem. Joan hadn't wanted just a man. Just Jack.

At this point he didn't care what she wanted. He wanted her and he was going to get her back. From what Tarak had told him thus far, it sounded dangerous. Jack knew he wouldn't have any trouble getting into the palace. It was getting out that was going to be difficult.

Jack hoped Joan was all right—that Omar hadn't done anything . . . Jack's hand tightened on the snapshot. If he'd done anything, touched one hair on her head . . .

Jack looked up at the moon again. Right now all he could do was pray.

Chapter Nine

JOAN GAZED AT THE SHIMMERING SILVER moon, thinking nothing could be that luminous. Strange, it was the same moon she'd looked at since she was a child; but ever since she'd met Jack, the moon was different somehow. Right now, she thought it the saddest thing she'd ever seen. She would give anything to feel Jack's arms around her right then and hear his voice. But that was an impossibility now. Jack didn't want her. At least he'd spared her the pain of not saying aloud that he didn't love her anymore. She knew those words would have haunted her all her life.

She wondered how many nights it would take to rid herself of the memory of him. She found she couldn't sleep in the bed. Every time she rolled over she put out her arms, thinking Jack would be there. But he wasn't. Last night she'd slept in the chaise. She would probably have to do the same tonight. And tomorrow night and all the nights until she finished Omar's book. The book...

There was no getting out of it now. She would have to make the best of the situation. She definitely saw

no way to escape. He'd posted another guard at her
door. As if five of those brutes weren't enough.

Joan leaned against the sill and looked at the moon
one last time before retiring. Just then she heard the
sound of a truck engine roaring into the square beyond
her tiny courtyard. Joan ran to the nightstand and flicked
off her lamp. She didn't want anyone to know she was
still awake. She went back to the window and peered
down at the square.

A big Jeep four-wheeler pulled into the square and
screeched to a halt. Quickly, it doused its headlights.
All the lights around the palace had been extinguished,
but by the light of the moon Joan could still see the
forms of two men as they hopped out of the Jeep. They
turned, and she could see their faces clearly. They were
Caucasian and both were in their mid-forties, she
guessed. They wore jumpsuits and baseball caps. Joan
thought them completely incongruent with everyone
else she'd seen since coming to Omar's palace.

A door below opened and two of Omar's guards
emerged, obviously to assist the other men. They went
around to the back of the Jeep and began unloading
equipment. There was a huge spool, nearly the size
of a kitchen table with thin wire wound on it. They
removed another spool and crates and cartons.

One of the men in jumpsuits dropped the spool he
was carrying, and barely missed his partner's foot.

"Goddamnit, J. T., get your head out of your ass,
boy," he shouted.

They were American! Joan nearly clapped her hands
in glee. She watched as they picked up the spools and
went about their chores.

At that moment Joan felt she had a big decision to

make. She could either sulk in her room thinking about Jack and refusing to do Omar's book, or she could go after the story she came here to write. Omar had wanted her to write about the "chosen one." It was obvious there was a story here, but it wasn't about Omar's spiritual powers.

Omar was a hoax, and she suspected he was more than just a bully. She sensed today, while he was being made up, that he would kill her if she got out of line. But Joan had no proof. A journalist, a real journalist, would find that proof. And then she would find a way to get out of this palace and expose Omar to the world.

Joan had told herself she wasn't a journalist, but she'd never really tried. Now was her chance. If her suspicions were correct, she had more to give the world than just a story. She might even be able to change events.

Joan crossed to the door and peeked out. All six guards snapped to attention. Quickly, she closed the door. She needed to investigate, but she'd already gone around with them once about letting her explore on her own.

She would have to find another way. She grabbed her Nikon camera, put it around her neck and climbed out her window onto the landing. She plastered her back against the wall. Suddenly, it looked a lot farther down to the ground than it had from inside. Cautiously, she edged her way along the landing to the staircase. Easing one foot at a time, Joan came to another window. She heard voices from inside—it was Omar and Rashid—and they were laughing.

She peeked into the room.

It was a large room, nearly twice the size of hers.

The walls were filled with pictures of Omar; a bronze bust of Omar sat on a marble pedestal in one corner and was lit with a spotlight. This wasn't a room, but a shrine.

The furniture was ornate Chinese with heavily black lacquered chests, desks and armoires everywhere. The bed was a monstrosity, rising ten feet high. It too was in the oriental motif. On the wall opposite her was a large map of the Sudan and Nile Valley. On the map were flag pins at several locations up and down the Nile.

Omar sat in a leather chair at his desk discussing the photographs in front of him. There were three stacks, but as yet Joan couldn't see them. Rashid peered over Omar's shoulder.

"Beautiful," Omar said, flipping through the pictures. "Beautiful." He flipped to another. "Ah, and this one. This is my favorite. If you didn't tell me that was once Rashid ben Amar, I would never know," he said, pleased.

Rashid laughed with him.

Omar took the photograph he liked so well and crossed to a bulletin board on the left wall. Joan had to lean a bit farther in to see what was happening, and when she did, she threw her hand over her mouth.

Omar pinned the picture next to another black-and-white glossy of a man hanging by a rope. It was ghastly. Next to that was a picture of a car in flames, another of a decapitated body. Omar not only hired political assassinations, he photographed them as well. He was more than demented, she thought. He was pure evil.

"Rashid, our enemies are gone. It's time to step forward and take the souls of the people."

A knock on the door was followed by Omar's signal for the person to enter. A guard peeked his head in.

"Are the Americans ready for me?" Omar asked, and the guard nodded.

"I will be right there," Omar said.

As the guard left, Omar glanced once again at his grisly gallery.

"This is still my favorite," he said to Rashid.

Then the two left the room.

Joan waited long enough to make certain the coast was clear. She climbed into the room and walked over to the map. These cities with the pins and flags must all mean something. The photographs were worse up close. Joan wanted to vomit, but instead, she took the cover off her camera lens and snapped as many shots of the map and photo gallery as she could. She peeked out the door, and seeing no guards to stop her, she made her way down the hall.

She saw no signs of Omar as she turned a corner and entered a large room. Her first thought was that he had come through here. She started across the parquet-floored room when suddenly she heard voices coming from the other side. Quickly, Joan ducked behind a column as almost a dozen women in beautiful chiffon and silk harem costumes entered the room. They were laughing and giggling. Joan was certain she had not been detected. One particularly gorgeous woman dashed to the far wall and pulled a cord. The long, flowing draperies parted to reveal a completely mirrored wall. The women began undressing. Their costumes fluttered into colorful puddles of fabric at their feet. To a woman, each was clad in tights and leotards—the latest in workout wear from America.

A woman dressed in fuchsia tights and a gray leotard opened an enormous wood cabinet.

She pushed a button, and out rolled a large Advent TV screen. She selected a videocassette, placed it in the recorder and turned the machine on.

Jane Fonda, pencil-thin and movie-star-gorgeous, filled the overly large television screen. Music filled the room along with Jane's voice leading her students in the workout.

Joan waited until the women had gone through the warmup and were sweating with the strenuous arm exercises before making her move. With the women engrossed in their workout, Joan raced to the next column and then the next until she was able to slip out of the room.

Once out of the workout room, Joan was able to make it across the courtyard without anyone's seeing her. It was deathly quiet, she thought, and there was no sign of Omar or Rashid. Joan peeked into a doorway, but saw no one down the open-air hallway. Just then that strange flute melody she'd heard the night before floated down from the high tower across the way.

Joan's curiosity about the music caused her to start toward the tower. She didn't think it had much to do with Omar, but the song was so sad. Then again, she thought, perhaps it had much to do with Omar.

She hadn't taken five steps when she heard a very strange mechanical buzzing coming from someplace below the palace. She turned and walked along the palace wall. The humming grew louder as she approached a grill almost at ground level. It was some kind of a basement, she thought as she knelt down.

The whirring noise was quite loud now. She peered into the grill.

Through the latticework, Joan saw part of a state-of-the-art, Rube Goldberg—like contraption. Bizarre-looking, it had disks, wheels, lights and wires coming out of it. She couldn't see where the wires went, only that there were hundreds of them. Red, blue, green and purple dials flashed off and on. Joan looked around the room. It was three times the size of the workout room in the palace. She guessed the N.Y. Knicks could hold their regional finals in this place.

There were three American technicians working on the monstrosity. Joan recognized the two from the Jeep, and now they were joined by another whom they called "Colt." He was adjusting wires. He took off his baseball cap, put on a pair of headphones and continued tinkering with the black and red wires.

The man Joan knew as J. T. held a remote control.

"How's that feel, Mr. Omar? Comfortable?"

Joan looked around, but she couldn't see Omar, though she heard his voice.

"The machine makes noise," Omar complained.

"With all the cheerin' and carryin' on, you'll never hear it," Colt assured Omar.

"Well, I think you're all set," Roy, the third man, said.

"I want you to have complete faith in us, Mr. Omar. We rigged the same basic effect for several motion pictures. In fact, Mr. Steve McQueen would not work without us." Colt proudly puffed out his chest when he spoke.

Joan strained her eyes. Omar had to be there some-where. If she could just see him, maybe she could figure out what was going on. She'd never seen a stereo set this huge. It reminded her of large twenty- or thirty-year-old computer data banks, but this wasn't a computer. She didn't know what it was.

"Did you ever meet Mr. McQueen?" Colt asked Omar, trying to keep it light.

"Get on with it," Omar boomed impatiently.

Colt made some adjustments to the remote control. "All right, Roy, take 'er away."

Roy twisted a dial on his remote control.

J. T. watched everything with a scrupulous eye. "Steady, steady . . ."

"Lookin' good. Lookin' good . . ." Colt said, encouraged.

Suddenly, there was a loud crash. Joan nearly jumped out of her skin.

"Aw, shit!" Roy slammed his hand against the dial and shut the machine down.

"Now, Mr. Omar, it's a delicate effect. You gotta give us a chance to work it out. I guarantee it's worked a hundred times."

Omar streaked into view, yelling.

"Rashid! I want to see him now!"

Joan quickly put her camera up against the grill and snapped a quick half-dozen pictures. No time for accuracy or focusing. She hoped just one would turn out. She could hear Omar and Rashid's thundering footsteps on some nearby stairs. Joan stood, and slammed her back against the wall just as Omar and Rashid emerged from the staircase that led underground. Joan didn't breathe as they strode past her and across the courtyard in the direction of the tower and the flute music.

She watched as they entered the wall below the tower. She hadn't seen the narrow door before, but now she raced toward it. Quietly, she entered the tower and shut the door behind her.

It was dark, almost too dark, and Joan stumbled twice trying to get to the first step. She was certain Omar and Rashid hadn't heard her, for they were still talking between them. Slowly, she followed them up the narrow, winding stairs, making certain she kept a good distance between them. She wanted to discover their destination, but she didn't want to be detected.

When she reached the top of the stairs, Joan saw a small hallway leading to a large wooden door with a tiny barred window in the door. It was a cell, a prison of some type. She wondered whom Omar would put in such a room. Who would be this important to Omar? She'd already seen that anyone he believed to be his enemy, he simply eliminated, much like pests. She could hear voices.

Omar and Rashid had gone inside the room, she thought. She decided not to go any closer. She circled around to the other side of the staircase and hid in the shadows. She strained her ears, trying to make out the conversation.

Omar's voice was excited and quite angry.

"Tell me how it is done!" he demanded.

Joan heard no answer. There was a loud slap. Then another. Still she heard nothing. She was certain Rashid was doing what he liked best, beating defenseless people.

"It's a miracle. It cannot be taught," a strained, though calm voice replied.

"I am losing patience!" Omar yelled.

Shoes scuffled and then the door to the cell opened. Joan panicked. There was no place to hide, and she'd waited too long to race down the stairs without being seen. The best she could do was shrink back into the shadows against the wall and pray they wouldn't see her.

With her back glued to the clay wall, Joan watched as Omar and Rashid left the cell, closed the door and headed down the stairs. She listened to their footsteps until she was certain they were at the end of the steps.

Slowly, she approached the door. She stood on her toes and peered through the tiny window. Sitting alone in the cell was a dark-skinned, bespectacled man. He was quite thin, with bare brown arms extending out of his soiled peasant shirt. He wore baggy pants that were tied with a rope around his narrow waist. She guessed him to be in his middle forties, though she wasn't sure at all. He could have been a hundred, for all she knew. His hair was thin, curly and unkempt. He sat cross-legged, playing his flute. He looked like one of the many snake charmers she'd seen in the bazaar that afternoon. He certainly didn't look like the kind of man who could threaten Omar.

Joan lifted her camera to take his picture. He had to have some kind of power, she thought. Perhaps he'd been kidnapped from some opposing tribe and Omar meant to ransom him. Joan couldn't help feeling sorry for him. Whoever he was, he was going to be Omar's next victim.

Just as she snapped the picture, a huge brown hand clamped down on her shoulder. Startled, Joan spun around to see Rashid standing over her. He ground his jaw, and when he did, his scar appeared to grow wider. His eyes were menacingly cruel as he glared at her.

Omar stood at Rashid's side.

"Joan, this is not the story I brought you to write."

Rashid grabbed Joan's camera off her neck and smashed it against the wall.

"Look, I'll just leave and not say anything." She knew this time there was no way out for her.

Omar's evil eyes were filled with disappointment. She sensed that, had she played by his rules, she might have been able to get out of here. She would have gone home to New York.

Suddenly, she saw Omar's expression change to one of shock. He was looking past her shoulder through the tiny window. Joan's curiosity forced her to look into the tower room.

Joan's eyes were saucer-wide as she looked around the empty room. THE MAN WAS GONE! Joan was beginning to think she'd stepped into the twilight zone. There was no sign of the man anywhere. She trembled as Omar stepped in front of her, unlocked the door and slowly let it swing open. Standing this close to him, she could feel Omar's anger rise like steam from his body. He whirled at her, his rage cutting through his studied deportment.

"Where is the Jewel?" he demanded of her.

"The jewel? I don't..." Joan was confused and frightened as Omar's eyes blazed with fury. Without warning, he raised his hand and slapped her across the face.

Joan's neck snapped back with the blow. Though the pain was great, Joan's first response was to fight back. She could feel tears sting her eyes and burn streaks down her face. But she didn't cry out. She clenched her fists, thinking how she'd like to beat him. Instead, she glared at him and bit her lip to keep it from trembling.

"The Jewel of the Nile. Do not cross me."

Joan kept her eyes riveted on Omar, but she refused to answer. She had no idea what he was talking about; but at that moment, she knew her silence would tell him otherwise. She didn't care what Omar thought, she just wanted a chance to get even. If he didn't have his bodyguard with him, she guessed Omar wouldn't be quite so confident.

As if reading her mind, Omar stepped to the side, leaving Joan to face Rashid's ugly, growling face.

Joan braced herself for the blows that were surely to come. Rashid raised his fists. She closed her eyes.

"Do not hurt her, Omar," a voice said in clear, British-accented tones.

Joan's eyes opened as she turned to see the prisoner step out from behind the door Omar had opened. He was smiling at Joan, but his eyes were defiant. When he spoke, his voice rang with authority and power. Joan was puzzled as to why she was afraid of him too. She glanced at Omar who was struggling with his anger and—fear?

Joan peered at the old man. "*You* have the jewel?"

Omar broke into a nervous laughter. "Miss Wilder . . . this *is* the Jewel."

The old man bowed gracefully to Joan as he clasped his hands to his forehead. It was a ceremonial bow she'd seen a dozen times in the little time she'd been in this country. All of this was making less sense with every passing minute. A man was a jewel or was it the jewel was a man? Whichever it—he—was, it could disappear and reappear at will. Joan shook her head. She had to be dreaming. She looked again as Rashid pulled out a knife and leveled it at her face.

Omar smiled sadistically. "Do I appear to be a fool?"

Joan held her breath. She was surrounded by maniacs and magic men.

"Please." She looked at Omar and then the knife. "Don't take this wrong, but I really think that you need some professional help. I know some wonderful therapists in New York..." Joan didn't know how to get herself out of this one, except that as long as she kept talking and she could hear her own voice, she knew she was still alive.

"It's a shame." Omar scowled. "I was so looking forward to working with you on this project."

"Don't do it. I've sold over five million books. If you kill me, there'll be people after you. There'll be a stink."

"What people? Your Jack perhaps?"

Joan gulped. Of all the people she knew ... yes ... she thought, Jack would come. He would know somehow.

"Jack will come for me." She smiled confidently.

"I should have told you. Jack is dead."

Joan felt every nerve in her body explode. She wanted to cry, scream, yell and shake all at once. This was hysteria.

"Don't be ridiculous. Jack would never die without telling me."

"Nevertheless, I took care of him in Monte Carlo."

Joan didn't believe him. He was bluffing—all con

men did that when the chips were down. His chips were down, weren't they?

"No . . . you couldn't—"

Omar nodded. His eyes gleamed with triumph. Joan couldn't stand it anymore. All her rage, terror and sorrow erupted within her. Without thinking, her hand swung up and slapped Omar's face.

"You bastard!"

Omar barely flinched. He smiled at her through gritted teeth. His eyes were red when he looked at her.

"Perhaps . . . but that will have to be our little secret."

Before Joan could say another word, Rashid grabbed her arm and hurled her inside the cell.

Joan tripped on one of the bricks in the floor and fell on her face. She pushed herself up and turned around in time to see the door close. She heard Rashid's wicked snicker as he locked the door. Omar looked at her through the tiny window and then he was gone.

Tasting blood, Joan realized she'd bitten her lip when she fell. She wiped her mouth with her hand. She turned to see the bespectacled prisoner sitting cross-legged, calmly inspecting her. He said nothing and his face was expressionless. Joan felt like an amoeba under a microscope, he scrutinized her so carefully.

"Hello. You're a very beautiful lady. Is that your natural hair color?"

"Pardon me?"

"I am getting personal too quickly. Forgive me."

"Who are you?"

"A prisoner," he said proudly. This time when he spoke, a smile spread over his face and his eyes came to life.

"How long have you been here?"

"About five years. It's starting to get boring. You can only meditate and count lice so much until the idle hours are no longer your friend. What is your name?"

"Joan Wilder. What's yours?"

"Abn al Ras . . . But most people know me as the Jewel."

Chapter Ten

THE MORNING SUN ROSE QUICKLY THE FOL-
lowing day, baking the land of Omar. The Suq was
especially crowded that day, for the shepherds had
come to town to auction their flocks. The vendors had
opened their stalls early, hoping for extra sales from
the families of the shepherds. The cafes were filled,
and people stood two rows thick around the fruit stalls,
the bread and cheese vendors. Lamb patties seasoned
with sage and curry were grilled on open fires. Their
aroma rose in the air and mingled with the stench from
the multitudes of sheep, unwashed humans and animal
dung.

When Jack and Ralph entered the village through
the large open gates, they had to elbow their way
through the crowd.

Not since Macy's Thanksgiving Day Parade in '78
had he seen this many people amassed in one place.
And the odor was nauseating. For years he'd dreamed
of visiting an exotic place like this. He glanced only
momentarily at the colorful tents, the fabulous brass
artworks, woven shawls, baskets and jewelry. He kept
pressing his way through the crowd. He heard the

shouts of a Sudanese auctioneer as he tried to entice the natives to bid on his flock of sheep. He heard villagers, nomads and vendors arguing over prices. He was beginning to understand a few words of Sudanese. As he passed the pottery stall, Jack was surprised to hear the merchant swear in English. Jack and Ralph continued. Jack didn't have time to waste, for today he couldn't think about the colorful bazaar or the souvenirs he'd like to buy. He could only think of Joan.

Ralph had been to a lot of weird places, but this was the worst. It definitely smelled the worst. From his vantage point—not quite five feet off the ground—Colombia had been paradise. Not two feet back there, he'd nearly stepped in a pile of camel dung. Where were the sanitation crews in these countries? No wonder they were riddled with disease and pestilence. Served them right.

Ralph looked around and then at Jack. "Nice place. Probably buy a swell two-bedroom townhouse here for five or six dollars. So, here's the plan. You get to your girl friend, I get the drop on Omar, he takes us to the jewel and we split."

"You're on your own. I just want Joan and what's coming to me," Jack said. The only reason he'd let Ralph come along was because he wanted his stake money back. Ralph could spend the next twenty years tracking down the Jewel of the Nile, the Star of India and any other gems he wanted. The only problem Jack could see was that Ralph was not likely to get the jewel and leave with his twenty grand to boot.

"Yeah, sure," Ralph replied. "Like I trust you.

"The same way I trust you."

"Comin' from a slime like you, that's a compliment."

Jack picked up his pace. At this rate it would take them all day just to make their way to the palace.

Joan looked mournfully out the window and wiped away another tear. She had cried all night, and she guessed she'd cry all day. It didn't seem possible, she thought, but knowing Omar's capabilities, Jack must be dead. She'd always thought she would know somehow: like some inner alarm would go off telling her he was *really* gone. But that had simply been a romantic notion, a device she'd used in her books. The reality was that Omar was a vicious murderer who was capable of anything. She couldn't doubt his word, not after seeing that gruesome portfolio in his office.

She folded her arms over her chest and leaned against the wall. She should be crying for herself, for there was no doubt in her mind that Omar would do as he'd said. It almost seemed pointless to mourn over Jack when she could be joining him soon.

She looked over at her cellmate. Jewel was playing his flute as he had every day for the past five years. He seemed totally unconcerned about their fate. He was just waiting for it to happen. They were both acting like sheep to the slaughter, she thought.

She hated being this powerless. But more important, she hated Omar for killing Jack. Omar had robbed her of her chance to make it up to Jack, to tell him she had been stupid and foolish. How could she have thought for one minute about writing when she'd been with Jack? She should have spent more time concentrating on him. She should have done a lot of things.

She slammed her fist against the wall. She wasn't going to let Omar get away with it, either. If she was already marked for death, she might as well give him a run for his money. She'd show him he couldn't kill her Jack and get away with it that easily. She might not get far, but she'd make his life hell trying to find her.

Joan went to the end of the cell, picked up a small stool and smashed it against the wall. She took one of the broken legs and looked at it carefully. Yes, this would do just fine, she thought. She went to the window and started pounding against one of the bricks in the wall.

Curious about her erratic behavior, the Jewel ceased playing his flute.

"What are you doing?" he finally asked.

"In *Angelina's Savage Secret* I had her escape from the old Tombstone jail by finding a loose brick in the wall. Once she got the brick out, she used her nail file to loosen the mortar around the other bricks until she was able to make a hole large enough to crawl out."

Jewel cocked his head to one side, then the other, trying to decide if her plan had merit.

"How long did this take? Twenty-two years?"

"Two pages." Joan continued pounding. She gnawed her lip in earnest. Yes, she could see the mortar loosening. "But I don't care if it takes a hundred years, I'm gonna get out of here and I'm gonna kill that man with my bare hands."

The more Joan thought of vengeance, the more driven she became. She envisioned herself, a Superwoman, choking Omar with the strength of ten men. She could see him beg for mercy, then his eyes pop out of his head and then . . . finally . . . die. She pounded with increased rigor.

Jewel considered her words. "I have a plan."

Joan stopped pounding and looked at him.

"It may not work, but we could try. I'll need your help."

"Anything." Joan knew the Jewel had been here a lot longer than she. Perhaps he knew of its idiosyncrasies. A trapdoor somewhere . . . ?

"Okay, stand up, put your hand against the wall and hold your fingers like this."

Jewel demonstrated what he wanted Joan to do. He pointed the tips of his index fingers together a few inches apart in front of his nose. Joan thought it looked like one of those tests the cops give drunks, but she did it anyway.

In one lightning-fast motion, the Jewel, seemingly out of nowhere, produced a roll of toilet paper and then hung it on Joan's fingers.

Joan looked at the toilet paper and then at the Jewel.

He was laughing uproariously. He had to hold his sides he was laughing so hard.

"I've been looking for a place to hang this," he finally said, still laughing. "Now, if I only had a pencil, I could write 'Help.'"

Joan was definitely not amused. She shoved the toilet paper at him.

"I'm sorry. I shouldn't joke at your expense. But after five years, you will do anything to amuse yourself."

Joan said nothing and picked up the stool leg and went back to her pounding. At least she could see some results now.

Jewel sat cross-legged once again and picked up his flute. He played only two notes and put it down again.

"In your book, did your character ever think of just shaking the bars?"

He got up and went to the window. He pulled at the end bar and it came off in his hand.

Joan was dumbfounded. Talk about idiosyncrasies! She knew she should have questioned him more. "I don't believe it. And you've been here five years?"

"Perhaps I wasn't ready to leave till now."

With a quizzical smile on his face, he twirled his hands in the air and produced a rose. He handed it to Joan. Joan took the rose, her eyes never leaving the Jewel. She smelled the rose. It was fragrant, the most beautiful shade of peach she'd ever seen, and it was real. Just who was this Jewel or Abn al Ras? What kind of man stayed in a jail cell for five years, knowing he could escape when he wanted? What puzzled her the most was that he would subject himself to Omar's abuse all those years. There had to be a purpose to actions. One thing was sure, Joan knew he was much more than just a magician. A lot more.

The Jewel smiled at Joan and pointed to the window. "Shall we?"

Joan nodded, and together they began tearing the bars out.

It was a good thing Jack had asked Tarak about the location of the palace, because he never would have believed this simple structure was the headquarters of one of the Middle East's most wealthy and dangerous men. There was nothing distinctive about it, especially the front doors that looked as if Ralph could ram them down without much trouble at all.

Jack knocked on the door. Nothing happened. He knocked again and then tried to force the door. Finally, the small sliding panel located at eye level slid open. On the other side were a pair of the angriest yellow eyes he'd ever seen.

"How you doin'? 'Name's Colton. I'm a friend of Joan Wilder's. Why don't you tell her I'm here and I'd like to see her?"

Jack kept smiling one of his nonchalant grins, but the guard did not react. He kept staring at Jack, his eyes narrowing more every second. Then, his eyes traveled downward to Ralph.

"I'm her brother," Ralph said.

The panel slammed shut. Jack and Ralph waited. They could hear mumbling voices and scuffling feet. But no one returned to the door. Ralph's stomach growled. He shifted his feet and then looked up at Jack.

"Let's not be in too much of a hurry here. Maybe Omar'll feed us first."

Jack sighed disgustedly. He must have been crazy to bring Ralph along. All he'd done since they started out was complain. If it wasn't the wrong brand of cigarettes, it was the food. He hated the wine, he wanted a toilet. His feet hurt from walking and his ass hurt from the camel ride. Jack couldn't believe Ralph had lasted six months in jail. It had to be a myth, Jack thought.

They must have waited a full ten minutes before the guard came back to the door. He slid the panel open and glared at them.

"I'm told she does not want to see you. Good day," the guard said and again slammed the panel shut.

For a split second Jack stood staring at the closed panel.

"Hey, wait a minute! What do you mean 'good day'?"

Jack lunged at the door and began banging on it with his fists. They weren't going to get rid of him that easily. He kept banging until he thought his skin would wear off.

"Nice work, lover boy. You know what they say. Once they've had a holy man, they never come back."

Jack glared at Ralph. He didn't need his snide remarks. Jack was more certain than ever that Joan was in trouble now. Joan wasn't the one keeping him out of the palace, Omar was.

"All right, there's gotta be another way in."

"Oh, yeah, Dr. Doom. I've got an idea. We'll go around to the back door, dress up in cat suits and ask for a saucer of milk."

"Up yours, shorty," Jack retorted. He'd had about all he could take.

Ralph gave Jack a look of mock hurt. "Oooooo."

Jack's anger and frustration were getting the better of him. "I'm the reason you're here," he reminded Ralph.

"Yeah, and for that I should kill you where you stand." Ralph wasn't above setting the record straight. He was sick of people always pushing him around. First it had been Ira, his cousin. God only knew where he was. But when Ralph did get his hands on that jewel, a meeting with Ira was the next family reunion Ralph would plan. In fact, if it weren't for trying to get that jewel, Ralph could have easily shot Jack and had his revenge. That they had to coexist didn't sit any better with him than it did with Jack. Jack would just have to learn, as Ira would, that nobody pushes Ralph around and gets away with it.

Jack walked around the palace, looking in windows and doorways. But the doors were closed and locked, and most of the windows were shuttered.

"She's gotta be in one of these windows somewhere." As he rounded the side of the palace, he found even more windows. These were open to allow the breezes to flow through, he guessed.

Ralph scanned the courtyard and some of the neighboring buildings. He looked up across the courtyard to the tall tower located at the end of the palace wall.

"There she is!" He pointed and yelled to Jack.

Joan crawled out of the tower window and onto a jagged ledge. She looked down. If it had been a hundred stories down, Joan didn't think she could be any more frightened. She threw her head back and kept her back close to the tower. Digging her fingers into the mortar between the bricks, Joan eased herself along the ledge. She worked her way to the left away from the courtyard and, she hoped, out of Omar's view, should he look out a palace window. Beneath her ran a narrow street, and across the street were many buildings. None were as high as the tower, but the closest was almost five stories high. From several of the village buildings, women had erected clotheslines which were bolted into the tower and then into the tallest building. That building must be some kind of an apartment house, she thought, for there were over a dozen clotheslines, all at various heights. It reminded her of New York.

Jack watched as Joan and some skinny man slowly worked their way around the tower. Just then, she nearly lost her footing as a loose brick tumbled to the ground.

"Hey, Joan Wilder, kind of goin' out of your way to duck me, aren't you?"

Joan stopped, and her back stiffened at the sound of his voice. Was that? No, but it was . . .

"Jack, you're alive!" she cried joyfully, looking down into the courtyard. She could feel his blue eyes riveting her all the way up here. She knew she should have trusted her instincts more. She knew she would have felt it if he'd really been dead. It wasn't a romantic notion at all—it was the bond of love between them that had brought him here.

He kept smiling at her as he nodded in answer to her statement. "No thanks to that swami of yours." Suddenly, he realized that she was on the outside of the window and not the inside. And who was that guy with her?

"What the hell are you doin' up there?"

"Not so loud. I'm escaping," she replied matter-of-factly.

"From what?"

"Omar."

"Didn't I warn you?"

He smiled. That was his Joan. Omar must have thought he had her neatly shut away. Jack could have told him better. Nothing ever stopped his Joan. Seeing her up there testing every inch of the way, fearlessly moving forward, reminded him of when they'd had to cross the gorge in Colombia. She'd grabbed ahold of that vine and gone swinging across. She'd surprised the hell out of him then. Now she was doing it again.

"Jack!" Joan yelled. Here she was probably a bazillion feet in the sky, trying to maintain her footing and escape from the clutches of a terrorist, and Jack wants to take the credit for being the better judge of character. Men.

Ralph snickered as he listened to the exchange between Jack and Joan. By the time they'd finished their bantering, Ralph burst into raucous laughter.

Jack looked down at him, a disgusted snarl curling his mouth. "What're you laughing at?"

"The both of you are losers."

Jack dismissed Ralph again and turned back to Joan. "Hang on, I'll get you down."

"This I gotta see." Ralph laughed.

Ralph shook his head. These two bimbos really deserved each other. It amazed him they'd gotten away with the stone in Colombia. Luckily for him, their mental capacities had deteriorated somewhat since South America. From all indications, Ralph was certain he'd have no trouble ducking Colton and his girl friend and retiring to Tahiti. He wanted to go someplace calm . . . and very far away.

Just then Joan heard a piercing cry from the wall of the palace. It was one of the guards that had stood watch at her room. He was calling to warn the other guards that an escape was being attempted. Joan felt her heart pounding. She tried to hurry, but each time she took another step, the old bricks crumbled a bit more. The mortar was becoming quite loose. She wasn't sure how much longer she could stay up there. It was obvious that she and the Jewel were too much stress on the ancient tower landing.

Joan looked over to the palace wall again. Several of the camouflage-suited guards were rushing up the stairs to their posts along the fortress wall. Their rifles gleamed in the sun, and she could hear them cocking the firing pins. She heard shouting and the sound of stomping feet as more guards hurried to the wall.

Another warning cry was sounded, and more shouting ensued.

Jack turned to Ralph.

"Get that gun out and cover me."

"What? We're gonna storm the palace? Hey, partner, you're on your own."

Ralph dropped the gun and walked across the courtyard. There was a little cafe around the corner he'd spied earlier. It seemed like a nice enough place to wait it out while Colton played John Barrymore. Ralph was not about to place himself in any more jeopardy than necessary. He wanted the jewel, but he wasn't this foolhardy.

Jack watched Ralph walk away. That little shit! He should have realized Ralph was the kind that didn't care about anybody except himself, and even that was a toss-up. Jack chided himself for feeling protective toward Ralph. He stooped over and picked up the revolver and shoved it in his belt. He looked up at Joan. That was his trouble, Jack thought, always being too sentimental.

Just then a number of Omar's men rushed into the square. They were dressed in full combat regalia. To a man they were furnished with the latest automatic repeating rifles, bullet belts and knives, and each man carried a revolver on his hip.

It was Jack's guess that everything, including the material for their uniforms and the visors on their caps was stamped *Made in USA*. It was a crazy world, he thought, made even crazier by politics.

Pandemonium reigned as the soldiers scanned the courtyard, trying to discern the enemy from the many villagers who were now ducking for cover. The soldiers seemed to momentarily be at a loss without their commandant to order them. Just then, Jack heard a loud voice booming orders to the soldiers as he raced into the square.

Jack dashed for a hay-filled ox cart. Looking over his shoulder one last time at the advancing soldiers, he sprang up to the roof of a one-story building. Misjudging the length of space between the cart and the edge of the roof, he nearly missed. Jack grabbed the edge, and for a long moment he dangled there—easy prey for Omar's highly skilled marksmen.

PING! The first shot ricocheted off the wall very near Jack's face. He turned his head away and tried to concentrate on pulling himself up. His lack of sleep the night before was doing him no good now. His body felt like lead, and try as he might, his arms refused to pull him up. Jack could hear more soldiers' shouting. He heard them exclaiming "American," and then he heard and saw more bullets being fired. "Come on, Jack," he mumbled to himself. If he could execute daredevil ski stunts, he sure as hell could conquer this roof.

A bullet hit the edge of the roof close to Jack's hand, and reflexively, he let go of the building. His other hand began slipping. Quickly he grabbed onto the roof again.

With a deep breath and great effort, Jack jerked himself up and onto the roof. He had just rolled onto his belly when half a dozen soldiers finally took aim. They pelted the entire wall and roof edge with gunfire, shearing away at least an inch of stone.

The courtyard below was mass confusion. Vendors, children and animals scurried everywhere, all of them disoriented. Flocks of sheep were spooked by the gunfire and took off running. They rammed into stall after stall and destroyed tents, wagons filled with provisions, and display carts of fruits and vegetables. Pottery smashed on the ground and brass lamps went tumbling from their shelves. A pair of oxen hitched to a large cart panicked along with the other animals. Bellowing with fear, the oxen trudged as fast as they could through the rabble, stomping over chickens and crates of doves. The oxen kept going, trampling everything in their path.

Children screamed for their mothers. A silk merchant tried to save his precious bolts of cloth as the sheep tore through his stall. The props were knocked out from his awning and the striped canvas came tumbling down. Two sheep were trapped inside the stall and could not escape. In their panic they kicked the man repeatedly. His screams mingled with those of others in the street.

From atop a particularly high sand dune, Tarak and his brothers awaited their signal from Jack in the village. Tarak had spent the morning pacing and focusing his binoculars. He could see nothing, though his vantage point was the best the land afforded.

Tarak had waited five years for this day to come. He was out of patience. Omar had kept their precious Jewel long enough. No longer could the tribes of Islam live in discord. He wasn't sure if the American could really help them. There was always the chance that Colton could make things worse. But Tarak was desperate. He would try anything.

He watched as nomads and villagers entered the city to trade at the bazaar. He wished there were another city for his people to conduct their business. He hated giving Omar this much control. It had been a bad year for the ranchers, shepherds and farmers. The drought had caused much suffering, and Tarak could only hope that, once united under the Jewel, the tribes would band together, share food and water with one another so that they all could live better. Tarak believed the Jewel could show them not only how to sustain their souls, but their bodies as well.

Tarak took out his binoculars again and peered down at the city. Suddenly, the sound of gunfire filled the Sahara. He could hear the sound of anguished human voices. He grabbed his rifle, lifted it above his head and sounded the dervish cry.

In response, his brothers and followers rose to their feet, screaming along with Tarak. The day of deliverance was upon them.

They raced to their horses and camels. One of the brothers dashed to a stockpile of rifles and began pitching them to the men. With rifles raised over their heads and screaming at the tops of their lungs, the dervishes galloped down the sand dune. Like a horde of desert raiders out of folklore, the nomads rode. Brightly colored tunics and neck scarves flew in the wind as the Arabian horses raced toward the walled city with Tarak in the lead.

They were racing toward destiny.

Chapter Eleven

INSIDE THE COURTYARD, RALPH NEVER GOT to the cafe where he'd planned to wait for Jack. Jack had been up and over the wall while Ralph was still frozen to the ground. Ralph kept staring at the multitudes of oncoming sheep. They looked like a white blanket, there were so many of them. It was the first time Ralph ever realized that rampaging sheep had red, angry eyes.

Ralph opened his mouth to scream for help, but it did him no good. The sheep thundered into the courtyard. Ralph turned and started to run. There was no escape. In seconds he was knocked down and trampled by the panicked sheep.

Joan's footing had become so precarious, she'd taken her only alternate route—the clothesline. Hearing all the shouting, the gunfire and stampeding sheep, she looked down. Jack was nowhere to be seen. She thought he'd gotten into that ox cart, but now the cart was gone and so was Jack.

Slowly, she moved hand over hand on the clothesline. She picked her way around clothes flapping in the breeze. One white cotton garment—an article of underwear, she thought—slapped her in the face and stung her eye. For a moment she couldn't see. She moved her right hand. She tried not to look down.

For someone as terrified of heights as she was, she'd certainly spent a lot of time up in the air—at least since she'd met Jack. Where was he, anyway?

She heard more gunfire. Jack must still be alive, otherwise they would have ceased fire. So far, no one had tried shooting at her. Joan's hands already stung from rope burns. Every time she let go with one hand, she was afraid she would fall. Her arms weren't that strong, but by sheer force of will she kept going.

She kept telling herself Jack was alive, for if she didn't she would lose all hope. Then, she would never make it.

Jack looked up at Joan from the rooftop. He'd made it over to the building nearest her, but he was still far, far below.

"Come on!" he yelled to her.

Joan opened her eyes again and looked down. He was there, waiting for her! He motioned with his arm for her to hurry. She moved her right hand over her left. She thought surely they must be bleeding by now. Again Jack yelled to her. He was very impatient.

"*You* try this!" she yelled back.

It was still another twenty feet before she was directly over the roof where Jack stood. She had to make it. She moved again. Her arms were tensed and quivering from the effort, but she managed another five feet.

Just then Joan heard the screaming dervish yell as Tarak and his men roared into the town waving their swords over their heads. Some rode with the reins clamped between their teeth, a sword in one hand, a rifle in the other.

The last of the sheep had stampeded through the bazaar, leaving a dazed and battered Ralph lying face-down on the ground. Once he realized the sheep were gone for good, he slowly got to his feet. He looked down at his shredded suit. There were clumps of mud, sand and dung trampled into the fabric. He took one whiff and nearly threw up. He dusted off his hat and turned.

Ralph's eyes widened to the size of saucers. Coming straight at him were the screaming, charging dervishes! He waved his arms to signal them to stop. The dervishes were annihilating anything and everything in their path.

Quickly, Ralph dove out of the way into a fruit stand, collapsing the cart and the neatly stacked pyramids of avocados, mangoes and pomegranates. Ralph opened his eyes and found himself face-to-face with three angry, sputtering owners. Cursing in Sudanese, they pounced on him, beating him with their fists. Ralph was so busy fending off their punches and jabs he was unaware of the thundering horses' hooves as the dervishes raced past.

The dervishes pounded through the Suq and up to the palace courtyard. From Joan's vantage point they looked like the cavalry coming to the rescue. She didn't know who they were, but they dove onto Omar's soldiers like seagulls diving into the ocean. Hand-to-hand combat ensued, with the nomads getting the better of the soldiers. Joan saw long swords whirling in the air, then striking their camouflaged-uniformed victims. Omar's soldiers raised their rifles, but never had a chance to fire as camel riders pounced on the soldiers' backs.

Joan was directly above Jack now.

"Jump!" he yelled to her, hoping she could hear him above the din.

"Will you catch me?"

"I'll catch you."

Joan took a deep breath and let go of the clothesline. She sailed through the air, wondering if she should have asked him how she was to land. Should she go in feet first, do a drop and roll, or bottom first? She chose the last, hoping he would indeed catch her.

She landed in his outstretched arms, but the force of her fall sent them both tumbling to the ground. Jack moaned, and for a moment she thought she'd hurt him.

"See?" he said, smiling at her.

Joan threw her arms around him. "Oh, God, you're alive!" He felt so good, so strong. She kissed his cheeks and neck and ears. She touched his hair and hugged him again. She'd been right—he did come for her. He must still care about her—a little.

Then she remembered that he hadn't come alone.

"Was that that dirty little man from Cartagena I saw you with?"

"It's a long story. Come on," he said, getting to his feet and pulling her up.

"No, I can't go without my friend."

"What friend?"

"There." Joan pointed up to the same clothesline she'd just dropped from.

Joan gaped at the sight of the Jewel walking across the clothesline like a tightrope walker. He had no pole to balance him, and yet he was clearly at ease as if he were walking down Main Street. In five more easy strides he reached the other side. He stood on the clothesline looking down at Jack and Joan with a big grin on his face. From out of nowhere he produced an umbrella which he quickly opened. He flitted off the clothesline and lazily floated down to the rooftop.

Jack was dumbstruck as he stared at the thin, brown little man.

"Who are you? Where'd you get that?"

With an impish grin Joan was coming to recognize, the Jewel brandished his hand in the air. "Same place I got this." He bowed to Jack and produced a bouquet of flowers out of nowhere.

Joan winked at the Jewel, her personal magician. Just then she heard more gunfire. This was no time for theatrics.

"Come on, I know where there are trucks."

With the Jewel and Jack behind her, they dashed across the rooftop and jumped onto another roof.

Just as Jack and Joan were about to spring onto another roof, Omar emerged from the palace. He scanned the clashing soldiers and dervishes. None of this would have happened if the Jewel were still safely locked up. Omar knew Tarak well. He would never storm the city gates if he didn't think he would ride away with the Jewel. Omar shielded his eyes from the sun and peered at the tower. The bars were missing! Quickly, he searched the neighboring buildings. There! On the roof he saw Jack, Joan and the Jewel.

"The Jewel! He has the Jewel!" Omar yelled to his guards.

Tarak, hearing Omar's cries, looked up from the

mêlée. He followed Omar's gaze to the rooftop. It was true.

"The Jewel!" Tarak exclaimed reverently.

Racing down the back alleys and passageways of the Suq and through the back gates, Jack and Joan made their way to the ordnance compound. Because the soldiers were inside the Suq battling with Tarak's men, they had left the compound completely unguarded.

"There." Joan pointed to the sea of military cars and trucks.

Jack slowed his speed when he saw the multitude of vehicles. Why, there was everything you could name. His first inclination was to grab one of those turbocharged Jeeps, but the desert half-track might get them farther. He followed Joan as she ran toward the trucks. Suddenly, Jack stopped.

There at the end of the runway was an F-16 being worked on by three engineers. The engine was running. It was his bet she was gassed up and ready to go.

"Trucks, hell! What about that baby?"

Joan's mouth fell open. "You don't know how to fly."

"How do you know?" Jack retorted.

"You do know how to fly?"

"Sort of."

"What do you mean, 'sort of'?"

Jack was indignant. That was the trouble with Joan. She always wanted background. Well, this time she was gonna get it good.

"I flew shotgun on a few smuggling runs to Mexico. Next step is jets." That should shut her up, he thought.

Just then the head engineer ordered his assistants to bring him more tools. They had just walked into the hangar when he noticed Jack, Joan and the Jewel coming toward the F-16. He climbed down off the wing, wiped his forehead with his sleeve. He yelled at them to clear the area, but they kept coming toward him. Angry that they would not heed his order, he walked up to Jack.

Jack smiled, and like a striking cobra, Jack's arm shot out and punched the engineer in the mouth. He fell like a ton of bricks.

"Sorry," Jack said.

Jack scrambled into the cockpit, with Joan helping the Jewel onto the wing.

Jack stared at the instrument panel while Joan fastened her seatbelt in the copilot's seat. For an instant she was afraid he didn't know what he was doing.

Jack rubbed his fingers together. "Okay . . . no problem."

He cranked up the F-16. Flipping switches and turning dials, Jack showed Joan what he could do. He pushed a blinking red button. With a giant *whoosh*, the exhaust from the plane literally blew down the hangar behind them.

Joan let out a victory yelp.

"Oh, my baby!" Jack cried and then turned the plane toward the runway.

Joan's eyes were glued to the runway. So far, so good. Jack eased the plane around in a perfect semicircle. She looked over at him and he winked confidently at her. Yes, she thought. He could fly this plane. Jack was taking them to safety.

Chapter Twelve

ENGINES ROARED AND WHEELS SCREECHED as Omar's soldiers climbed into jeeps, armored trucks and half-tracks and raced to the end of the runway ahead of Jack. Shouting orders and frantically waving his arm, the lieutenant signaled to his men to form a roadblock. One by one the vehicles rooster-tailed in the sand and came to a halt. Forming a wall of steel machines, the soldiers stood inside the jeeps and open-bed trucks with rifles aimed at the F-16.

The dark-eyed lieutenant held his arm ready to signal his men to fire. He had armed them with the new shipment of mini-14 semiautomatic rifles. At 223 calibers, they could penetrate quarter-inch steel at 3600 feet. Unlike the M16's Omar's personal guards used, which were meant only to maim—the bullet buzz-sawing through the body, wreaking havoc—the mini-14 was invented to kill. The lieutenant liked the new rifles best.

The F-16 had no place to go and would have to shut down its engines. The lieutenant thought of the bright red and gold ribbon Omar would award him for capturing the Americans. He pulled his own mini-14 to his shoulder. More than ever he wanted the Americans.

Jack kept flipping levers and braking the plane first right, then left. It jerked and bounced but went nowhere. The roar of the blasting engines was deafening despite Jack's effort to turn them down.

Joan held onto her seat to keep from going through the windshield. She should have known not to trust Jack. This was no single-engine Cessna he was piloting. This was an F-16. She'd read *Newsweek*. She knew about these rockets disguised as planes. Their "G-force" was so great that, when ascending, the plane went so fast that it drove the blood from the brain down into the body, causing the pilot—or passengers like her—to pass out. She looked at Jack while he nonchalantly pushed buttons and lowered levers. She could tell he hadn't read the same article.

"Shit!... If I can get to the road, I can take off."

"Don't take off!" Joan cried, thinking again of the G-force.

"You wanna drive?"

Frustrated, Jack rammed his foot against the brake. The F-16 took a sharp turn and spun almost completely around. When he eased off the brake, the F-16 was now headed toward the compound. Between Jack and the compound were three clusters of bivouac tents. Frantically, Jack pressed on the brakes, trying to maneuver the plane back toward the runway. He failed.

Suddenly, Jack's expertise in piloting had put them in the middle of the tents. The plane kept spinning around even though Jack was sure he'd cut the engines. But that little green light kept blinking at him when it should have cut off. The wings of the F-16 sheared the canvas, ripping one tent after another into shreds. Those that escaped Jack's vego-matic tactics were incinerated by the rocket blast from the exhaust.

Joan screamed as she saw the tents behind and beside them burst into flames. They looked like giant matches flaming against the brilliant blue sky. In seconds, the tents were reduced to smoking cinders.

Not able to guide the plane to the runway, Jack saw the Suq straight ahead. The entrance gates were wide open. Jack held up his hands as if measuring the distance between the gates. He looked at the left wing and then the right.

"It's gonna be tight!" he announced to Joan.

Joan looked at Jack, trying to understand what he was talking about. Just then, he revved the engines again and let off the brake. This time, the plane did not spin around, but went straight as an arrow toward the Suq. Joan threw her hands over her eyes, then slowly let them fall. He wasn't going to try driving through the Suq, was he?

Letting the rockets roar, Jack zoomed the F-16 through the gates. Just as the nose passed through, he realized he'd misjudged the opening—the left wing was completely mangled. Jack peered out the window to see shredded steel, dangling wires and sparks flying everywhere. He smiled, though, for he'd taken half the wall down.

The dervishes were holding their own against Omar's men. Tarak raised his sword to his opponent who was trying to fend him off with his rifle butt. With a lightning-swift flash, Tarak cut the man's arm off, relieving him of his weapon. Screaming and clutching his bloody stump, the soldier dropped to his knees. At that instant a soldier dropped onto Tarak's back from a high ledge. Tarak threw the man over his shoulder and lunged into his belly with his sword. Tarak pulled away and quickly scanned the courtyard. Omar's men kept coming in droves from inside the palace. He could hear the whir of dervish swords as they rose into the air and then fell against the enemy. Omar's men may have had the latest in weaponry, rifles and grenades, but Tarak's men were warriors. Dervishes never allowed the opponents a chance to shoulder their rifles, much less fire them. Dervishes had The Unseen on their side. Omar, Tarak knew, was a false prophet. He would never win.

Omar frantically looked around. Though his men were holding off the dervishes, he still was no closer to finding Jack and Joan. He raced to the palace doors just as another platoon of his men were thundering down the hall. He signaled to them.

"Look in those houses! Check the streets!" he commanded as he pointed to the opposite end of the courtyard. Suddenly, he stopped dead still; his mouth gaped open in shock.

Headed straight toward the main square was an F-16. Omar's F-16. And its left wing had been sheared off. The plane picked up speed as it howled through the Suq. Though the wingspan was shorter now, it still could not pass through the narrow streets without creating havoc.

Ripping clay awnings off buildings, knocking over vegetable stalls and pottery shelves, the F-16 destroyed everything in its path. Jack whooped with delight as he stared directly into Omar's stunned face.

Joan jumped up and down in her seat and hugged the Jewel. She took back every bad thought she'd had about Jack. He didn't need to fly the F-16. He was doing just great on the ground! She hoped she would never forget the look on Omar's face. He was in their power now. She wondered what he felt like, being crushed as he'd crushed so many others.

The F-16 roared on, dragging clotheslines, small carts, canvas and mangled baskets in its wake. People raced away screaming, and sheep scattered everywhere. It was pandemonium, Joan thought. She looked at Omar again. It was poetic justice.

Tarak heard the defeaning roar behind him but fighting for his life against a bull of a man, he'd had to ignore everything but his opponent. Knocking the man unconscious, he turned to see the F-16 roar past him. He looked inside the cockpit. It was Jack with his American girl friend, and with them was—

"The Jewel! I see the Jewel! Follow them, he's taking the Jewel!"

Oblivious to everything except the fruit-stand owner who was still pummeling him with enormous fists, Ralph suddenly heard Tarak's voice. Rising more confidently to his own defense, Ralph delivered two severe blows of his own and managed to get to his feet.

"The Jewel!"

Ralph looked up just as the F-16 sped past him. Ralph's eye was beginning to swell, and everything seemed a blur. But he definitely could see Jack at the helm.

"Colton! You dirty double-crossin' son-of-a-bitch! You did it to me again!"

Just then half a dozen armored trucks and jeeps raced into the Suq in pursuit of the F-16.

Tarak let out the dervish cry and signaled to his men. Landing final blows to stun the soldiers, the dervishes raced to their camels and horses. Tarak mounted his black stallion and raised his rifle over his head. His horse reared up and then galloped off in the direction of the plane.

Ralph scrambled away from the fruit-stand vendor and dashed into the street. He tried to stop several of the dervishes, hanging onto the bridles of their camels, but they wouldn't stop.

"Hey, fellas, wait for me."

The dervishes ignored Ralph, their minds on only the Jewel.

Jack had executed a perfect turn, and now the plane was heading back toward the village gates. Omar's men were now racing behind him in jeeps and were firing their rifles at the plane. Jack looked up to see the soldiers closing the entrance gates. Damn! He hadn't ripped enough of the wall down. The gates were iron and wood. He knew he didn't have enough runway room to pick up enough speed to blast through them. If he tried to bash them down, he would only succeed in killing himself, Joan and her . . . friend.

Joan was frantic. "Turn the plane! Turn it!"

"To where?" Jack yelled. They were trapped in this narrow street.

"Oh, noooooo!" Joan screamed and hid her eyes. They were going to die this time, she knew it.

The Jewel smiled. Lackadaisically, he peered out the window as if he were sightseeing.

"You know, this is my very first time in a plane."

Jack spun around and looked at him. Who was this guy? Jack had to do something. He scanned the control panel once again and spotted a large red button.

"I got it!" He exclaimed.

Jack fired one of the wing missiles. In less than a second the gates were blown away, and in a full second the F-16 passed through the flaming opening and into the safety of the desert.

As the plane roared out of the village, Omar signaled to his men to follow. He watched as they zoomed into the desert. Quickly, Omar shouted to Rashid and then they raced into the palace.

The dervishes whooped and shouted as they charged through the village gates behind Omar's army.

Finally, on a broken-down donkey, Ralph rode out of town through the smoldering gates. He coughed and choked on the swirl of smoke and dust and everyone else had left behind. He swatted the donkey's flanks, and for the hundredth time in the last fifteen minutes, he cursed Jack Colton.

Like a deadly tarantula, Omar's black helicopter crept across the sky. Rashid angled the chopper to the east. Omar peered through high-powered binoculars at the long stream of dust and sand below. Though the F-16 was moving fast, his men were directly behind. The American should have known he was out of his element dealing with one as powerful as he, Omar thought. He hoped his men didn't get trigger-happy and kill Jack and Joan. Omar wanted them alive. He had plans for Joan. She would be a lovely addition to his secret harem—not the one composed of his legal wives—the white harem, the one he'd paid so dearly for. He signaled to Rashid, who then accelerated the helicopter and raced toward the F-16.

Jack barreled the F-16 down the desert trail. He was feeling confident about his prowess with this plane. If only he could figure out how to leave the ground. But, as he thought about it, he was probably better off on land.

Heading south toward the village on the same desert trail was a rickety old bus. It was the 11:00 bus, and as usual, every seat was taken by local passengers, their children and their animals. It was a noisy, stinking vehicle, but the driver didn't care. He made a good living. He couldn't complain.

It was drawing close to twelve, for the heat had intensified. The driver wiped his neck with a bandanna. He peered into the distance. Heat rose in swaying sheets from the sand, creating an odd-looking mirage. He wiped the sweat from his eyes. He was seeing things, wasn't he? It looked like a rocket heading straight for him.

Suddenly, the driver realized that the roar in his ears was from the F-16, and he'd been in the desert long enough to know that mirages did not make noise. Just as the bus and plane were about to clash, the bus driver jerked the bus to the right and swerved out of the F-16's path.

His passengers cheered and patted him on the back. Dazed, the driver stared at the stream of armored trucks following the plane. Nothing like this had ever been penciled into his schedule.

Joan let out a sigh of relief as they passed the bus. It had appeared out of nowhere. Were they really going that fast?

As they sped along, the wind picked up, making tiny swirls in the sand. The swirls became larger and more forceful, creating funnels that rose from the ground and whipped into the plane. The F-16 rattled and shook as the wind battered it from every side. Joan tightened her seatbelt and said a prayer.

Wildly, the plane skipped along the rocky terrain, spinning on sand and leaping over intermittent sand dunes. Joan thought her teeth were being rattled right out of her head. Skimming over dried-up and cracked streams and riverbeds, the plane jostled to and fro. Joan feared that precious speed was being lost.

The jeeps and desert trucks took advantage of the F-16's plight and opened their engines. Careering down the trail, jumping rocks and skittering past trees, Omar's men closed the gap. The lieutenant radioed the vehicles behind him to overtake the plane. He checked his mini-14. It was fully loaded.

Jack saw one of Omar's jeeps race up on his left side. He'd lost more speed than he'd thought. Instantly, Jack hit the afterburners. The rocket engines exploded, sending Jack and Joan into the dunes. There was plenty of distance between him and the soldiers now, Jack thought. Out here in the dunes he could go much faster.

The force from the afterburners plastered Joan against her seat. It was a long moment before she convinced herself she was not as terrified as her heart told her she was. They were jetting across the desert at an incredible speed.

"Where're we going?"

Jack turned to her with a quizzical look on his face. "Are you kidding? I don't even know what the hell I'm doin'!"

"Jack..." the Jewel said calmly.

"Yeah," Jack snapped.

"Joan tells me you have a passing knowledge of tropical birds. Perhaps later we can sit and talk. I've never been to the tropics, and I would love to hear your stories."

Flabbergasted at this man's offhanded attempts at humor, Jack turned completely around and stared at Joan's friend.

"Who is this guy?"

Suddenly, Joan screamed. She pointed in front of them.

"Jack!"

The nose of the plane started lifting and dropping. It was as if they were on a teeter-totter.

"What are you doing?" Joan asked.

"Nothing!" Jack retorted, but quickly checked the instrument panel to double-check. No, he hadn't accidentally pushed the wrong buttons. He wondered if this was some kind of aftermath from the afterburners.

"Why is it doing that?" she demanded.

Just then Jewel pointed in front of them.

"Habo'ob."

"Ha-what?" Jack asked.

"Sandstorm. Tough luck," Jewel said in that nonchalant manner that was about to drive Jack crazy.

Joan followed the Jewel's finger to the horizon. A huge churning brown cloud rose from behind the largest sand dune like dawn. Even over the noise of the rockets she could hear its deadly roar. In seconds it filled the sky, the earth, and surrounded them. It cut off the sun, making everything look like dusk.

"Jesus Christ!" Jack cried as the sandstorm embraced them.

"A good time to bring him up," the Jewel said.

Joan peered at the Jewel. There must be something to meditation—nothing seemed to bother the Jewel. He was as calm now as he'd been in the tower cell.

Suddenly, Joan felt as if she were riding the roller coaster. They zoomed, slowed, bobbed and swayed. Finally, the F-16 lifted off the ground.

"We're taking off!" she cried, thinking of the G-force. Jack didn't know how to pilot this plane at all. How could he know when to slow them down so they wouldn't black out? Joan knew there was nothing to save them now. If the sandstorm didn't cause them to crash, they would die from the G-force.

Omar's black helicopter zoomed ahead of his ground troops. Rashid bore down on the rudder, turning the craft to a more northerly direction. Suddenly, Omar dropped his binoculars, his eyes were huge as he spied the sandstorm.

"Turn back! Turn back!"

"It's too late!" Rashid exclaimed as he fought with the rudder. The winds had taken over.

The helicopter began to shake violently, defying all Rashid's efforts to land the plane. Struggling with the controls, Rashid pitched back and forth in his seat despite being belted in. Exhausted, he finally threw caution to the wind. The helicopter headed straight into the sandstorm.

On the ground the string of Omar's jeeps and desert trucks raced toward the horizon. The lieutenant stared at the sandstorm looming in front of him. He glanced at the speedometer. They were going over 90. Even if they were turned in the opposite direction riding away from the storm, they could never outrun it. Their fate was sealed.

When the F-16, the helicopter and the jeeps were swallowed by the sandstorm, it was like Jonah entering the whale.

Chapter Thirteen

CRYSTAL-BLUE SKIES SPREAD OVER THE Sahara, defying all knowledge of the sandstorm. The wind was calm as tiny insects and reptiles scurried about the sand in search of food. Two scorpions, yellowish brown in color and about two inches in length, slowly climbed over pieces of black twisted metal in search of small insects. Coming upon a small spider, the scorpions circled the prey, then stung it to death. Together, they devoured the lunch. The scorpions trudged over the metal, back to the sand and away from the two men standing next to the wreckage.

His clothes dirty, stained and otherwise disheveled, Omar threw up his hands.

"My helicopter, my beautiful jet. Both destroyed in one morning. It's not enough that I kill them. I want to know their relatives, their friends, anyone they have ever met."

Rashid turned away, his steely eyes scanning the desert.

"We will find them."

* * *

Three sand dunes away, the F-16 had buried itself nose down into the sand so that only the tail protruded into the air. It looked like a great metal ostrich. Inside the plane, Jack was frantically going through the survival kits and gear. It was eerie inside the cockpit, stuck under the earth the way it was, Jack thought. He could see nothing but sand from all the windows. It was miracle they were still alive. There was little on board that would help them.

"This pilot traveled light. Water, a gun and a prayer rug." Jack shrugged his shoulders. In desolate land like this, he wondered which of the three was most vital. Then decided it was a toss-up.

Joan sat under the F-16's wing, enjoying the little bit of relief the shade offered. She felt completely spent, as if every bone in her body were groaning from the endurance ride she'd just completed. Now here they were in the middle of the desert with no means of transportation. Everywhere she looked, she saw only sand. The golden sun blared down on them, and its golden rays were reflected by the golden sands. She never wanted to see that color again! What she wouldn't give for a good rainy month in New York where the skies were glorious gray. She ran her hand through her hair. It was a mass of sweaty snarls. She had no comb or brush, and worst of all—she thought as she squinted at the sun—she had no nosekote.

Beside Joan sat the Jewel, calm and utterly serene. She wished she could find that kind of total unconcern. Instead, her stomach was still pitching a fit just as it had from the moment she engineered her escape, through Jack's rescue and the "plane flight." She wished she had her nerve pills—even more than the nosekote.

Looking again to the monstrous sand dunes, Joan thought this must be "eternity." She felt as if she were staring death in the face—but a slow death, one that came with parched skin, dehydration and, finally, the vultures would pick her bones clean. She shivered.

"Where do we go from here?"

The Jewel pointed toward the late afternoon sun.

"You head in that direction. West. It will take you to the Nile. A day, maybe a day and a half. The Hamars have a well along the way. Say hello for me."

Joan looked to the west. A day and a half? Could she live that long under this Sahara sun? How much ground could she cover before she fainted from sunstroke? Would her very tender, fair skin blister, then crack and bleed? What if the Hamars would not allow her to drink from their well? It sounded dangerous. Even more dangerous than G-force.

She looked at the Jewel. She was getting attached to this funny fellow. For some reason, she felt a tug at her heartstrings, knowing he meant for them to part. She almost felt as if he were her good-luck charm. She didn't want to leave him. He was her friend.

"Where are you going?"

The Jewel pointed in the opposite direction.

"Over those mountains. To the city of Khadir. It is only a day before Omar proclaims himself there. Now that you have been kind enough to free me, I can stop him."

"All alone?"

"You could come along, but I am not one to impose. Good-bye, Joan."

Joan thought she would cry; instead, she smiled at the Jewel. He clasped her hand, and without saying a word, she felt everything he wanted to say. Friends who've been through great trials or dangers are always the strongest bonds, she remembered her mother telling her. That was how Joan felt about the Jewel. From the first moment she'd seen him sitting in that tower cell, Joan knew he was no ordinary man. He was saintly. He did have a great mission in his life. They had escaped death together and had defied Omar. Two days ago she would have said that was impossible. She didn't want the Jewel to leave and go back. She might never see him again.

The Jewel stood, opened his umbrella, and with a wink and smile he started off across the desert. The Sahara, the killer desert, Joan thought.

"He has an army. You can't stop him with an umbrella," she yelled to the Jewel, but he did not acknowledge her words. He continued walking. He didn't look back.

Jack emerged from the cockpit and stuck his head out of the doorway.

"All right, let's get goin'."

He jumped down from the wing of the plane and stood next to Joan.

"I'll tell you, lady, you sure know how to pick 'em. Great guy, that Omar. Did I mention that he blew up my boat?"

Joan stared after the Jewel. He looked tiny and frail against the massive sand dunes. He had to be crazy. Surely there was something she could do, but they were only a holy man and a woman against all of Omar's forces. She looked at Jack. He couldn't help the Jewel any more than she could. And what was he babbling about? Something about the *Angelina*—Omar had blown up his boat. Joan looked at the Jewel again. Would Omar kill him, too?

"No . . ." Joan finally answered. "I'm sorry."

"Well, I'm gonna get that sucker right where he lives. The tribesmen that brought us over told us about a jewel Omar stole. Jewel of the Nile. Some precious, holy stone."

Jack smiled determinedly at her. Now that Joan was safe from Omar and with him again, where she belonged, Jack wanted only revenge. Omar had destroyed the *Angelina*—Jack's dream. If there was a chance to get even, Jack wanted to do it. If he could find this Jewel of the Nile, then he could put all the pieces of their life back together again. Maybe then Joan would love him again.

Joan couldn't believe what Jack was saying. They had narrowly escaped death more than twice that morning, were now faced with a dangerous trek across the desert, and Jack was thinking about stolen jewels. Jack was never going to change. He would always be mercenary. He only wanted her when there was treasure to be had.

"Really?" she said, not trying to hide the tinge of sarcasm in her voice.

"That's right. And I'm gonna go back, gonna find out where it is; then I'll take it, buy the *Angelina Two*, and sail off to Greece. You can come too, if you'd like. I warn you, though, it might mean the good life."

Jack tried to deliver his words with a devil-may-care ring to them, but instead he came off sounding callous. He wished he could rearrange them somehow, but he'd always had a hard time saying the right thing to Joan.

He wondered why it was so hard for him to tell her he loved her. Or to ask her flat out why she didn't want him. He could understand it if she wavered a bit now, since he had no money; no boat. Possessions, social standing and all that stuff were important to women. He wanted to give her the best because Joan was the best. She was the only important thing in his life.

Joan nearly gasped. Jack acted as if he were doing a favor by asking her to go to Greece with him. And how long would that last? Until he decided to race off in search of another treasure? She could tell by the way he asked her that she was only a second thought. She could kick herself for the mournful face she wore. She didn't want Jack to know how rejected she felt. She wanted him to think she was strong; tough— like him.

"No thank you," Joan said after mustering her courage. She pointed to the Jewel. "I'm going with him."

"Where's he goin'?"

Joan stood and brushed the sand off her clothes. She flashed Jack a hard, steely look. She wondered how he could always look so vulnerable when he wanted something from her. He had always managed to get his own way by looking at her with those soulful blue eyes. She'd fallen for it too many times. He was a great actor, she thought. She knew herself well enough to know that Jack would always be able to break her heart. She was no more than a lump of modeling clay to Jack. It was her bet that the only reason he wanted her back was because he missed his favorite toy. She'd been such a fool! She wanted to get away from him before she burst into tears.

"To the holy city to stop Omar."

"Wait a minute! You're crazy! What'd that Omar do to you?"

Suddenly, Jack was frantic. What had happened to Joan that she would throw all caution aside like this? What defense did she have against Omar with all his guns, men and machines? Did she hate him so much she'd rather risk death than be with him? They couldn't have gotten that far apart. He would've had to do something terrible for her to hate him. Maybe the desert heat had rotted her brain. This wasn't like Joan at all. Couldn't she see that she was better off with him? There was no danger if she stayed with him. He would protect her, care for her. Though right now, that statement was straining the truth a bit. He had nothing but the clothes on his back—and a heart full of love.

Joan was not to be swayed. She started off to follow the Jewel. "Thank you for coming. You were a very big help," she said to Jack as she walked away. "I do hope you find your jewel and that it is everything you imagine."

Joan felt her shoes filling with hot sand already and she wasn't twenty feet away. But she didn't care. She *had* to get Jack out of her system. She needed to find someone who thought of something besides money. Someone who thought about *her* once in a while.

Jack watched her go. At least when she left with Omar, Jack told himself that Joan had never had a chance. Omar was so handsome, rich, charming and powerful, any woman, even Joan, would have been sick not to fall for him. Jack was just an ordinary guy—nothin' special about Jack T. Colton. But now, this was different. If there was any doubt Joan was rejecting him and only him, she had erased that doubt.

It was as plain as the nose on his face and he'd been too dumb to see it. Joan was some kind of adventure freak. She liked living on the edge of death. She wanted all the hairpin curves life could throw her. And she got her jollies out of watching him risk his ass for her. He'd heard Hemingway had lived his life like that. Bullfights, drunken brawls, weekends in the slammer. Writers. Maybe Joan felt she had to "experience" this crap in order to write about it. If that was the case, then she was a real sicko.

She was leaving him. Try as he might, he could never deny that he loved her. He wanted her to love him back.

"Hold on! You're gonna follow some little bagman you found in that jail? You want goddamn adventure? Come on with me!"

Joan never stopped walking. She could hear him yelling to her. By now tears were streaming down her cheeks. The Sahara wind dried them before they reached her chin. She was glad. She didn't want Jack to know he could upset her like this; that he meant this much to her. She thought she'd gotten to the point that he couldn't hurt her anymore, but he'd fooled her again. She didn't want much in this world. She just wanted to be loved for herself. If she went back, she would just be delaying the inevitable. Sooner or later, he would run out of treasures. He would run out of his need for her.

Jack felt as if he were cracking in half. "Okay, fine! Go! I didn't come here for you anyway!" he yelled, thinking that was a lie. "I came to get rich! I came for that jewel!" He shook his fist at her. He'd like to shake her from head to toe.

Upon hearing Jack's last words, the Jewel stopped in his tracks and turned to face Jack.

"If you want the Jewel, you better follow us. I know where it is."

Stunned, Jack stood for a full second with his mouth open. Not only did this guy know how to make Joan follow him, he was the key to the treasure he wanted. For a second he didn't believe it. But now it made too much sense. Maybe Joan wasn't leaving *him* after all. Maybe she was after this Jewel of the Nile, too. Of course, that had to be it! She didn't hate him. She wasn't real pleased with him at this moment, but he could straighten that out. There was hope! Many a mountain had been climbed in this world on sheer hope alone. Jack Colton was not one to discount anything he could use as leverage. The only thing was, if Joan really didn't want him, this time he was sure to find out. The thought sat restlessly on his mind.

"Damnit!" Jack swore as he slung the survival kit over his shoulder. Like it or not, he was throwing himself up for the big kill once again. He must be some kind of masochist. Normal guys didn't act like this about a woman. Of course, he couldn't think of that many guys he'd ever known who'd ever *really* fallen in love. It was something to think about. Jack started after Joan and her friend. Suddenly, he stopped and looked back at the plane with its hind end jutted up into the air. He might not have the chance to get his digs into Omar later. But this plane, Omar's pet possession, would do rather nicely.

"Oh, yeah."

Jack opened the survival kit and withdrew the .45. He took careful aim at the plane and squeezed the trigger, relishing every ounce of his revenge. He'd teach Omar to take his girl away—and to blow up his *Angelina*.

At the top of his lungs, Jack shouted, "Hey, Omar, your mama!"

Jack pulled the trigger. His aim was dead-perfect. Instantly the F-16 caught fire. Jack watched as the flames spread through the fuselage. Quickly, Jack took off running toward Joan. He'd just made it to her side and pulled her to the ground when the plane exploded.

Like venomous reptiles, the desert half-tracks, tanks and jeeps slithered over the crescent-shaped sand dune. The Soviet-made T-62 armed with high-velocity 115-millimeter guns led the brigade. Because of its light weight, it sped across the sand as if it were flying.

Omar watched as his forces came to him. He wished he'd been able to buy the American-made M-60. If he'd had that air-cooled diesel engine that could outrun anything in the desert, armed with the ballistically superior British-made 120-millimeter gun, he could have stopped Jack. But he hadn't been fast enough. He needed a faster helicopter; he needed better weaponry. If someone like Jack Colton could cause him this much aggravation, he was in trouble. More than ever, Omar knew he'd been right to stifle his people's education. Perhaps he should ban all American television broadcasts. It was not good for them to be exposed to Western technology: they would become more difficult to control.

Omar started walking toward the convoy, all the

while wondering how he could convince the American
military that he "deserved" their beneficence. He hadn't
wanted anything as much as that M-60 since he'd paid
the Moroccan thieves to steal his Mercedes.

Rashid heard the convoy behind him, but did not
turn around. His eyes were too busy scrutinizing every
inch of the horizon. Colton was out there somewhere.
And Rashid wanted him—badly. He pulled at his ripped
tunic. It was bloodstained from the deep gash he'd
received in the crash. Rashid didn't like scars. One
was enough, and he'd chopped his assailant into four-
teen pieces—he'd counted them, one by one. Rashid
touched the tender spot on his head. His eyelid flickered as the pain shot through his skull. Rashid's eyes
narrowed and came to rest on a single point on the
horizon. He stretched out his aching arm and pointed.

"There!" Rashid yelled to Omar.

Omar stopped walking and turned at the sound of
Rashid's voice. He followed Rashid's gaze. There,
over the farthest dune, rose a thin funnel of black
smoke. If Colton had run up a flag, he couldn't have
done a better job of marking his position. Omar smiled.
Colton's inevitable death would be sweet.

Chapter Fourteen

WITH SAND NESTLED IN THE CRAGS OF HIS face, coating his beard and embedded in his clothes, Tarak looked like a mutant creature born of the Sahara. Tarak drew heavily on his pipe and exhaled the smoke. He passed the pipe to one of his brothers seated beside him on the sand. Perched on this highest dune, Tarak could see half the Sahara, he thought. His men had ridden out the sandstorm, not the worst they had ever encountered. Dervishes were a strong people and could survive many hardships, he thought to himself as he looked at his equally disheveled brothers. They had formed a semicircle and now were carefully observing the horizon, looking for anything—a flash of sunlight off the metal wing, an unusual movement— something to give them hope again.

Tarak could not believe his Jewel was dead. He, his brothers and the other tribes of the Sudan desperately needed their spiritual leader, the true prophet, to fight Omar's oppression. Dervishes did not have Russian tanks, American jets and French bullets to fight Omar. They only had strong constitutions and brave hearts. With the blessing from the Jewel to protect them, Tarak believed he had the strongest army in the world.

Suddenly, one of the brothers stood. He cried out, and all rose to see the funnel of black smoke on the horizon.

"A sign! He's alive!" Tarak proclaimed.

To a man, they leapt into the air, whirling and crying the dervish cry. Tarak led them in a chant as he hugged his brothers and praised the Unseen. He spun around in the ritual dance of the dervishes, his brothers clapping their hands. They fell to their knees and gave homage in the centuries-old bow. Then they stretched out fully in the prone bow, giving the greatest reverence to the Unseen.

Instantly, Tarak was on his feet, yelling to his men to mount their steeds. Tarak grabbed the mane of his mighty black stallion. He raised his rifle over his head. His smile was wide and victorious. He turned around to see that all his men were mounted when, suddenly, he stopped and peered into the distance.

On the sand dune directly behind the band of dervishes appeared a little man. His clothes were tattered and sandblasted. He was swaying from right to left as he staggered to the peak of the dune. The little man paused for a moment, then his knees gave way and he fell to the ground. He tried to shout, but his throat was filled with sand, as was every pore and crevice in his body. His head reeled back. Tarak thought he'd passed out from the heat. The little man rolled down the sand dune and came to a stop at the dervishes' feet.

It was Ralph.

* * *

The wreckage of the F-16 was still smoking when Omar arrived. He ordered the half-tracks and more expensive vehicles to remain back while he and Rashid investigated. Should there be another explosion, Omar didn't want to lose any of his precious tanks.

Little remained of his once proud F-16. Metal scraps, the tail and smoking ashes were strewn everywhere. The cockpit was nearly intact since it was still embedded in the sand.

Omar could only think of the years, the conniving, the persuasion it had taken to wrench this plane from the American military. He thought of the promises he'd made not to deal with the Russians when he'd placed his order for Russian tanks only three months before. And now an American had taken his prize and destroyed it.

Rashid climbed out of the cockpit. He'd been checking for bodies. When he emerged, his face was solemn, the anger still flaring in his eyes.

"They are gone."

Omar was stunned. This was impossible. The Jewel, Colton, Joan—had all escaped? Omar looked at the smoking debris. It wasn't Colton who had saved their lives, it was the Jewel and his almighty power. For five years Omar had kept the Jewel safely locked away in the tower while he built his army and established himself as ruler. The Jewel had always known his fate was death. It had only been a matter of time. No one had ever defied him till now. Just when he was on the verge of becoming spiritual and political ruler of all the tribes, Omar's plans were being thwarted, his power challenged. The Jewel had never taken steps to stop him. Was it possible Colton and Joan were more of an influence than he'd thought?

If the Jewel had died in the plane crash, it would have slowed his progress, made his inauguration less triumphant. But he could have turned the Jewel's death to his favor, citing to the people that the will of the Unseen had been done. He, Omar, was the one true leader.

With Joan and Colton's intervention, the course of history was being changed. It was imperative Omar find them. If he were to be ruler, he could not allow any of the trio to live.

Omar thought for only a second. The Jewel's plans were simple to decipher.

"He'll go to the city."

Rashid nodded. "Then he must go over the mountains. We will have him by tonight."

"Bring them to me at the Khadir."

Rashid headed for the half-tracks. They would make the best time over the craggy terrain between the desert and the city. Rashid gave orders to the drivers before seating himself in the lead half-track. He called for a count of ammunition. He ordered all the soldiers to check their rifles and make certain they were fully loaded. Rashid wanted no surprises. Not this time. He gave the signal and the engines started.

Omar climbed into the T-62. He took one last look at the smoking fuselage. Being a child of the Nile himself, when given to fear, he believed in superstition just as much as one of his illiterate villagers. There was a chance the destruction of the F-16 was an omen. Perhaps it was a sign meant to test his courage, his intellect. His eyes narrowed. Omar could not afford these feelings of doubt. If he should waver in his conviction, his strength, then all was surely lost.

With conviction, he bellowed his orders to the driver. He would go back to Khadir and await Rashid's return—with their prisoners.

As if walking from one movie set to another, Jack, Joan and the Jewel left the desert behind and entered a striking mountain pass.

It was like a Garden of Eden, Joan thought as she passed a prolifically growing plant with wide flat green leaves. Jewel told her it was called "kat" and was chewed by the natives for a mildly stimulating effect. "A popular boost for field-workers," he'd quipped. She saw markh, a leafless, thornless tree with bare branches and slender twigs. There were over a hundred different grasses growing here, the Jewel said, with Spanish reeds growing near the water. As they walked he pointed to the Acacia trees, a poincianna with spectacular orange and scarlet flowers and the eucalyptus with its aromatic leaves. There were several palms, including the doum palm whose leaves were used by natives to make the traditional African fan.

Confidently, the Jewel led the way through the foothills, pointing out the wonders of his native land to Joan. Several times, she had stopped to inspect a particular plant he'd mentioned and now she was having trouble keeping up. Jack was lagging far behind.

Jack wiped the sweat from his forehead. Just look at them, he thought. Joan and her friend were acting as if this were a Sunday walk in the park. And since when did Joan become a botanical freak? He heaved the survival kit to his left shoulder. He was glad they were getting out of the goddamn desert. He thought if he ever saw sand again it would be too soon.

Jack was glad they were rid of Omar. He was nothing but bad news for Joan. Maybe now after her little escapade in the tower, she would agree with him. He didn't know about Joan. Sometimes she acted like a halfwit. He hadn't decided if it was her natural optimism or foolhardiness that caused her to throw herself into these life-and-death situations without any thought as to the outcome. It was probably both. She was her own worst enemy.

He looked up to see her bend down and pick some odd-looking flower. She never looked back, but he knew she wanted him there. He watched her hips as they swayed when she walked. He wondered how long he could go without making love to her. Not long, he knew. He wondered if that thought ever entered her mind. Did she want him anymore—even sexually, if nothing else. Jack sighed. It was best he try not to think about it. He needed his energy to survive.

Jack paused for a moment. "You know where in the hell you're goin', mister?"

The Jewel kept walking, but called over his shoulder, "Oh, yes. Over the mountain."

"Well, that eases my mind considerably."

"Jack, keep up," Joan said, turning to see how far behind he was.

Jack glared at her. "Hey, don't worry about me, okay?" He knew *that* wouldn't be too hard for her.

Jack stubbed his foot on a rock. The pain shot up his leg. Sweat was pouring down his neck, back and chest. He was certain now the jungle in Colombia was a piece of cake compared to this blast furnace.

"'We're goin' over the mountain,'" he mumbled Jewel's words to himself. "No wonder this country is so goddamn backwards . . . in three thousand years no one's ever given a straight answer."

It had taken almost an hour to make their way through the foothills to the base of the mountains. Joan looked up and wondered if it would get any cooler up there. Her jumpsuit was plastered to her skin and she thought she would never get all the sand out from between her teeth. What she wouldn't do for a bath. She'd done just about everything she could think of to keep her mind off the heat and the danger. But she'd run out of questions about the trees and flowers. She thought she knew every subterranean layer of rock, soil and sediment ever unearthed in Africa.

She looked at the Jewel. Nothing bothered him. Not the heat, the blazing sun or Omar.

Well, she'd really done it this time. She had been such a fool to come here. She should have listened to Jack and stayed on the boat. Maybe he didn't love her, but at least she would have been alive at the end of the year. At this point she almost felt they were doomed. Sure, they kept walking, but sooner or later Omar would swoop down on them in his helicopter or pop up from some sand dune and shoot her. Kill Jack.

She trembled. She didn't want to think about it. She couldn't. The only thing that kept her going was the belief that they would get away. She didn't know how, but she knew they would. She had to believe in something. At this point there wasn't much to believe in.

She didn't believe in love anymore, that was for sure. She had Jack to thank for that. She knew now that it was the loss of that hope, that dream of love in her life that had stifled her writing. Hell, it had killed it. Joan wondered if she would ever be able to write again. When she thought about it, she felt hollow inside. There were no ideas, no stories, no heart left in her. She would never be the same again and it was all Jack's fault.

Climbing the craggy mountain was not so easy as it looked, Jack thought. It was slow going because there were no bushes or limbs to grab onto to pull himself up. The terrain was rocky and desolate. This was the windward side of the mountain that received little rain.

Jack stopped to wipe his forehead again. He'd never be able to make it up the mountainside at this rate. He was exhausted already. He didn't think he could move another step. He looked at his watch. They had been traveling for hours, and yet Jack would have sworn it was less than one hour. What was happening to his sense of time? He'd always prided himself on his tracking abilities. He dropped the survival pack to the ground and took out the canteen. He took a long drink, and as he wiped his mouth, he looked at the vast desert floor beneath him. It was miles back to the plane wreckage. It seemed impossible they had come this far, but they had. He looked up to the Jewel. There was something about that funny, skinny man that he couldn't quite put his finger on. It was almost as if he were a sorcerer of some kind. Jack wondered if Joan's little friend had anything to do with Jack's lost sense of time. He chuckled to himself. Maybe he was Aladdin's great-grandson.

Jack put the cap back on the canteen and took one

last look at the desert. Suddenly, his head jerked forward and he shielded his eyes for a better view. There was long trail of dust weaving its way toward the mountains.

"Hey, take a look at this," he called to Joan and her friend.

Joan and the Jewel stopped and looked to where Jack was pointing. Joan knew in an instant it was Omar. As they watched, they could hear the screech of the half-tracks as they churned up the desert.

"What the hell did you do to that guy?" Jack demanded of Joan. "Why does he want you so bad?"

Jack almost didn't want the answer to his question. In a burst of energy, he grabbed the survival kit and took off down the path to the next area of clear footholds.

Joan dug her heels into the mountainside and kept climbing. She glanced back again to see the half-tracks gaining on them. She picked up the pace.

Jack shook his head. "It's my fault. When you first started talkin' about coming here, I shoulda tied you to the mast and put right out to sea. You woulda bitched for a couple of days, but I had enough beer, I coulda handled it."

Joan snorted. "Will you stop complaining? You didn't have to come with us." Why did she say that? Wouldn't she ever learn not to reach for a commitment from Jack? Every chance she got she stuck her foot in, and every time he shot her down. Fools never learned.

"Hey, I'm just here to protect my interests," he said, but decided it wasn't the right time to tell her *she* was the only "interest" he really cared about. "And don't you get pissy with me. I saved your sorry ass."

"We were doing just fine, thank you, till you came screaming into town."

"Well, excuse me for livin'!"

"You know," the Jewel said, "finding love is the same as climbing a mountain. It is very hard going up, but when you get to the top, you can see the way back clearly."

"What?" Jack asked.

"It worked well in my head, but now that I hear it, I don't know what it means, either."

Just then, they heard a rumbling from below. The half-tracks were nearly to the foothills.

Jack turned to Joan. "Can your little friend run?"

Rashid sat in the lead vehicle holding on to the dashboard as they roared over the rocky ground. He took out his binoculars to make certain of the American's position. He pointed to the driver to veer more to the left. He wanted to avoid that narrow path. They would take the wider route—there were more boulders—but the half-tracks could make it. Rashid checked his revolver. He would like to kill Colton himself, but he knew Omar would not allow it. He must bring them back alive to face Omar. Their death would be slow, tortured and painful. Rashid smiled. He hoped Omar would let him watch.

Jack grabbed Joan's arm, pulling her alongside him. They were moving faster now than ever before, and still the half-tracks were gaining on them. Even Joan's friend was scurrying as fast as he could.

Joan held onto Jack's hand. She tried to make her legs go faster, and pull herself up the steep incline. But it was a losing battle.

Jack grabbed onto a rock and pulled himself up. He slipped. The half-tracks were bearing down on them.

"Well, why don't *you two* get us out of this one?"

"I'm sure it is not my destiny to die on a mountainside," the Jewel said.

"What about us?" Joan asked.

"Hmmm . . . now that is a whole other ballgame."

Jack finally pulled himself up onto what looked to be a ledge that ran around the side of the mountain. He reached down and helped Joan up, then the Jewel.

It was narrow, not more than a foot wide and filled with rocks. Joan's foot slipped on one rock after another. Carefully, she placed her foot before allowing all her weight. One false move and she would go tumbling over the mountainside.

Joan gulped as she looked down to see the half-tracks pull to a halt at the base of the mountain. She jerked her head up and plastered her back against the mountain wall. She dug her hands into the wall to keep her balance. With Jack in front of her and the Jewel behind her, she should have felt safe, but she didn't. They should have one of those ropes tied around their waists such as real mountain climbers used. What was she thinking? She'd never dreamed she would be climbing a mountain. She didn't even know they had mountains in North Africa.

Slowly Joan made her way, following Jack's lead. She watched the position of his feet and followed suit. Just when she thought there might be a chance for them, rocks began trickling down the mountain around them. They were small stones, but they kept pelting her head and shoulders. She didn't dare look up for fear one would hit her in the eye.

Rashid stood next to the parked half-track as he observed the trio through his binoculars. He knew if he did not stop the Americans and bring the Jewel back to Omar now, he might lose them, for the ledge circled the mountain to another pass on the other side. This was Rashid's chance. He would take it.

Rashid went to the back of the half-track and opened a compartment. He extracted a light anti-tank weapon. This had been one of the guns Rashid himself had pressed Omar to order. Made in Germany, they were dependable and packable. Best of all, they were lethal. Rashid activated the long three-inch-wide cylinder that looked like a mini-bazooka. He aimed at the ledge, but his vantage was poor. He jogged backward in order to achieve perfect aim. He stopped and leveled the gun on his shoulder. This time his angle was perfect. He would not be able to bring them back alive, as Omar had requested, but the situation was desperate. He was using desperate measures.

Rashid fired the gun. He smiled, thinking he would return with the dead bodies. He would be commended.

Joan looked down in time to see some kind of rocket go flying from Rashid's shoulder toward the mountain. Toward her! Joan screamed just as the rocket zoomed into the mountain fifty yards below them and exploded.

She was still alive!

Suddenly, it felt as if the entire mountain had been shattered. The rocks slipped under Joan's feet and the wall at her back trembled. She could hear a horrid rumbling beneath her, but she couldn't see what had happened. The din grew louder and the ledge shook with greater force. Then, she realized it was a rock slide. The mountain below them had been destroyed.

Huge boulders, hunks of stone and tons of gravel tumbled down the mountain to the foothills. Rocks flew everywhere. Joan wondered how long they would last on this precarious ledge before it too fell to the earth below.

Just then, Joan realized that Rashid and his men were still at the base of the mountain. She looked down to see the half-tracks being buried by the rocks. She could hear the soldiers screaming as they scrambled inside the half-tracks for safety. They pulled some of the vehicles away in time to avoid damage.

Jack was whooping with delight. He'd never seen a prettier sight. He turned his posterior to Rashid and called out to him.

"Hey, Omar, kiss my ass!"

Rashid, standing at the rear of the half-tracks, and devoid of any injury, glared at Colton. He couldn't hear what Colton was saying but he had a good idea. Omar may want the Jewel back, but Rashid swore to himself that Colton would be his to deal with. There was nothing he would like more than to feel Colton's throat beneath his hands as he slowly squeezed the life out of him.

Jack looked down at Rashid's malicious face. It didn't take a genius to know what that ugly son-of-a-bitch was thinking. Jack couldn't help laughing, though. They had outsmarted Rashid and Omar again. Jack liked this feeling of victory that ran through his veins.

He felt as if the world were his once again. Nothing could hold back Jack T. Colton.

Joan wished Jack wouldn't laugh in Rashid's face like that. She had a feeling it was bad luck. After all, Rashid was still alive. He could still come after them. She looked in front of them and saw that the ledge— their passage to safety—was gone. It must have been blown away in the blast or the rock slide.

"Now what do we do?" she asked Jack.

"Up the mountain, darlin'."

"What mountain?"

Jack turned and looked at the broken ledge. Suddenly, his humor left him. There was no place to go but back—to Rashid. That was just as deadly as trying to scale the shattered ledge.

"Well," the Jewel said, "I suppose we'll just have to find another way up the mountain."

Jack looked at Joan's friend, wondering whom he was trying to kid.

Just then, from high above, a rope fell right in front of Joan. She blinked twice, wondering if there were mirages in the mountains.

The Jewel grabbed it. "Like this, perhaps," he said lightly as if he'd expected the rope to appear.

Joan shook her head, trying to make sense of this . . . magic trick of his. First it was toilet paper, then flowers, then parachute umbrellas. Why not a rope?

She looked at Jack. Maybe he knew what to make of this.

Jack shrugged his shoulders.

"Take it," he said.

Gingerly, Joan reached out and grabbed the rope.

She pulled on it—hard. Amazingly, it held. She was more stunned than ever. The Jewel's mirages were real.

Knowing it was their only chance for escape, Joan began climbing the rope. Hand over hand, she inched her way upward. Suddenly, the rope started moving. Frightened, Joan nearly let go. What kind of rope was this that could move of its own accord?

"Hang on!" Jack yelled to her.

Then Jack and the Jewel grabbed on below Joan. Slowly, all three were hoisted up the mountainside.

This was the craziest escape Jack had ever seen. He was beginning to wonder about Joan's friend. There were too many unexplained coincidences since he'd met this guy. Maybe he hadn't been too far off, guessing this guy was related to Aladdin. Maybe there was something to those stories about genies and lamps and magic carpets. Not that he'd ever really believe in magic, but this rope . . .

"Who'd you say you were?" Jack asked him.

"I didn't."

Joan reached the top of the mountain and slid over the ledge. Jack and the Jewel followed her.

Joan stood on unsteady feet gazing at a dozen ebony faces framed by massive hayricks of dung-greased hair, tangles of dreadlocks and kinky swirls. Some of their faces had been painted with a while chalk or clay, making them look even more bizarre. Their hollow dark eyes stared at her, scrutinizing her clothes, her jewelry and her hair. They touched her arm and then jumped back, they more frightened than she. Slowly, they moved closer, inspecting Jack. They were scantily dressed with odd-colored loincloths, bare chests and many necklaces of bones and teeth. Two of the more muscular youths carried spears decorated with feathers.

They looked fearsome, but their manner was childlike. Joan held her breath as one of them lifted her hand and inspected her red nail lacquer. His faint smile told her he approved.

"These are Nubians," the Jewel said. "The people time has forgotten."

Chapter Fifteen

DUSK SETTLED A COOL BLANKET OVER THE desert as Ralph began to stir from his dream. He was in an enormous suite at the Plaza Hotel; Room Service had just brought him filet mignon, baked potato, Caesar salad and a six-pack. There was a blonde lying on the bed watching him light the candles. Later, they would go out to a nightclub in his chauffeur-driven limousine.

Ralph smiled in his sleep, and then suddenly he awoke with a start. He blinked. He should have known it was a dream. He was still stuck in the desert. The Plaza was a long way down the road for Ralph.

The dervishes were seated in a semicircle around him. He rose up on an elbow. They were all staring at him with blank expressions. He had a queasy feeling in his stomach, as if he were the main course. They didn't look too pleased with the way things were going.

Ralph tried to smile at them, but it was a miserable attempt. He could tell they were camped for the night, since the camels and horses were tied up behind him. Maybe it was time he made more of an effort to be their friend. Especially since they looked at him as if he were the one who'd brought them all their bad luck.

"Hey, thanks. I thought I was dead meat out there. I owe you a real solid. When you fellas come to New York and drive cabs, I want you to head up to the Bronx. My blessed mother makes sausage and peppers like you never had."

He smiled again. Their faces were unchanged. They weren't buying it. One of them even reached for his knife, unsheathed it and toyed with the blade. Ralph swallowed deeply. He'd have to do better.

"How about that double-crossin' Colton runnin' off with the jewel? He's gonna hold out for the highest bidder. He's screwed us, boys, but we'll get him. We'll ride together. All of us. Brothers. I'm feelin' a real sympatico here. Like I'm one of you."

To a man the brothers all laughed in Ralph's face.

Ralph couldn't understand it. He thought he'd sounded sincere. He would have listened to him. That was the trouble with these half-baked desert-brains. They never knew a good line when they heard it.

"What's so funny?" Ralph demanded.

"You think you can be one of us?"

"What, is it a restricted club?" Ralph taunted. "Is there some kind of initiation? Some kind of test? Fine, test me. Gettin' you guys back your jewel is that important to me."

Ralph smiled at the brothers and they smiled back. Finally, he had them on his side. And so easily, too. After all, how bad could their initiation be?

Nestled in the crook of three mountains and protected from invasion from all four sides, the Nubians had founded their colony over a thousand years ago. The mountains supplied them with clear drinking water, grasses to graze their oxen and sheep; and through age-old teachings they knew how to cultivate the land until it bore its maximum in fruits and grain. They knew how to irrigate the land by digging round wells in the desert. They made a honeycomb of salt pans on the edge of the Sahara to supplement the cattle's diet. The salt pans were filled with saline water, and when evaporated, would leave behind thick salt deposits that would form into cakes. The cakes could be transported wherever the Nubians wanted.

The Nubian huts were elongated to provide for large families. After his first marriage, arranged for by his parents, a Nubian male could take as many as three wives during his lifetime. The first wife always retained her position of power and lived in the more elaborate daub-and-wattle hut. Each male arranged his main hut and the smaller huts of his other wives into a circle forming his own "family."

As Joan, Jack and the Jewel were led along the mountain crest to the top, the villagers gathered to greet them. Joan was fascinated with their costumes. The women wore heavily embroidered blouses and striped wraparound skirts. On their heads were headpieces made of many scarves, all twisted and wrapped around the head and then adorned with strings of beads. They wore eight huge gold loops in each ear. They were a tall, slender people. Above all, Joan was struck with how the most beautiful men and women were allowed to come forward first; the others stayed to the rear of the crowd.

The Jewel explained that Nubians had an exacting

ideal of beauty and they spent long hours adorning their bodies, making ceremonial clothes, jewels and headpieces. The men were even more concerned with beauty than the women.

As Joan drew closer to camp, she noticed that the Nubians were all smiles at their arrival. Needlessly, she had feared they would be looked upon as invaders.

The Nubians surrounded them, their brightly painted faces beaming with delight as they touched Joan. They seemed fascinated with her light—untanned—skin. Almost to the last man and woman, everyone stroked her arm and peered closely at her face. She was flattered. Joan thought she would never buy another bottle of Coppertone again.

The Jewel spoke to the Nubians in their language as the villagers inspected Joan's belt, her shoes and stud earrings. Joan took one earring out and handed it to one of the young girls. The girl squealed with delight and placed it in one of the eight holes pierced in her ear.

The Jewel finished his conversation with the good-looking man wearing the most jewelry and the largest white-feather headdress. Joan assumed the man was the leader.

"It's amazing," Joan said to the Jewel. "Where did you learn to speak this?"

"To live in the Sudan you must know many languages. It's a lot stranger that I speak English."

Jack was ear-to-ear grins with relief now that they were out of danger. He was surrounded by four men about his age but all six inches taller. They spoke all at one time and Jack sensed they were filled with questions about their journey here. They were fascinated with his survival kit, and so Jack handed it to them to investigate. Jack tried to explain his gear to them, but the language barrier was a tough one to overcome. He resorted to sign language and gestures. It helped.

"Thank 'em for us," Jack said to the Jewel. "You big, bad wonderful people. I love ya, Nubians!"

Reacting to Jack's exuberance, one of the tribesmen reached out an arm to Jack in the traditional arm shake. Jack slapped the man's hand giving him "five," forgetting momentarily this wasn't New York.

"My man!"

The native looked at his hand, totally confused by the gesture. Jack smiled and watched as a slow smile once again filled the young man's face.

Several of the village women were chattering among themselves and then turned to Joan and babbled some more.

"What are they saying?" she asked the Jewel.

"They want to know if the two of you are married."

Joan was taken aback. Why couldn't they ask something simple, like where she bought her jumpsuit? It was a simple question, she thought. At that moment Joan realized fully her dilemma. There was nothing the matter with her writing. There never had been. She didn't need challenges or direction. The incompleteness she'd felt was because, in her heart, *she was married to Jack*. She'd tried to be modern and blasé about their arrangement, but Joan wasn't *that* contemporary. She could never leave Jack, because she loved him. She was his till the day she died. What bothered her was the simple fact that their union was not legal.

As long as they went on as they did, she was an

expendable item to Jack. Joan wanted more than that from him. She wanted "forever." It wasn't an unreasonable demand, she thought. Not if he loved her. Of that, she was not sure.

Jack had said he'd come here after the jewel, after revenge. He'd told her that she was not the reason. But, Joan wanted not to believe him. Too often, she'd seen that pleading look in his eyes, that vulnerability that allowed her to delve into his soul. He thought he was being smart, not giving in to her and keeping her at a distance.

Now, Joan knew why she'd made such a big deal about doing a book on Omar. She'd wanted Jack to stand up for himself. She'd wanted him to take her away on the *Angelina* despite her protests. She'd wanted him to put his claim on her; his name on her. She wanted to be his, and she wanted him to be all hers. She didn't want to lose Jack. She didn't want to wake up one morning and find he'd sailed away—without her.

Joan looked at the Nubian woman who'd asked the question and was waiting for an answer. Sadly, Joan looked away. She didn't have what she wanted.

In nearly inaudible tones she said, "No, hardly."

Joan had no more said the words when the tallest and most handsome Nubian male grabbed her by the arm. He smiled. Instantly, Joan panicked.

"Wait, what is he doing?"

The native spoke to the Jewel. Joan waited for the Jewel to translate for her. The exchange continued. She was growing nervous. This man had a firm grip on her arm—a very possessive grip. The Jewel spoke again. The Nubian nodded. The Jewel smiled. Joan was beginning to think this was the SALT peace talks. Would they ever finish?

Finally, the Jewel turned to her.

"I'm afraid if you're not married the tribe leader— this gentleman here—can claim you for his own."

Jack burst out laughing. Joan looked scared to death. Served her right after ditching him in Monte Carlo. She was really taking this thing too seriously, he thought, watching her eyes grow wide.

"We're married, we're married! Jack, tell them!"

Jack tried to ignore the pleading look in her green eyes. . . .

"Well, we sailed together for six months . . ."

"Jack!" Joan was beside herself. She'd get him back for this.

Jack smiled. He'd known all along there was no danger of Joan becoming this man's wife. He guessed he'd let her sweat long enough.

"We're married," Jack said.

The Jewel laughed along with Jack. He turned to the Nubian leader who was looking at Joan with wide, expressive eyes. He translated and pointed to Jack. Dejectedly, the Nubian released Joan. Still, he continued to stare at her. He reached out a hand and touched her cheek. Joan's smile was wan and she trembled slightly.

Joan shot Jack a vicious look, but he only chuckled at her. Jack loved to tease her, but she wished he would be more careful about his timing. They didn't know these people and their ways. One wrong move, or the wrong word, and she could have ended up herding cattle and weaving baskets for the rest of her life.

Just then, the Nubian turned away from Joan and grabbed Jack's arm. Gruffly, he spoke to the Jewel.

"What's this?" Jack exclaimed, thinking this guy's grip wasn't as friendly as he thought it should be.

"Since you are married, the only way he can have her is to wrestle you and beat your brains in." The Jewel smiled at Jack.

Joan smiled too, relishing Jack's discomfort. Turnabout was fair play.

"You gotta be kiddin'," Jack said nervously, looking up a good eight inches at the painted Nubian. Suddenly, he realized this guy was deadly serious.

The Jewel shrugged his shoulders and smiled at the Nubian. He leaned over to Jack.

"They love their wrestling."

As Jack was being dragged away, Joan called after him, "Good luck, dear."

In the center of the village was a ceremonial ring painted in the dry earth. Inside that was a smaller painted ring, this one used for wrestling. Jack wondered if they followed the Wrestling Commission's rules.

The villagers rushed to the wrestling ring and surrounded the duo. Anxiously, they awaited the beginning call to be given by the high priest, Mokao.

"Okay," Jack said to the Nubian. "But not in the face."

Chanting a high-pitched bird cry, Mokao then rammed his decorated spear into the ground. The match commenced.

Jack hunched down and circled his opponent, but the Nubian remained erect. This was going to be a piece of cake, Jack thought. Suddenly, the Nubian charged him and landed him with a flying tackle.

Joan stood on the sideline and Jack fell at her feet. She could almost hear the wind gush out of his chest. Jack landed face first, and she could tell he'd gotten dirt and sand in his eyes. He tried to wipe them, but the Nubian grabbed his arms. Half blind, Jack was unable to land a successful blow. He scrambled on the ground, but his maneuvers were ineffective. Joan crossed and uncrossed her arms, then nervously chewed on her nails.

With every move, Jack got more twisted until he looked like a pretzel. Joan couldn't tell if the Nubian was that good of a wrestler, or if Jack was simply that bad. She heard Jack moan and grunt as he tried to break loose from the Nubian's hold. Joan distinctly heard a SNAP! when the Nubian jerked Jack's neck back.

The crowd was going crazy as they cheered the local wrestling champ. They chanted and raised their fists in the air.

Jack had bitten his lip, and blood spurted out of his mouth. The Nubian grabbed him by the hair and rammed his face down on the ground repeatedly. Jack was dizzy and couldn't plan a strategy. He tensed his leg muscles, trying to flip himself out of this painful hold. But nothing worked. Again, he felt his head pummeling the ground. His ears were ringing.

Joan's eyes filled with tears and she was frantic.

"He's going to kill him," she said to the Jewel.

"Yes, I think your Jack is quite a good sport, don't you?"

Joan gazed at him wide-eyed. This was no laughing matter anymore.

"Stop them!"

"I was planning to, silly girl."

The Jewel grabbed a young boy of about eight or nine from the crowd and, together, they crossed to the ring. He picked the boy up and began flipping him in the air. The Jewel spun him over his shoulders and around his body. He tossed him in the air and then caught him just before he hit the ground. Joan and the crowd watched spellbound as the Jewel flipped and tossed the boy as if he were nothing more than a baton. The boy laughed with delight.

The crowd turned away from the wrestling match and began laughing at the Jewel and his antics. They clapped as the boy went shooting under the Jewel's legs, and then went over his shoulders and down again.

The Nubian had lifted a screaming Jack to his shoulders, then over his head and was about to slam him to the ground when, suddenly he too noticed the Jewel. He stopped mid-motion and began laughing along with the crowd.

Joan couldn't laugh at anything, seeing Jack's panicked face. Jack could easily have his spine broken if the Nubian continued. The Nubian continued laughing and was unable to hold Jack any longer. He dropped Jack like a sack of potatoes.

Jack hit the ground with a thud, but he was not badly injured. While his opponent was in the midst of hysterics, Jack reared back and coldcocked the Nubian on the side of the head. Like a falling tree, the man hit the ground.

Victorious, Jack dropped to one knee, out of breath but smiling at Joan.

"Yeah, I got him . . . I got him . . ."

Seeing that Jack was safe now, the Jewel completed his performance with the boy. The natives cheered him wildly as he took one bow after another.

Joan rushed over and hugged Jack. She looked back at the Jewel. He'd saved Jack—and her—more than once in less than a day. She would never forget this day—nor the man.

Chapter Sixteen

THE SILENT MIDNIGHT-BLUE DESERT NIGHT was broken by a distant sound of a pack of jackals crying for food. Their pathetic cry was absorbed by the sand dunes and forgotten.

A blazing bonfire crackled and sent millions of sparks into the sky. One of the dervishes threw another log onto the fire, then shielded his face from the intense heat. He backed away.

Tarak stood before Ralph with a deadly serious look on his face. Tarak did not take ceremonial matters lightly. It was an honor to be a dervish.

Only twice in Tarak's lifetime had his family allowed an outsider to be put to the dervish test. Great legends had arisen over the centuries about those who survived the dervish ritual. In the past, those who had failed had placed curses on the dervishes. But always, the curses had been reversed and visited themselves upon the ones who had spoken them. Dervishes were a magical people. Dervishes knew that. Outsiders were disbelievers. It took a strong man, of body, soul and mind, to undergo the ritual. One must have great desire and faith to become a dervish. It took an extraordinary man.

Ralph had professed such a desire to Tarak and his brothers. But Tarak had his doubts. This test would decide if Tarak's doubts were founded.

He faced Ralph.

"To be one of us, you must see with your heart's eyes, not with the eyes in your head."

Ralph nodded. It sounded simple enough. "Gotcha."

Tarak raised his voice. Ralph thought he sounded like an evangelist he'd heard once on television.

"Your heart will never bring you fear or pain, if you know our way."

Ah, that was it, Ralph thought. Their "way" must be the magic Tarak always spoke about. 'Course, he'd seen enough of these crazy dervishes to know they could do some pretty weird things. Suddenly, he wasn't so sure.

Tarak was amused. "Just your heart. You must learn to trust your heart."

Then, one of the brothers took a torch from the bonfire and walked over to the darkened area where the brothers had all gathered. There on the ground they had laid a path of wood, stones, grasses and twigs. Tarak whispered it was "the pathway of fire." Ralph gulped deeply as the brother bent down and placed the torch to the grasses. In seconds a long lane of fire extended a full fifteen or more feet.

"What the hell's that for?" Ralph demanded.

"You are looking with your eyes," Tarak said.

The brothers burst into revelry, chanting ritualistic songs and diving over the pathway of fire. Several brothers dashed to the camels and brought back their juggling balls and bats. They whooped and sang as they juggled the balls to each other over the flames. They took out their swords and brandished them over their heads as they let out the dervish cry.

The desert night was filled with song and solemn chants. The jackals ceased their cry and fled from the area.

One of the brothers tied up his tunic and walked across the burning path barefooted while the other brothers swung their swords in the air around him. When he completed his walk, they cheered him and patted him on the shoulders. They kissed his cheeks. He was one of them.

"Hey, keep your friggin' jewel." Ralph turned away. They weren't going to make shish kebab out of him!

Instantly, Tarak pulled out his knife. It gleamed in the firelight. He pointed it at Ralph's neck. Tarak had gone to a great deal of trouble for Ralph.

"Are you afraid?"

"Damn right I'm afraid! I'm always afraid."

"You believe in your fears. If you *believe* something will hurt you, it will hurt you."

Ralph looked down at the fire, then back at the knife. This guy talked a good game, but Ralph was too practical, too urban for this "faith" nonsense. He wasn't born yesterday. There had to be more to it than that.

"It's a trick, right? You put some kind of crap on your feet, what? What's the secret?"

"Secret?" Tarak leaned down to Ralph and whispered conspiratorially. "Don't say 'ouch.'"

Ralph smiled wanly as Tarak pointed his very sharp, shiny knife toward the fire. He placed a forceful hand on Ralph's back and gave him a nudge. Reluctantly, Ralph followed Tarak to the flaming pathway.

Ralph could hear his own heart as it slammed against his chest. He knew if his knees shook any more he'd get bruises. He'd been scared before, but not like this. Somehow, he thought he should be able to get himself out of this.

The brothers lined either side of the pathway. Their faces were illuminated by the fire, showing anticipation and a wild glaze in their eyes as they chanted. Four of the brothers continued their juggling. Ralph wondered if that was part of the initiation. Would he have to learn to juggle? Why couldn't he take those lessons first, and do the "fire walk" later?

He looked back at Tarak.

"What is the worst that could happen to you?"

"That I end up cherries jubilee."

"And what is the best that can happen?"

"I make it out alive and get the jewel."

Tarak nodded. "The choice is yours."

Ralph looked back at the fire—his death. He'd always thought the worst way to die was by fire and the best was by drowning. Why couldn't he have picked a beach band of dervishes? Ralph took a deep breath. He raised his foot over the coals. Instantly, he jerked his foot back. The heat was more intense than he'd thought.

He looked again at Tarak and his shiny knife. What was it he'd said? Believe and you'll make it. Look only with your heart. At this point Ralph figured he couldn't lose anything by trying.

Ralph had never believed in anything in his whole life—especially not in himself. The first thing Ralph's old man had ever told him was that he was a loser. And Ralph believed him. Throughout his entire life, Ralph had done everything to prove his old man was right. Now, Tarak was telling him to try a different way of thinking.

Staring at the means of his annihilation, Ralph had nothing to lose by trying Tarak's way. He closed his eyes and concentrated on living. If he didn't live, he'd never find the jewel. He would never be rich. And Ralph wanted to be rich.

With his eyes squeezed shut, thinking of a giant jewel, Ralph jumped onto the hot coals. He hippity-hopped as fast as his short legs could take him down the path. He screamed from the top of his lungs, but he never opened his eyes. He kept screaming, jumping and believing until he got to the end. He instantly dove into the sand and rolled around, just in case his pants had caught fire.

He grabbed his feet and blew on them. Suddenly, he realized that they were not badly burned at all. They were red, but not charred, not destroyed. He was alive! He'd gone through the initiation.

"I did it!" he exclaimed.

Ralph jumped to his feet and strutted around like a popinjay as the brothers cheered him. Tarak smiled and sheathed his knife.

This was the greatest night of his life. Ralph had achieved something; though it wasn't tangible, it meant more to him than he thought it would. He was proud of himself. For the first time in his life he was proud.

"I did it! Oh, yeah, I believe! I believe!"

Chapter Seventeen

MAAGANI, JOAN LEARNED, WAS THE KNOWL-edge of secret potions the Nubians used to enhance their beauty. The gift of *maagani* is feared by other tribes. Still others wish to steal this power from the Nubians. These secret formulas are concocted from the leaves of the *eedi* tree and the seeds of the *roogo* plant. Some formulas were said to induce madness and keep away evil spirits.

Tonight, as the Nubians prepared for the ritualistic love dance, there was no talk of evil spirits. In her hut, Joan watched as the young girls applied a pale yellow powder to their faces to lighten the skin. They outlined their eyes with black kohl and also their mouths so as to make the teeth appear whiter. A long painted yellow line was drawn from forehead down the nose and to the chin.

They wore their most elaborate headdresses and many bejeweled earrings. The girls oiled each other's breasts, backs, arms and shoulders with scented liquids. They wore no blouses, only heavily embroidered skirts that were tied low on the hips.

They gave Joan a modest ceremonial white wraparound dress of thinnest cotton gauze. They twirled her around as they tied her into her garment. There was a breast sash of gold silklike material that had been embroidered in deep pinks and reds. Joan thought it the loveliest handwork she'd ever seen. Around her waist was another sash embroidered with ancient symbols looking curiously like Egyptian hieroglyphics.

While the Nubians finished dressing her, Joan looked out of the hut to see that the celebration had begun. Three stilt-walkers danced by an enormous bonfire. Their bodies glowed in the crimson firelight as they shouted and chanted native songs. Beneath their stilts, a sea of red feathers fluttered in the breeze. Slowly, the waves of red feathers rose and fell to the music; and then with a great, joyous cry, the feathers fell away to reveal more dancers. They pranced about the fire, their cloaks of feathers swirling over their heads.

As the music reached crescendo, the Nubian women from the hut dashed outside, leaving Joan to follow them. The women, moving in a sensual dance, sidled up to the stilt-walkers. In the firelight, their painted faces seemed to change colors. Their oiled bodies gleamed and looked almost ethereal.

Joan watched as the men, seated in a semicircle, were mesmerized by the beautiful Nubian girls. As the girls gyrated their hips and extended their arms gracefully over their heads, Joan marveled at these women. They knew little about the civilized world. They had to transport water by oxen, heat their huts by bonfire and weave their own cloth. By every standard, they were considered a backward, illiterate people. But Joan realized these women knew more about life than she did. When they wanted a man, they took him. They didn't wait around until he was ready. They played none of the silly, wasteful games that she and Jack did. They were not only braver than she, they were smarter.

Joan spied Jack sitting in the center of the semicircle, and she started toward him. Suddenly, she found herself walking next to the Jewel. She blinked. He seemed to have appeared out of nowhere.

As they walked, the Nubians smiled and nodded at her.

"Everyone's so friendly now . . ." she said, thinking of the wrestling match earlier. She had feared the Nubians wanted Jack dead.

"The Nubians are hopeless romantics. It was not the fight they sought . . . only the expression of love." The Jewel smiled at Joan.

The stilt-walker glided past them as he twirled a long, fiery torch. He turned, laughed loudly and then stepped directly over Joan and the Jewel. Joan felt as if she were walking under a moving ladder. As the stilt-walker passed, Joan noticed embers fall from his torch. One particularly large ember floated down and landed on the Jewel's arm.

Joan screamed and hurried to brush it off. Quickly, she stomped the ember into the ground. She checked the Jewel's arm. Such a burn could scar for life. But as she gazed at his arm in the firelight, Joan was amazed to see it wasn't even scorched. It was impossible!

"Your skin didn't burn!"

"A small test. There will be greater ones for all of us."

Joan couldn't figure out what he was talking about.

She'd known from the moment she met him that he was an unusual man; she sensed he was a holy man. Now she had seen the strength of his power. Perhaps he was not of this earth; perhaps a spirit. She wasn't sure she should be the recipient of such knowledge. It made her feel unworthy.

"Then shouldn't we tell Jack?"

The Jewel cut her off. "You will know the right time," he said and then walked away.

Jack was sitting in the middle of the semicircle, watching the dancing. The young men of the village were talking and gesturing among themselves. Jack was stripped to the waist, and his chest had been oiled with the same perfumed concoction all the Nubians used. He wore a brightly colored sash around his waist.

He looked up as Joan sat down. Instantly, he noticed that she did not sit next to him. She had left a space—too great of a space to suit Jack. He'd wanted her next to him.

She was beautiful, he thought as the firelight danced off her creamy skin. Her hair sparkled with a life all its own. She glanced at him and paused. Her eyes bore into him. For a long moment she held him spellbound. As always, he cursed those eyes that could turn him to jelly. There were times when Jack was positive Joan possessed his very soul. She had an uncannny ability to read his mind, know his needs before he did. As much as he'd tried to fight it, Joan owned him. And God help him, he didn't want it any other way. He only wished she would want him, too. He started to slide over next to her when the Jewel sat down between them.

Jack glared angrily at the Jewel and was about to

say something when the sound of the drums, clanging pieces of wood and odd-sounding wooden clackers burst into rhythm.

Suddenly, the young girls came dashing into the center of the painted circle. The dancers were shoulder to shoulder as the music picked up tempo. They quivered forward on tiptoe and then broke into a series of exaggerated facial expressions. The Jewel explained they would be judged on charm, magnetism and personality in this dance. The facial expressions were essential.

Joan watched as eyes rolled and teeth flashed. Their faces contorted into wild-looking grimaces and smiles. Suddenly, someone—one of the elders, Joan thought— shouted "Yeeehoo" and the dancers stopped.

The music changed to a more exotic melody, and slowly the dancers broke formation and moved gracefully about the circle.

Joan stole a look at Jack. Her tensions started to melt away as the music soothed her. She wished she had sat next to him. She wanted to touch him, feel his hand on her leg. She wanted to lean over and tell him that she loved him. She wished with all her heart he would want her back. But that was another of her fantasies; she'd indulged herself too much. Jack would never commit to her. Marriage was something he ran from as if it were a disease. She looked at him again— she wished she could run from Jack, but she couldn't. He would always be in her heart.

The Jewel noticed the sad look in Joan's eyes and signaled with a wink to the Nubian girls. The girls rushed over to Joan and coaxed her to join them in the dance.

Joan was hesitant. Her uncoordination must be national news by now, she thought. But then she remembered a night—a particularly romantic night in Colombia when Jack had taught her to dance. She remembered the way he'd held her and moved his body with hers. It had been the first time they'd kissed. She remembered all his kisses had been like that—for months—until Lisbon. It wasn't until then that Joan realized how much she loved Jack. This wasn't a bi-annual cruise for her. When she'd seen that young couple being married in the piazza, Joan had known then she wanted to be Jack's bride. But he'd dragged her away from the wedding and back to the ship so fast she'd thought they'd get jet lag. The love they'd made that night was earth-shattering. She knew she'd never forget it. She had thought it was a new beginning for them, but he never mentioned the wedding again—nor had he proposed. Joan didn't have to read between any lines. Jack's message to her was clear and simple. He was not the marrying kind.

The giggling girls grabbed Joan's arm and pulled her into the circle.

Jack clapped as Joan began dancing. Looking just past her, he noticed that, just outside the circle, the big son of the chief—whom he'd fought earlier—was beginning to wake up. All this time he'd been stretched out on the ground, oblivious to the music and revelry. Jack watched as the Nubian sat up and looked around, surprised to see the party that was going on. Slowly, the Nubian's eyes rolled back in his head. He dropped to the earth again, out cold.

Jack smiled and puffed out his chest. Never let it

be said that Jack T. Colton couldn't hold his own against a Nubian.

Just then the Jewel nudged Jack and handed him a strange black root. The Jewel began chewing it and Jack followed suit.

"What is this stuff?" Jack asked.

"That is *mokassa* root."

Jack tore off another hunk and chewed voraciously. "Really tasty."

"Yes . . . and the Nubians believe it is a strong aphrodisiac."

As Jack nodded, he realized he was light-headed. He watched as Joan whirled about in front of him. She was erotic, swaying her hips and tossing her arms over her head. The firelight caught in her golden hair, making it appear alive. Shafts of light darted off the blue, green and yellow beads she wore around her hips. Her skirts whirled into a fluffy white cloud around her legs. He could see her feet, then ankles, knees, then thighs as the skirt rose higher and higher. Joan spun around the circle like a firefly.

A thin film of perspiration broke out on Jack's forehead. He wiped his face. If he'd been out there dancing, he couldn't have been any hotter. He smiled as Joan moved in perfect rhythm to the music.

Joan felt that electricity again, knowing Jack's eyes were on her. She kept dancing. She wanted to go to him, but she needed a sign from him that he still wanted her. She didn't want to be just a means to find his jewel. There was always that doubt in her mind, just as there had been in Colombia. She had never known for sure that he wanted her. Until he showed up in New York. But now it was different, more crucial. If he didn't come to her now—tonight—she knew there was no future for them. And how she wanted a future with Jack.

Jack looked at Joan. The firelight shone through the thin gauze dress, outlining her breasts, hips and long legs. Never had she been this beautiful and never had he wanted her this much. But he was afraid. He feared she didn't really love him, that she wouldn't give herself fully to him. If he went to her, what was to keep her from walking out on him again? He'd pretended all this time in escaping Omar that Joan still wanted him, even though everything she had said to him told him differently. Did she love him?

Jack watched as Joan's creamy thigh swooped past his face. When she had looked at him just then, he had seen love in her eyes. Was it possible he was only being foolish? Had he wasted days and nights unnecessarily? As he looked into her eyes, he could feel himself succumbing to her. She had such power over him. Before tonight, it had mattered that he not relinquish control to her. He didn't know if it was the *mokassa* root he chewed or Joan, but now, nothing mattered anymore. He finally admitted to himself that what frightened him most was not Joan, but a life without her.

Joan whirled in a final last spin before coming to a halt. Panting and out of breath, she stared at Jack. He didn't make a move, only stared at her with those wide saucer eyes. Her heart was slamming against her chest and her eyes were filling with tears. Please, come to me, Jack, she thought. Couldn't he tell she loved him? She would do anything for him, if he would only ask. She guessed she would always be a fool for Jack. She thought of the years she dreamed of being in love, really in love. Never had she thought it would hurt this much.

Sensing this night was a turning point for them, Joan slowly, sensuously lowered her arms. She flipped her wild mane of blond hair back and smiled at him. She lowered her eyes seductively. She parted her lips and wetted them with the tip of her tongue. She picked up her skirt, turned her back to him, and just as she darted out of the circle, she raised her skirt even higher to reveal nearly all of her long, slender legs.

Jack sprang to his feet, tossed the *mokassa* root to the Jewel and dashed after Joan. He knew damn well he needed no other aphrodisiac than his Joan.

The hut was decorated with beautiful Nubian tapestries on the walls. A single candle flickered as Jack peeled off Joan's breast sash, hip beads and then the gauze dress. He touched her shoulders, then her breasts, reveling in their creamy color and satiny touch. He kissed the crook of her neck.

Joan felt her legs sag beneath her. She always reacted like that when Jack kissed her there. She leaned into him and kissed his ear. She untied his waist sash and unzipped his pants. She pushed them down. She put her arms around his neck and pulled him closer. She could feel his heart beating rapidly against her skin. She felt his hands as they caressed her back, hips and buttocks. He squeezed her derriere and Joan chuckled lightly—she had him back. She wished they would never have to leave this place. She wanted this night to last forever. She wanted them to last forever.

They fell to the floor.

Lying naked on a thick handmade mattress, Jack took his time as he caressed every inch of Joan's body. She quivered as his hand roamed to her stomach and came to rest. The musky, spicy scent of the Nubian oil filled Joan's nostrils as she let her hands wander across his chest and down his muscular arms. She felt her heart nearly explode. How she had needed him, wanted him. She wanted to make him see that she never really wanted anyone or anything but him. His love and their life together were all that mattered to Joan. For without him, she had nothing. He kissed her again and Joan felt the fire surge inside her. With his tongue he explored her lips and mouth, igniting every nerve ending in her body. With a hunger only Jack could create inside her, Joan kissed him back, taking from him the passion he gave. The time for hesitation was over the moment he'd swept her into his arms. With every inch of her body Joan told Jack she was his. He kissed her back with a determination she'd never felt from Jack. Joan thought his kiss had never been this possessive.

She placed her hands on his head and pulled him to her breasts. For long, lazy moments, he lingered there, teasing and sucking until Joan thought she would scream from the pleasure. She tingled from head to toe with a torrid, urgent desire. Never had she felt like this, as if she would perish if she did not take from him all that she could. It was some ancient, inner voice that told her it was her love that would keep him strong, give him courage. Joan kissed him with increased ardor, hoping to infuse him with all the love she felt.

Gingerly, he moved over her; and as he did, he could see her green eyes filled with soft, unspoken words of love. What he saw in her eyes at that moment told him that all he'd hoped for, dreamed of, was his for the taking. Joan was his love, his only love. He would never lose Joan unless he pushed her away.

He kissed the base of neck where the skin was especially soft and sweet. She moaned and he felt her arms tighten around his back. What a fool he'd been. Though he'd told himself he'd given Joan everything, he realized now that he'd given her everything but what counted most. A commitment. They were not an ordinary couple. They were special. Their love was rare. And he'd nearly lost it all by his stupidity.

No wonder Joan had left him. He should have seen how asinine he'd been, but he'd been too blind, too self-centered.

He put his arms under her shoulders and kissed her neck again. Effortlessly, he entered her. Her sharp intake of breath excited him beyond all reason.

Every time Jack penetrated her, Joan raised her hips to him. She wanted him deep inside her where he couldn't go away again. She felt tears sting her closed eyes as her passion mounted. Her breath caught in her chest and throat.

Together, they left the earth and rode the constellations. Joan felt herself rising and falling and then finally pitched into a spinning whirlpool that pulled her down. When she climaxed, she screamed and buried her mouth in Jack's shoulder. Suddenly, he shuddered and moaned and fell against her.

Their passion spent, they clung to each other, neither saying a word, but knowing they had never communicated so totally.

*   *   *

Jack awoke in the middle of the night and realized the candle was still burning. He got up and was about to extinguish it when he spied several vials and pots in the corner. Thinking it was refreshment, he investigated and found they contained the body and face paints the Nubians had used earlier that night. He picked one up and then looked over at a sleeping Joan.

He gathered the colors and went back to bed. While she slept he dipped his finger in the yellow paint and began finger-painting tiny flowers on Joan's stomach. She began to stir.

"What are you doing?"

"Making you beautiful, Nubian style."

Joan looked down at the green and yellow vine he'd painted on her stomach and thighs. She smiled, took one of the pots and began painting Jack's face with an iridescent green color.

She painted butterflies, bees, ships and waves on his chest. She drew two interlocking hearts and wrote her name on one. He followed her lead and drew the same hearts over her breasts and wrote his name on her.

When he looked into her eyes, he realized how vulnerable she was. He put the pots aside and took her into his arms. He pulled her on top of him.

"Always . . . Joan."

"Forever . . ." she whispered as she kissed him.

Jack made love to Joan again. As their bodies mingled, breast to breast and thigh to thigh, the paints became smeared and formed a strange pattern on their bodies.

Jack kissed Joan a hundred times and held her even closer.

Joan was filled with so much joy, she allowed her tears to stream down her cheeks. Jack kissed her eyes, her ears and nose. He smoothed her fears and promised they would never part. Finally, he convinced her that the only treasure he needed in his life was her.

For hours they talked, caressed each other's bodies and wove their dreams for the future. When they finally fell asleep, Joan noticed that the sweat from their love-making had washed away all the paints, save for the hearts with Jack's name on her breast, and her name on his chest.

Chapter Eighteen

DAWN BURST OVER THE MOUNTAINS, SPLASH-
ing the sky with brilliant oranges, pinks and reds. Birds
soared into the air, calling to their mates as they
swooped down into the valley in search of food. The
Nubians' cattle and oxen awakened and their animal
sounds mingled with those of the village women as
they chatted with each other while preparing the first
meal of the day.

Joan stretched her arms over her head as the morning
sun warmed her face. She turned and saw Jack staring
at her. He hadn't been awake long, she could tell, for
there was sleep in his eyes—and a great deal of love.
She kissed him and nuzzled her face in his neck. Never
had she felt this safe, this positive about the future.
She hoped she could always feel this peacefulness that
seemed to blanket them.

Jack held her closer as they looked out of the expan-
sive hut opening. The fertile Nile valley below them
exploded into a multitude of colors. For a moment
Joan thought it looked like a kaleidoscope. Flowering
trees in fabulous rust, crimsons and oranges grew in
long winding bands down the mountainsides. It looked

as if someone had dumped huge cans of paint from the sky, she thought. There must have been over a hundred different greens ranging from emerald to turquoise to celedon.

Joan thought of all the times she'd dreamed of the Nile, read about it, studied it in school. Until this moment she'd never been so filled with awe. It was along this river that man had been born and civilization was created. All the wonders of ancient Egypt and the splendor of nineteenth-century "darkest Africa" were to be found along the Nile.

It was amazing that this tiny tribe of Nubians still existed. Since 1512 B.C. it was believed all aspects of Nubian culture had been assimilated into the Egyptian when Thutmose I conquered the Northern Sudan. For their sakes, Joan was glad the Nubians had isolated themselves from the rest of the world. Otherwise, she and Jack would never have escaped Rashid.

She touched Jack's chest and kissed his cheek. It had been a long time since she'd felt this sure about them.

"We haven't had a night like this since Colombia."

Jack put his arm around Joan and rested his head on her shoulder. He was deeply contented. He felt as if he'd been given back his life.

"Funny how gunfire seems to bring back the old magic," he said. He guessed they had both needed a bit of shock treatment to make them see the light.

"Not your average couple," she said, thinking no one had ever loved a man as much as she loved Jack.

He smiled and pulled her closer. "You keep me young, Joan Wilder."

Joan fell against him, kissing him, breathing his

breath. They were one again. Her biggest regret was that they had wasted so many days, so many nights with this insane struggle over commitment. They should have realized the outcome. They should have been smarter. "What fools these mortals be," she thought to herself.

Jack pressed her closer to him, knowing they were of one heart, one soul. He wished it were possible to be of one body. He felt like dancing for joy, for he had everything—he had Joan.

As he breathed in the fragrance of her hair, he thought of where they would go from here. They had no *Angelina* to go back to, no house in Connecticut, no villa in Rome. They had no *place*, and he wanted something they could call home. They needed a base. They needed money to buy a base.

Playfully, he whacked her lightly on her naked fanny.

"What do you say we round up your little friend and go after that jewel?"

"Jack, there's something you should know about the Jewel . . ."

"Yeah?"

Suddenly, they heard a loud commotion outside the hut. Then they heard the frantic cries of the Nubians, and animals barking, squawking and yelping. Then they heard gunfire.

Jack was instantly on his feet. He grabbed his pants and raced to the hut opening.

"The bad guys."

Joan hastily grabbed a flowing native wraparound dress, one that was more manageable. In seconds, she was dressed.

Jack started out the opening when Joan stopped him.

"Wait, I've gotta get the Jewel."

Confused, Jack followed her out. Had Joan known all along the jewel was here? Had this village always been their final destination? Once again he had to hand it to Joan. Just when he had her figured out, she surprised him again.

There was pandemonium everywhere as Omar's guards crisscrossed the village searching every hut for the Jewel. Chickens and pheasants scattered as children ran everywhere screaming for their parents. Mothers grabbed children and scurried away from malicious-looking uniformed soldiers. Most had never seen a rifle, much less an automatic one. But already they knew the death these men held in the long cylindrical rods. Nubian men, young and old, were being held at gunpoint. Those that tried to run away were shot at.

Joan ran through the mêlée looking for the Jewel. From what she could see, one Nubian youth had been killed. It was the man Jack had wrestled. Upon seeing his body, she slammed her hand over her mouth to stifle her scream. But she kept running from hut to hut.

Jack glanced at the menacing soldiers as they darted around and through the crowd, following Joan.

"The jewel is here?"

"Yes," Joan yelled back.

"Where is it?"

"I can't find him," she said, checking one of the last two huts.

"The little guy?"

"The Jewel."

"The little guy's got the jewel?"

"He is the Jewel."

"Hey, honey, you're not makin' sense."

"You're not listening," Joan shouted as they dodged bullets and chickens.

"Start over," Jack said, sliding behind a hut in time to miss a round of bullets.

He pulled Joan close to him and peered into her eyes. She wasn't making any sense at all.

Just then Joan heard a familiar voice. It was the Jewel.

"There he is!" She pointed around the hut.

The Jewel was being dragged into a half-track by one of Omar's guards. The soldier was a burly man and no match for the emaciated-looking Jewel.

"Come on," Jack said as he took off running.

Jack barreled his body against the guard and knocked him to the ground. While Jack was struggling with the guard, Joan grabbed the Jewel and they took off down the mountainside. Jack pulled back his fist and knocked the dazed guard cold. Without losing a second, Jack spun around and followed Joan.

Joan found a path across the mountain face, but it was barely navigable. The ground was rocky; it seemed that every time she placed her foot, the rocks slid out from under her. Joan had the uncanny sensation that she was on roller skates. This side of the mountain was more fertile, and there were long stretches of green grass with soft earth beneath. Finally, however, Joan decided those easily crossed areas were placed there only to lull her into thinking all the ground was smooth. As soon as she took the terrain for granted, a sharp rock would jut out of nowhere and stab her foot. Twice in the first few minutes, Joan found herself flat on her fanny. She got up and started off again, only to slip, fall and then slide a good distance down the mountain.

Joan felt her arm being scratched by the grasses and her "dress" hike up nearly to her hips. She tumbled over and over, thinking not of broken arms or legs but of propriety and constantly kept yanking at her skirt. Finally, she gave up and concentrated on braking her fall. She grabbed a tree limb and slowed herself to a stop. When she stood, looking back to Jack and the Jewel, she realized both her shins were badly cut and her palms were bleeding.

Finally, Jack and the Jewel caught up to her. They kept up the pace.

Jack dug his feet in and kept on going. His thigh muscles ached already—and it was long way down this mountain. He was still puzzled by what Joan had said.

Jack turned to the Jewel. "Do you have the jewel?"

Joan heard him and yelled back, "He *is* the Jewel."

"That's right," Jewel said. "I am me."

"What're you talkin' about? Omar stole a jewel."

"The Jewel is not a jewel," Joan retorted exasperatedly. "The Jewel is a man."

Jack turned back to the little man. "Omar stole you?"

"I am the Jewel." He nodded happily as he slipped on a patch of wet grass.

Joan looked at Jack's confused face as he slowly realized the impact of what they were telling him. Joan burst into laughter. The Jewel laughed, too.

"Shit!" Jack exclaimed, and then he too slipped on the same patch of grass. He went sliding down the mountain on his backside. With his hands over his head, unable to grab onto anything more than a flower or two, Jack couldn't stop laughing. The ground became more densely planted and Jack's slide slowed. He rolled over twice before coming to a stop near a eucalyptus tree. He stood, brushed himself off, and looked back at Joan who was tumbling after him.

"Yeah," he mumbled to himself. "Sure . . . the Jewel . . . Yeah, what the hell? . . . The Jewel . . . right, right . . . How did I miss it? . . . Hey, Omar, I got your Jewel."

The Jewel came skittering down toward Jack and Joan. Joan looked at him, thinking he looked much as he had when he was walking the clothesline out of their tower cell. She wondered why he didn't make his magic umbrella appear. He hopped and skipped and, finally, they were all together again. This time they held hands as they continued to scramble and laugh their way down the mountainside.

They were nearly to the bottom of the mountain. Joan hadn't thought about where they would go from here. She really didn't care, as long as it was away from Rashid and Omar's men.

Just then, she heard the sound of two blasts from a train. Joan looked at Jack and then the Jewel. She had been with the Jewel long enough to know that he could make a train appear out of nowhere. Even more astonishing—he could make certain an existing train was on time.

Chapter Nineteen

CIRCLING AROUND THE MOUNTAIN BASE spewing black smoke, the rickety train chugged as fast as its battered engine could go. It was caked with sand and dirt from too many days in the desert and too few washings. The windows that remained intact were open, allowing the sultry breeze to fan a baby's face, to cool a woman's brow. The train was filled with natives all bound for Khadir and Omar's holy anointing.

Joan, Jack and the Jewel peered down at the fifty-year-old train as it slowed and came to a stop at a small station. Next to the station was a cluster of small clay buildings. Joan knew this was not a town, only an outpost, since she could not see any other buildings.

The Jewel pointed to the train.

"The White Nile. It will be carrying the people to meet their new redeemer."

Quickly, the trio hurried down the mountain. Joan kept slipping on the thick grasses, but Jack helped her along. They had no time to lose, Joan thought, as she investigated the station area more closely. There was no fuel area, no water tower. The train would only stop for a few short minutes, take its passengers and leave. Joan ran faster.

The train was halted in the station as Jack, Joan and the Jewel came racing off the mountain. Joan thought her lungs would burst from the exertion. She thought it marvelous her ears hadn't popped during their quick descent.

Jack led the way over the flatland with Joan quick on his heels. Joan had just emerged from a clump of tall grasses onto the dusty road area when, suddenly, a jeep came roaring past her and almost knocked her over. Her heart lurched when she recognized the man driving. It was one of Omar's men. She darted over to Jack just as one of Omar's trucks whizzed by.

Jack grabbed Joan's hand, and with the Jewel the three ducked behind a large flowering bush.

Joan watched as Omar's soldiers scanned the area. How had they gotten here so fast? she wondered.

A crowd of over a hundred villagers, both Moslem and African, wedged their way onto the already crowded train. A family with six children and carrying as many makeshift bundles pushed and prodded everyone out of their way. The children bellowed as loudly as their arrogant and rude father, but they all managed to find a seat. With dirty, beaming faces, the six children waited while the rest of the angry passengers boarded.

Approximately a hundred yards from the train and the station, Tarak and his brothers watered their camels at a well. Tarak's face was grim as he surveyed the boarding passengers. Twenty minutes of personally inspecting every man, woman and child in the crowd had revealed no sign of his precious Jewel, nor of the Americans.

Tarak was not discouraged. Nothing would deter him from finding the holy leader. Tarak and his brothers had come too far, risked too much to give up now. If there was a way, the Unseen would guide them. He adjusted his tunic as he leaned over to dip his copper ladle into the cool water. Tarak believed as his father had and his father before him. Tarak was not a perfect man, but he always tried to do the right thing. Just as there was always water in abundance when he had need of it, so too would the Unseen deliver the Jewel back to his people.

Suddenly, Tarak heard his name being called by his newest "brother."

Ralph tromped toward the well. He wore the traditional dervish garb. The ends of his twisted turban kept falling in his face, slapping his neck and cheeks. Ralph slapped at the material, but it evaded his wishes. His caftan caught between his bowlegs, and it had taken him half the night to learn how to walk in these skirts and not trip over his feet. Ralph had been determined to conquer the caftan, for he'd landed on his face one time too many. Ralph never wanted to taste sand in his mouth again.

Upon seeing Ralph, Tarak dropped the ladle and stood. His eyes were earnest.

Ralph shrugged his shoulders.

"They're not there. I checked every face, looked up every skirt. Nothin'."

Easing their way around the back of the train, Joan, Jack and the Jewel merged into the crowd. Joan stole a long scarf from a hastily tied bundle a young girl was carrying and wrapped it around her head. Jack crouched down so as not to be so conspicuously tall. The Jewel eased his way around the people, chatting nonchalantly and brightly to everyone.

Joan kept her head down as they inched their way forward onto the train. She glanced over to Jack and realized he had disappeared. Panicked, she scanned the crowd and found him over to her left beneath one of the train-station posts. The poster waving in the breeze caught her eye and she took a step back to see it more clearly. With a gulp, Joan looked at a picture of herself!

It was the picture from her book jacket, and there were Arabic letters beneath her name. Quickly, she worked her way to Jack and the Jewel.

"Look," she said, indicating the poster.

Jack pulled her scarf over her mouth and nose to disguise her, and glanced behind him.

Omar's guards were checking the people as they boarded the train.

"Just keep moving," Jack said, hoping for the best.

With heads down, Jack, Joan and the Jewel crept through the crowd and away from the train.

With a last glance at the poster, Joan said, "I always hated that picture."

Exerting every ounce of power its antique pistons could muster, the locomotive pulled from the station. Natives hung out of the windows as the morning sun rose in the sky. Children sat on their mother's laps, for there was not enough room. Animals, chickens and pets confined inside homemade crates filled the aisles, making it impossible for anyone but the conductor to pass. Nearly wobbling from the overload, the train moved at a turtle's pace.

From a rock that jutted out from the mountainside, Joan watched the train struggle to build up steam. Her plan would work, she knew it. She signaled to Jack and the Jewel as the train began to pull away.

They stood up and began to run alongside the train above the train on a narrow pass. The pass curved into an overpass that arched above the tracks.

With precision timing, they reached the overpass and Joan readied herself to jump.

"All aboard," Jack yelled as he jumped first. He landed in a crouch and looked up to Joan.

Holding her breath and her nose as if she were diving into a river, Joan jumped onto the slow-moving train.

The Jewel reached the edge of the overpass, but then he hesitated.

Joan stood up and smiled at Jack.

"And you didn't think it would work."

Just then the unsuspecting Joan was hooked by a height-measuring bar.

"Jack!" she screamed with the last breath in her lungs. The metal bar had slammed into her with enough force to knock the wind out of her. She felt as if her chest were on fire. She wanted to call out to Jack again, but couldn't. Her eyes were wide with fear as he slowly kept moving away from her. She reached out for him, but he was too far away.

Jack leapt to his feet and began running toward Joan. The train was moving at only five miles an hour, he guessed, but it was enough to keep him away from Joan. It was like those horrid nightmares he'd had as a child. He kept running toward something he wanted very, very badly, but the hell of the dream was that it always stayed just inches from his grasp. He reached out his hand, but their fingers never touched. She was frightened, he could tell—and so was he.

Joan finally regained her voice and yelled again. "Jack, help!"

At that precise moment the locomotive changed gears and there was a tiny space where the engine made no noise. Joan's voice could have carried for miles had it not been for the reflecting mountain walls. Her echoes were deafening.

Tarak, watering his camel, instantly dropped the goatskin bag and looked up. Ralph stopped whipping away at his turban tails and listened. His grin was wide and hopeful. Every time he'd ever given up on Joan Wilder, she had always popped up. He should have remembered that from Colombia. She had never disappointed him.

Nearly a dozen soldiers raised their heads. To a man, they spotted their prey hanging from the measuring bar above the train.

Jack was drenched with sweat as the train picked up speed. Willing his legs to move faster, Jack poured it on. He jumped from car to car, but he knew he might as well be standing still. Joan was no closer now than she was before. Another car was coming up. Jack jumped onto the next car and lost his footing. He slipped and nearly fell off the train. His thighs stung with hot pain. Still, he managed to regain his speed.

He ran and wiped the sweat from his face with his sleeve. Joan was terrified. He had to save her.

The Jewel looked down at the moving cars beneath him. He didn't like looking down from high places at moving things below him. It reminded him of snakes, and he hated snakes. He kept telling himself that if Joan and Jack could perform this trick, so could he.

Mustering his courage, he closed his eyes and pitched himself forward onto the train. As he landed on the train, he collided with Joan.

Jack had finally built up so much inertia that he could not stop running. He saw the Jewel land on the train and then slam into Joan. Jack tried to slow himself, but couldn't. He knocked Joan and the Jewel down at the same time.

Shouting orders to his men, Omar's lieutenant jumped into the nearest truck. The driver revved the engine and started after the train.

At the same moment, the dervishes, on the other side of the train, mounted their camels and horses. Thundering over the station's loading area and onto the tracks, Tarak and his men raced alongside the train. Ralph, now an experienced camel jockey, urged his mount on. In no time, Ralph was directly behind Tarak. The dervishes cried the shrill desert cry of their ancestors as they rode toward their Jewel.

Hearing all the commotion, the fifty-two-year-old engineer turned around to see what could be so important about his run—one he'd made every year since he was fifteen. He saw nomads on camelback on his right side and soldiers in modern camouflage uniforms on his left. He scratched his head. Nothing like this had ever happened on his run before. The engineer didn't like disturbances. He had an unblemished work sheet. He intended to keep it that way. He turned to the guard beside him.

The guard was dressed in the new military dress of the Sudan. It marked him as a member of Omar's army.

The guard turned around and investigated. He could see no one on the roof of the train, nor on the left. But when he looked to the right, he saw the American man and woman and the Jewel climbing down the side of the train and into one of the cars.

The guard climbed onto the next car, which was loaded with long wooden posts. He burst into the first passenger car. He yelled to two other guards standing at the rear of the car. They shouted a reply in their native tongue. All three left the wondering passengers behind as they pursued the "criminals."

Indicating that the next car held their prey, the first guard flung the door open dramatically. He cocked his rifle, relishing this moment of power in his otherwise dreary life. He and his companions scanned the crowded car.

They saw men, women and children filling every seat and blocking the aisle. There were Africans, Sudanese and Moslems. They saw baggage that looked like people and people that looked like baggage. Chickens cackled and pigs grunted. It was hot, dusty and smelled of sweat—it was normal, and nowhere did they see the Americans.

Angered, the first guard cursed in his native language. Starting with the first row, he began tearing *koffias* off each person to reveal his identity. He unveiled women whose skin had never seen the light. One irate husband lifted his hand to strike the guard, but after looking down the barrel of the guard's rifle, he thought better of the chivalrous gesture.

The guards moved forward, but they received much taunting and opposition from the passengers.

Jack kept his eyes on the approaching guards as he motioned to Joan and the Jewel to enter the car behind them. There was nowhere for them to go. The train had picked up speed. Jack knew if they tried to jump, they would be seriously injured. The guards moved down the aisle and toward the door.

Jack spun around and entered the last car.

The caboose was lavishly decorated in white with linen-covered walls, and with velvet draperies on the windows and in the back to designate a sleeping area, he supposed. It was air-conditioned, with piped-in stereo music and indirect lighting. The furniture was gilded and French—the kind that once sat in palaces. There were expensive silk flower arrangements, a lush, well-stocked bar and a lighted oil painting. Suddenly, Jack felt chills sink into the marrow of his bones. There was only one person in the Sudan who could afford luxury like this.

Joan and the Jewel nervously looked at him.

Just then, two guards stepped in behind Jack and trained their guns on him.

Omar stepped out from the white velvet draperies.

"Thank you for returning the Jewel of the Nile."

Chapter Twenty

THE ANCIENT CITY OF KHADIR STRETCHED its remaining tall columns toward the setting sun. The last golden rays of sunlight mingled with the first silver moonbeams, casting an eerie glow over the ruins. For over two thousand years, the city of Khadir had been a gathering place for higher learning, culture, art and commerce. At one time, it had been host to Ramses II, Nefertiti, Alexander the Great and several of the Roman Caesars. The city reached its zenith during the early Arab rule in 639. It was during this time the Islamic culture spread over the Sudan. But as the centuries rolled on and the Arabs left and the Turks came, and then the French and Britons, the city of Khadir was abandoned as the professors and scholars moved to Khartoum.

It was fitting Omar would choose this place to perform his "miracle," for Khadir was known as a spiritual place and a place where men of all beliefs and cultures could gather to find peace. In those ancient days, as today, the Sudan had chosen a path of mediation and synthesis between the Islamic and African traditions. To show his people that he was the true leader, Omar needed the mystical backdrop of Khadir to convince his followers.

In the center of the city stood the remains of a once ornate temple. Its walls were intact, but the golden dome no longer reflected the sun. Gone were the blue glass windows that soared forty feet high. The tapestries that had taken a hundred years and thousands of hands to weave had been stolen or burned or destroyed by the elements. Jewel-encrusted candelabra, crystal lamps and gold chairs had been sold in auctions to pay for the living costs of the few holy men who had remained in Khadir when the Turks ruled the land. Finally, the temple had crumbled, not so much from inattention and lack of maintenance as from irreverence.

Folklore told of the ancient holy men who still roamed the city, praying for the redeemer. Their souls could not rest, for they believed no mortal men would carry on their work. They reasoned that if the city of Khadir had been abandoned, so had their religion. There were those who believed that once the redeemer was brought to them, the walls of Khadir would no longer cry in the desert night over the loss of believers.

On this night, thousands of pilgrims had gathered at Khadir to see Omar proclaim himself their leader. From the tribes of the White Nile, the Congo and the Red Sea Hills they had come. From the highlands of Darfur and the Ethiopian Highlands they had traveled on foot and camelback. From the volcanic pile of the Jabal Marrah had come seven tribes of farmers, all with their children, wives and animals. From the modern cities, small towns and remote farming villages, they had come by train.

They spoke in different languages and lived by different customs. Few shared physical similarities. They were more diverse than any nation in the world. But they all believed in the redeemer.

Outside the city each tribe set up small camps with clusters of tents surrounding a communal bonfire. Some of the tents were extremely elaborate, reminiscent of a time when warring sheiks ruled the sudan.

Filing into the city, dressed in robes similar to the other pilgrims, were Tarak, Sarak, Barak, Ralph and the other dervishes. Ralph peered around him at the throng as they chanted religious-sounding cries. Passing several of Omar's guards, Ralph pulled the end of his scarf over his face. Ralph knew this was no time to get caught. He was too close to the jewel. As they walked under an arch that led into the temple, Ralph noticed the guards were distributing guns among their ranks. For the first time, Ralph wondered what kind of jewel this was.

He'd seen El Corazon, held it even, but this—he glanced again at an automatic rifle—this must be a plate-sized pearl! Or a fist-sized ruby. Maybe it was a diamond the size of a headlight. Ralph gulped. It was going to take a lot for him to pull this off.

Inside the temple, Tarak stopped. Ralph nearly ran into him. Tarak looked down at Ralph and pointed.

A quick head count told Ralph there were over five thousand fierce-looking warriors facing a giant stage that had been erected between crumbling columns and dusty relics of perished kingdoms. Above their heads was a giant replica of Omar's insignia. Ralph frowned. Omar's ego was more inflated than he'd thought. He was going to enjoy taking him down a peg or two.

As the sun fell behind the mountains stealing its golden light, the electricity in the crowd grew. Arguments and scuffles broke out among tribesmen. Men raised their guns, flaunting them in the air above their heads, each trying to make a show of power. Young boys flicked knives up, over and around their bodies, showing their skill, intimidating their enemies.

Though the dream of a redeemer was universal among these people, thousands of wars, years of bickering and jealousy had been well ingrained.

The moon ascended farther into the heavens, casting a green-silver light on two men working high up on the temple wall.

Dressed in *gallabahs*, one of the men withdrew a pair of binoculars and scanned the crowd below. The other man checked his watch and nervously tapped his foot.

The first man put the binoculars away, lifted his robes and reached into the pocket of his jumpsuit and pulled out a pack of cigarettes.

Placing the cigarette in his mouth, J. T. lit it with his Bic lighter. He inhaled deeply and rechecked the wires at his feet. Perfect. He looked at the moon one last time before he and Colt hurried out of sight.

Scratching, sniffing, then scurrying away, the rats bolted down the dank corridors of the temple catacombs.

Out of the pitch blackness crept a yellow ball of light. Illuminating the rats and their tomb-mates—the skeletons of ancient martyrs—Rashid hurried with the torch toward the cell containing the Americans.

* * *

It smelled like five thousand years of putrefaction, Joan thought, as she looked up at the rope tied around her hands. Her arms were extended over her head and the rope tied to a beam on the ceiling. The rope cut into her skin, burning and making the skin raw. She tried not to move, but whenever she saw one of those red-eyed rats sniffing at her feet, she couldn't help flinching.

From the light given off by the torch in the wall, Joan could see that the beam they were tied to was sturdy. There was no chance of its being rotted enough to collapse. She looked over to Jack who was hanging next to her.

He was staring down a rat the size of a kitten as it stalked them. Jack wrestled with his ropes but only managed to cut his skin. With no other weapon, Jack spit at the rat. Jack's aim was deadly. The rat scurried away.

Joan felt guilty and depressed—not to mention frightened. All of this was her fault. She had placed them in peril, and there had been no need. She chided herself for falling victim to Omar's flattery. She had been vulnerable at the time—thinking Jack didn't love her—and Omar had taken advantage of her. He had appealed to her vanity, reinforcing her notion that she could become a journalist. She had been wrong to belittle her novels—her work. She was good at what she did. There was no reason to change. She had made a lot of mistakes in her life, but she would never forgive herself for exposing Jack to—she kicked at the rat who was nibbling at her foot—death.

She looked at him. His eyes were filled with love.

She would have given anything to put her arms around him—comfort him—and draw strength from him. She tried to smile.

"Sure beats the hell out of Greece." She felt tears in her eyes. "I'm sorry."

"Don't be. You came here to write history. And you came damn close to *changing* it."

Just then, the iron grate that had sealed them into this tomb slowly slid open. Rashid entered, his menacing scar looking crimson in the torchlight. Joan winced as he leered at her.

"Excuse me," Jack said, "whom do we talk to about the accommodations."

Rashid ignored Jack and climbed onto the ledge above their heads. Joan twisted around, trying to see what he was doing, but it was too dark. She wanted to think he was untying their ropes.

"What's he doing?"

An eerie cold air engulfed the cell as Omar entered. His smile was malicious. Joan thought it incredible she'd ever thought this horrid, demented-looking man was handsome. Now that she knew him, she realized his cheekbones were much too high, making him look sinister; his smile was too tight and his eyes were not ebony but darkest blood red. He was the devil.

"Rashid applies goat's blood to Mr. Colton's rope. It is a scent well known to the inhabitants of the catacombs."

Joan gasped and again scolded herself for being "hopeful."

The sound of scratching claws reverberated off the stone walls. Suddenly, the room was filled with the sound of squeaking rats as they scurried down the many halls that led to their cell.

"Rats..." Jack said, looking at Joan.

"They will eat through the rope. And then..."

Omar smiled sardonically at Joan, relishing her plight. He bent down to the floor and kicked away the gravel with his shoe. He pulled back a wooden covering.

Joan looked down to see a huge black pit yawn at her. She held her breath as Omar picked up a rock and hurled it into the pit. They waited, but she heard nothing. A full minute passed, and still nothing. Joan looked at Jack, still his devil-may-care self; he harrumphed at Omar.

"Oh, Jack..." Joan sighed.

"Don't worry," Jack retorted sarcastically, "I'll land on my feet."

"Oh, but you shall not be alone, Mr. Colton. Rashid is placing a vial of acid that will drip slowly through Miss Wilder's rope."

"Only a sick, perverted mind would take the trouble to do this, Omar. Why don't you just shoot us?"

"Jack..." Joan tried to cut him off.

Jack was insistent. "What kind of demented psychopath could even think this up?"

Omar's maliciously thin smile grew on his face. He bowed theatrically to Joan.

She sighed and looked pleadingly at Jack.

"The Savage Secret..." Joan was nearly in tears as her guilt flew inside her like bats in a cage. More than ever, she realized she was not only responsible for bringing them here, but the mode of their death was also her creation. "... it was my biggest seller."

Jack cringed at the sobriety of her words. "Well, did either of them survive?"

Joan looked away. "She did."

Placing an urn of acid on its side next to Joan's rope, Rashid finished his macabre task and climbed down off the ledge. Joan watched as he stood next to Omar. She gulped as she looked into the gaping abyss at her feet. They still had not heard the rock hit bottom. She hoped it had landed on a ledge, or perhaps was lying on the ground and they just hadn't heard it. Joan kept staring into the black hole as Omar spoke.

"No man has ever heard the bottom of the temple well."

He and Rashid both bowed again.

"It will be your last adventure. Good-bye. My people await me."

Whirling around in his white silk and gold robes, Omar turned to go.

"Omar . . . WAIT!" Jack called, but Omar kept walking.

"Marry us!" Jack yelled.

Joan's mouth flew open in shock. Never had she been so moved. Her tears cascaded down her cheeks as she realized they would be united for eternity. She had been feeling sorry for herself, thinking of all the things she would miss by dying this young. She had wanted a wedding with a white gown and flowers. She had wanted to bake her best pumpkin cheesecake for Jack. She had wanted to join an aerobics class, write at least five dozen more books; she wanted a baby, maybe two; she wanted to watch Jack teach his child to ski; and she had wanted to grow old with Jack . . . very old.

Jack filled his eyes with this image of loving, tearful Joan. She didn't have to say anything, for he knew what was in her heart. She had told him with her body and with words that she loved him. He should have realized a long time ago that Joan was as old-fashioned as he. She was a romantic; she would never make the first move. He should've been more forthright with her and proposed a long time ago. He'd been looking for signs from her, and all along she had been waiting for a sign from him. They could have avoided a lot of pain if he'd only have opened his mouth. He sensed Joan was punishing herself for the situation they were in, but Jack knew it wasn't her fault . . . it was his. If he'd been more honest with himself and with Joan, she never would have felt the need to leave him. But, he'd been afraid. Joan had been right to leave him— he'd needed some sense knocked into his head.

Jack turned back to the retreating Omar. "Let the Jewel marry us!" he yelled into the darkness.

Omar's scuffling feet stopped abruptly. Jack could barely make out the white form in the shadows. Omar took a step forward into the torchlight, but all Jack could see was Omar's head and his repulsive, cynical grin.

"But you're about to die. . . . You want to marry?"

Jack looked at Joan as he beat down the last of his doubts. "If she'll have me."

Joan stared at Jack. Even in the dim light, his blue eyes blazed with love and honesty. So many times she'd looked into that face she loved and seen one thing in his eyes, and yet his lack of commitment or his blasé words told her something else. Her heart told her that he loved her, perhaps even more than she loved him; but her intellect—that part that weighed reality in a scientific, emotionless manner—told her that Jack could never commit. He was a free spirit, devoid of responsibilities and ties. She wanted something entirely different. Was he saying all this only because they were about to die?

Jack's face was covered in nervous perspiration as he pressed Omar.

"For God's sake . . . let the Jewel marry us. What difference could it make?"

Omar paused momentarily and considered Jack's words. He glanced at the acid on Joan's rope as it sizzled and smoked. The hemp was deteriorating quickly. He barked an order to Rashid in Arabic. Rashid rushed away into the darkness. Omar turned again to Jack and Joan.

"A fitting end for Miss Wilder. I'm sorry I will not be here to give the bride away." Again he bowed to them. "Omar's blessing." He grinned tauntingly and left.

Joan watched as more rats scurried down the beam, following the scent of the blood. She watched as their red eyes—much like Omar's, she thought—shone menacingly in the torchlight. They sniffed the beam with tiny noses as they headed toward the rope. The sound of their gnawing on Jack's rope nearly drove her insane. She wanted to scream as she watched his rope jerk as the fibers of the hemp loosened.

Terror struck Joan as she realized they wouldn't live long enough to say "I do."

Chapter Twenty-One

AT THE MOMENT OF TWILIGHT, JUST BEFORE
the city of Khadir was bathed in midnight blue, Omar's
guards lit a multitude of torches and placed them along
the ancient temple walls. Though the ruins were crumbling and the carvings of long-passed kingdoms of the
Lower Nile were worn, the pilgrims paid homage to
their ancestors. They passed stories among themselves
of the glories that were to be theirs once Omar could
lead them. Their dreams of regaining the fame of their
fathers would be reality. They talked of palaces of gold
and silver they would build to Omar, of the end of
hunger and disease and of the Cadillacs they would
order from America. Omar would bring paradise.

As the stories circulated from tribe to tribe, the
crowd became inflamed with zeal. They were impatient to begin the new order. They were weary of the
past with its faults and imperfections.

Omar's men shuffled through the crowds disguised
in the clothing of the different tribes, whispering to
the tribal leaders the words Omar had carefully chosen
that would ignite the passion of the people.

In low, reverent chants, the people began repeating

Omar's name. The chant spread from tribe to tribe and grew in crescendo. Omar's men raised their voices in more bellicose shouts to agitate the crowd.

"Omar! Omar! Omar!"

The people demanded their redeemer.

Making their way to the catacombs was like working through a maze, Ralph thought. People were packed so closely together, all he could see was a wall of caftans and tunics. Finally, they had made their way to the opening to the tombs.

Ralph looked down into the oval, gaping opening that led to the tunnels beneath the city. He heard echoes of strange noises. He distinctly heard the rush of water. Peering farther, the stench nearly pitched him backward. There was no telling what kind of sanitation laws existed here.

Tarak looked around him at the excited masses. He saw weapons of all kinds emerge from beneath tunics. There were enough semiautomatic rifles in the temple to annihilate half the Sudan. It was a bleak day for his country. Tarak knew if Omar succeeded, his power would be great indeed. Tarak realized—though his countrymen did not—that should Omar gain control, there would be no freedom, personal or political, ever again for his people. Omar must be stopped. Only the Jewel could do that.

"Omar prepares the tribes for wars of conquest against our neighbors."

Ralph leaned a bit closer and whispered to Tarak.

"So, we got to find the jewel, right?"

"It would take a lifetime to search the tombs beneath the temple. But we must try."

Tarak and the dervishes started to enter the catacombs when, suddenly, Ralph froze.

He should have recognized those sounds before! How could he ever forget?

Just in front of him was a large rat—nearly a five-pounder, Ralph thought, as the rodent blocked his way.

Impatient, Tarak barked at Ralph, "Hurry!"

"I . . . I can't. I was on a boat. . . . Anything but rats."

Ralph was literally shivering in his shoes as Tarak took out a dagger and spun it at the rat. It sank into the rat with a thud. Aghast, Ralph watched as the rat did not die, but only tumbled away with the knife in its belly.

Ralph knew an omen when he saw one. That rat had to be immortal. What if he ran into living mummies in these tombs? He wasn't illiterate; he'd read about Egyptian curses and the consequences to those that invaded sacred tombs. He opened his mouth to protest to Tarak, but the dervish brothers grabbed his arms and pulled him inside.

Joan smelled death all around her. The rats chewed viciously on Jack's lifeline, causing it to snap, shake and then drop a bit.

"Don't go before me, Jack!" she screamed.

Jack looked down into the endless pit.

"Don't worry, I'll probably die of natural causes before I hit bottom."

He looked up to see even more rats scurrying toward the blood-soaked rope. The rats on the beam were fighting with each other for territorial rights. Two particularly large rats had mangled each other quite badly.

Jack's hopes soared. If he could hold out long enough for the rats to kill each other...

Just then Joan screamed. The acid was eating into her rope at a much faster pace than the rats. TSST! The acid dripped from the urn and ate not only the rope but the beam. Joan smelled its acrid smoke. Suddenly, her rope dropped over two inches. She was hanging lower than Jack.

She tried to be cheerful, but her voice cracked. "I spoke too soon."

"Well... will you?" Jack asked. Timbres of fear were in his words, though he kept trying to be brave.

"Will I what?" Joan asked, still staring down into the pit.

"*Marry me* ... I'd get on my knees..." He waited, but she said nothing. She only looked at him with those sad, loving eyes. She tried to smile, and he could see her dimples in the light. He smiled back.

"Hey, I don't regret a day with you, Joan Wilder."

Regrets, Joan thought, she had a million regrets. She wished she had the time to list them all. She regretted those nights she'd felt separated from Jack only because she wouldn't tell him what was on her mind. She regretted leaving him in Monte Carlo and thinking her writing was more important than he. But she never regretted loving him. He was the best thing that had ever happened to her—the only person that mattered.

"If I had it to do over, I'd give up all of my ambitions and sail around the world with you."

"No, no! *I'd* give it all up. Who needs the boat? I'd take typing lessons and move to New York and be your secretary!"

Joan thought her heart would burst. He'd told her he would do anything for her once before, but he hadn't meant it. Now he did. She believed that if by some miracle they would live beyond today, Jack would carry out his promise to her. But she couldn't do that to him. She didn't want him to change. She loved him the way he was.

"Then you wouldn't be Jack Colton."

"And you wouldn't be Joan Wilder."

Just then the cell door opened. With a gruff push, Rashid shoved the Jewel inside. With thick rope, Rashid bound the Jewel to an iron ring that was bolted into the stone wall.

Joan looked over to the Jewel who was gasping at the bottomless pit beneath Jack and Joan's dangling feet. Clearly, he was frightened for them. Joan felt a new rash of chills eat into her skin.

Jack turned his head to the Jewel.

"I hope you got a trick to get us out of this."

"Magic is just hope in the face of disaster," the Jewel said with a wan smile.

Joan gulped. Somehow she had thought . . . prayed . . . he was a holy man, but he was a man, not a god.

"You'd better make it a short ceremony," she said as the acid burned into the hemp and jerked again. Joan dropped another inch.

The Jewel's face was solemn and his eyes were filled with admiration for this courageous pair. They had become friends to him. He would always remember them with fondness.

"I am very honored."

Chapter Twenty-Two

BATHED IN A SNOWY, ELECTRIC-WHITE TUNIC with a gold turban on his head, Omar looked to be in a trance. He closed his eyes and meditated briefly. He opened his arms in a ceremonial gesture of faith and love and then closed them over his chest. Suddenly, his eyes sprang open and he observed himself in the full-length mirror. He wondered if perhaps he should raise his eyes to heaven first before closing them. He wasn't certain which gesture would look the most authentic. He wanted to be convincing, not theatrical.

From outside he could hear the people chanting his name. They had come from great distances, and when he'd looked at the thousand of followers he had inspired, even he was stricken with his own power. Omar had always known his destiny was a special one. Perhaps it had been the Unseen's way of telling him he was more than just a man.

Omar's thoughts of glory were interrupted by the voices of the two American special-effects men he'd hired. J. T. was busily painting his robes and body with an anti-inflammant coating. The odor was pungent, but they assured Omar it would dissipate once the coating dried.

Omar knew of some tribes of the Sudan who claimed they could walk on fire, but he was convinced it was either folklore or a trick. From ancient times, the nomads and tribes of the Nile had been fascinated with fire. The Egyptians had worshiped the sun as god and built temples to it. Many tribes knew that fire was a source of life and great power. Fire warded off night beasts, cooked their food and kept them from freezing on cold desert nights. It was believed the fires on earth were descendants of the fire god, the sun.

Drawing upon ancient superstitions and religious beliefs, it was fitting that Omar utilize fire to perform his "miracle." It was a medium even the simplest mind could comprehend. And with J. T. and Colt's help, Omar knew his people would be awestricken.

J. T. finished the painting and put his utensils away.

"Remember you got thirty seconds," he reminded Omar.

Just then, the room was filled with even more voices chanting Omar's name. There was an excitement in the air, a fever pitch that was contagious. Omar's smile was broad and his eyes took on the glassy look of a zealot.

Suddenly, Omar forgot his need for military power. He did not think of guns, jets and army tanks. He did not think of the forces he would need to control his people. He envisioned himself as he was now, resplendent in his ethereal robes, a ruler not only of earth but of heaven. He was the Redeemer. He was omnipotent. He could perform the miracle they had come to see. He could bring rain to the parched land;

he could end hunger, pain and poverty. He would give all his subjects a home to live in, food on their tables, and guarantee them a healthier life. He was Omar. He could do anything. He was God.

"Don't you feel the power! I will *be* the Jewel. Do not be surprised if I refuse your tricks!"

J. T. glanced at Colt and rolled his eyes. This guy was really looney-tunes. There was nothing worse than working with an actor who suddenly believed his own movies. They might have big trouble with Omar if J. T.'s hunch was correct. This was no time for a change in game plans. If Omar didn't do just as they had instructed him, Omar would be reduced to a burnt offering. Time was running out. They'd tried several tricks, trying to give Omar his "miracle." The levitation thing didn't work out, nor did the manufactured celestial explosions. The "comet" they rigged up wouldn't shoot high enough to look real. This fire gag was their last shot.

Colt grew nervous as he watched the rapt expression on Omar's face while he listened to his name being chanted. He'd seen the same look on rock stars just before going onstage. Especially the ones who couldn't sing and whose only "draw" was the light show J. T. and he were hired to create. Colt hated dealing with these super-egos. But the money was good.

"Great, great, but when you get to that fire, do *exactly* what we said. Walk straight down the middle. We'll be waiting with the extinguishers," Colt reminded him.

Omar nodded, but it was apparent he was more interested in hearing his name being chanted and sung in the temple.

* * *

By torchlight the dervishes entered a main burial room. Tall columns rose to the ceiling. They were beautifully carved with hieroglyphics and scrollwork. Several curved openings branched out from the room. Three were painted with gold lettering in ancient symbols and the other three were painted only with cobalt-blue figures and pink borders edged in silver. To Ralph, they all looked like tunnels to nowhere.

Ralph could tell from the look on Tarak's face he didn't know which one held the jewel. It was a crapshot.

One by one the dervishes split up to investigate the various tunnels. Tarak and Ralph took the tunnel straight ahead, thinking it looked like the one most traveled. If there was a precious jewel at the end of it, it made sense to him that Omar would have gone to look at his treasure many times. Ralph knew he would have.

As they progressed, the tunnel grew darker and more fetid. Ralph took out his trusty lighter. Though he could see better, it did not eliminate the stench. Ralph held his breath as he continued.

Suddenly, Tarak stopped. The tunnel took a curve and forked in two directions.

"You will be on your own, brother. Leave fear behind!" Tarak said and disappeared into the other tunnel.

Ralph peered into the absolute blackness. Gulping, Ralph took a step, then another. He raised his lighter to see stacks of human bones. As he passed a line of skeletons hanging from the ceiling, one of them was jarred by his movement and crashed to the ground. Startled, Ralph jumped to the side and backed into another skeleton. Its hand fell onto Ralph's shoulder. Ralph jammed his fist into his mouth to keep from screaming. He felt something roll across his shoe. Ever so slowly, he lowered his lighter to the ground. He'd thought it would be another skull.

Rats! There must have been dozens. Ralph jumped back and nearly dropped his lighter. This was his worst nightmare. Ever since his first experience with a rat in a tenement in New York at the age of five, Ralph had been deathly afraid of rats. Then there had been those awful days in the cell in Colombia, the rat-infested ship on the way to Africa. Ralph could handle anything—snakes, spiders, what have you, but rats . . . Ralph wanted to puke.

"The Mother Superior warned me I'd end up here."

The chanting had turned to a restless, angry cry. The tribal warriors raised their guns and swords as they shouted Omar's name.

Suddenly, there was a huge explosion followed by a streaking whistle. The crowd raised their faces to the heavens in time to see shimmering red, green, blue, silver and gold lights fill the midnight blue skies. Against the backdrop of the moon, more fireballs soared into the air and exploded, showering the temple and grounds with magnificent lights. Like the light of a thousand candles, the fireballs spewed their color across the heavens and turned night into day.

The crowd was awestricken as unexplained lights illuminated the temple, statues and ruins. On the ground, smaller fireballs spun on posts and whizzed green and silver embers across the temple. More colored lights raced into the sky, their booming sounds shaking the earth and exacting sounds of wonder from Omar's followers.

As the kaleidoscope patterns sparkled and then floated to the earth and died, a massive blast of trumpets sounded. Collectively, the crowd turned their faces toward the hundred trumpeters on stage.

Like a ray of sun, the spotlight clicked on, illuminating Omar in his white robes. He stretched out his arms as if to embrace all his people. He stood above them, a solemn smile on his face. He looked heavenward as the last of the fireworks and laser lights dimmed. He was not disappointed with the work the Americans had done for him. Perhaps it was a bit showy, but he'd needed to impress. He closed his eyes as he waited for the din to hush. He could feel their eyes on him as they waited for him to perform the greatest miracle of all.

When the crowd was completely quieted, Omar extended his arms full-length toward the heavens and then slowly lowered them out to the people. A mighty roar shattered the silence and reverberated off the temple walls. Five thousand warriors shouted Omar's name once again in their lustiest voice. Surely, the heavens could fall under the impact, Omar thought as he looked out to see the warriors raise their guns. Their adoration was all-important to him. Omar knew at that moment that they were his, miracle or no. These men were prepared to give him the ultimate sacrifice. They were willing to die for Omar—for the Holy War he intended to instigate.

The crowd quieted and Omar spoke.

"Out of the Past, from the first dawn to The Last Sunset,

from the darkness of ancient times to The
Light at The End of the World, I come to
you, oh my people, as your servant,
humble, proud, asking only your
blessings for the great task that lies
ahead! Once our people ruled from the
wide blue seas of Agadir to the ports of
Aden and Mocha. We Cast a Giant
Shadow across the mother
of continents. Once invincible!
Once mighty! Once worshiped by slave
and freeman! But Once is not Enough!
The Brotherhood of our tribes has
disintegrated like the lost villages of the
Sudd. Where are our Paths of Glory?
Even the walls of
Jericho
fell beneath the will of the faithful.
Where is our faith now? Where is our
Lust for Life? Lonely Are the

Brave people of the river. The Devil's
Disciple had taught
us to live like women, tending sheep,
making blankets to hide
from the cold of the desert winds! What
is this way of life? What more than A
Lovely Way to
Die? For Seven Days
in May, I fasted by the mother Nile. Like
Ulysses I listened for the siren's call. A
voice came to me from Twenty Thousand
Leagues Under the Sea and it called to

me ... Omar! Omar! Abandon not your
people. Come to Khartoum and be
Champion. Not for Love or Money, but
for glory! Fear not your enemies, for
what are they but a Glass Menagerie!
Tonight as I look across this reverend
ground I see The Way West, the way to
restore our rightful empire! We have
not gathered to cry, but to
celebrate! Look to the Big Sky! The stars
tell us to reclaim our heritage. No longer
shall we be Strangers When We Meet. We
have a new Arrangement! Unified in
battle! Fellow soldiers of the sword! From
Omdurman and Sodiri, from Dilling and
El Abbasiya, from Lake Nuba and
Muglad, from Qala, Umm Ruwaba,
Gallabat and Ghazal, from Kordofan,
Juba, Loka, Ayod, Abu Zabad, and

Jebel Oda, from Akasha and Halaib, from
North and South I summon you. The War
Wagon will chase our Moneychangers!
We are one, blood of my blood, like
Spartacus, each man called by the same
name. No longer do I Walk Alone.
Destiny is our Ace in the Hole! Like
Joshua, the Young Man With A Horn,
hear my clarion call! Trust not a Man
Without a Star! But be my Posse. The
large and the small. The poor and the rich
The Bad and the Beautiful. All! Follow
me to holy war! Be fierce as Vikings!

And in terrible unity we will restore the
great empire of our father's fathers. Lift
up your arms! Let loose your voices!
Listen for the Last Train from Gun Hill!
It calls for you! And the call is . . . Omar!

Joan watched as another drop of acid slid out of the
urn and onto her rope. It sizzled upon contact with the
twisted hemp, and Joan dropped a fraction of an inch.
Another drop of acid rolled over the edge of the ledge
and was about to drip onto the rope when Jack swung
his arm into its path. He caught the drop on his shirt,
and though it burned his skin and he flinched, he
prepared himself for the next drop.

"Jack, you can't!" Joan pleaded with him. There
was enough acid in that urn to burn both of them—
given enough time. Jack was being irrational if he
thought he could prevent her death. She loved him all
the more for being this gallant. But she didn't want a
hero, she wanted a man; she wanted him alive. She
wished she could hold him one more time, feel his
arms around her. Of all the hells she was going through,
perhaps that was the worst. She wasn't afraid of dying
anymore. She could think of worse things. She could
think of living without Jack.

Jack turned back to Jewel.

"Go on!" Jack demanded. Jack was superstitious
enough to believe that if he didn't make it official,
there might be a chance she would be someplace in
the hereafter where he couldn't find her. It was one
thing to go tromping around South America and gallop
over half the Sahara for Joan, but who knew what
Heaven was like?

The Jewel eyed Rashid, who was barely breathing.

Rashid was ready to pounce at the slightest movement. He was well trained as a bodyguard, and his instincts told him this was a trick. The Jewel's reputation for trickery, magic and sorcery was legendary. Rashid glowered at Jack and Joan.

The Jewel began the ceremony.

"The marriage sacrament is an ancient and holy one . . ." It was difficult for the Jewel to continue, as his attention was drawn to a niche near the outside of the cell. The door was wide open, as Rashid had left it so that the Jewel could see the passageway clearly. Five years in prison had taught his eyes to accustom themselves to very dim light.

The Jewel tried not to call Rashid's attention to himself as he peered at the little man just outside the cell.

Ralph's back was slammed against the wet stone wall in the hall just outside the cell. He was standing face-to-face with the biggest rat in history. Its red beady eyes were staring into Ralph's frightened beady eyes. Ralph broke out in a nervous sweat. His hands trembled and he could feel his knees knocking.

"Rrrrrrrats. Not rats . . ." he mumbled to himself.

Of all the enemies in the world, Ralph would rather take on the Mafia than this rat. Ralph had never been frightened of Omar or his army during his trek through the desert and into Omar's village. Ralph was no dummy. This king-sized rodent was a carrier for rabies, the bubonic plague, typhoid and a thousand other diseases. Rats were the scourge of the earth and had no purpose in this life except to frighten him.

Upon seeing Ralph's predicament, the Jewel turned

away and spoke again. This time, his voice carried a new, mystical timbre to it.

". . . as ancient as the dervishes, people without fear, courageous and mighty . . ."

Ralph wasn't paying attention to anything but the rat. He thought about taking out his lighter and shining it in the rat's face, but he was afraid the rat would bite him. He tried to force his feet to move around the wall, circling the rat and escaping him. Concentrating on his legs for a long moment, Ralph still had not moved. He felt cemented to the ground. He was afraid he would remain here forever. Now he knew where all those skeletons had come from. The rats had picked the bones clean. Ralph clutched his stomach.

Just as he was about to vomit, Ralph heard the voice from inside the cell as it rose in pitch. The sound reverberated off the walls of the tunnel. It rang in his ears, causing him to look past the rat to the man who was speaking.

The Jewel raised his voice even more now that he had Ralph's attention.

". . . to you I say, 'I COMMAND YOU TO COME FORWARD! I COMMAND YOU TO BE STRONG!'"

Joan looked at Jack as she realized something was wrong. This was no ordinary wedding ceremony. For a moment she completely forgot about the acid, the rats and the ropes. She wondered if the Jewel was trying to give them a message in some secret code. She struggled with it a moment but failed to decipher its meaning. The Jewel's voice rose even more. Now, Joan realized that Rashid was at full attention. He didn't trust any of them at all.

Just then Jack's eyes flew open as he dropped another inch.

"Jack, hold onto me!" she screamed.

The rats had eaten all the way through the rope. The hemp spun in a tiny whirl and then . . . the rope broke.

Jack began to drop into the pit, but with lightning dexterity, Joan swung her legs out in time for Jack to grab on.

Clinging to Joan's legs, Jack glanced down into the black hole. He shuddered as he prepared himself to fall into oblivion. Jack knew the acid would eat through Joan's rope even faster now that it was being pulled so taut.

Just then, they heard the rumble of something striking bottom. The echoes sent chills up Joan's spine.

"My God, what was that!"

"Omar's stone. It *is* a long way down!" Jack gulped.

At that moment, the sound of Omar's voice filled the caverns. The words were muffled, but Joan was well aware of his intent. She could hear the crowd cheering him. There must be thousands, she thought. If she'd ever been able to do anything with her life, she would have given everything to have stopped that madman. She pitied the people of this country, for they were being conned into a war they really didn't want and all for nothing . . . only for the glory of Omar.

Rashid was growing impatient with all of this. He saw no reason to allow the Americans another breath. He would have enjoyed killing them with his bare hands rather than watch these stupid rats eat away at a rope. Sometimes, Omar's theatrics were more than he could take. Rashid cocked his gun. He saw no reason not to hurry things up a bit.

Just then the Jewel began speaking again.

"COME TO ME!" he commanded Ralph as he stared directly at the frightened little man outside the cell.

Willing his heart to stop hammering, Ralph gathered up his courage and let out the fiercest scream he could. He bolted past the evil rat and raced into the cell.

Rashid whirled around to face Ralph and raised his rifle.

In an instant, Ralph raised his lighter to his face.

"Need a light?"

He held the lighter to his mouth and exhaled just like one of the dervishes. A giant tongue of flame shot out of his mouth and into Rashid's ugly face. Rashid screamed in agony, dropped his rifle and covered his burning face with his hands. He stumbled backward, still in agony. He lost his footing and fell into the bottomless pit.

Joan gasped as Rashid's screams faded away into oblivion. She closed her eyes.

Just then, Joan dropped another inch. She looked up to see the acid was doing its work.

"Do something!" Jack yelled to Ralph, who was peering into the pit.

"The jewel," Ralph demanded. "Where is it?"

"Behind you!" Joan said angrily. Why was he asking questions when they had only seconds until she and Jack joined Rashid?

Ralph turned around, but only saw a strange-looking skinny man.

"This ain't no time for tricks!"

"Damnit, he can take you to the jewel!" Jack bellowed.

"Who?" Ralph asked anxiously.

"Him! Help us!" Jack yelled as his hands slipped on Joan's ankles. There had been enough slack in the rope between his tied hands for him to grab onto Joan's ankles. He realized he couldn't hold on for long with his hands still bound. Jack used his teeth to untie the rope. It was a painstaking process, but he managed to get it off. He spit the piece of rope into the pit. He was sure his weight was wrenching Joan's legs out of her hip sockets. She didn't cry out from the pain. Jack slipped another inch. He kept looking at Ralph, willing him to come to their aid.

"We're going to fall!" Joan screamed as the acid ate further into the hemp.

"I'll let go," Jack said, looking up and seeing her pained face. Sweat and tears mingled on her cheeks. She was in agony. "You hold on."

"No!" she screamed, thinking they couldn't die. Not when they'd just found each other again. It wasn't fair. They were meant to be . . . just like the heroines in her novels. She wished she could be brave, as they were . . . and smarter. If she were Angelina, she'd think of some way to escape death.

That was it! she thought.

"Jack, try to swing. I wrote a circus book—Swing!" Joan knew it was a long shot, but they had nothing to lose.

Jack arched his back and then threw out his stomach. He didn't move much at all. He tried again, and moved a few inches. He arched harder this time and threw his legs into it. This time they moved a full six inches.

Jack increased his efforts and pushed harder and quicker.

Joan used her thigh muscles to push Jack back when he arched, and she arched her own back keeping rhythm with him. Their weight kept the momentum up, and soon they were swinging like a pendulum over the abyss.

With each swing they moved closer to the side of the pit. Jack tried to catch onto the side with his legs. Twice he tried, but failed.

This time when they swung, Jack raised his legs, trying to get them over the edge of the hole. It didn't work. He was hanging too far down. He shimmied up Joan's legs a few inches, knowing now his positioning was better.

Joan groaned as Jack worked his way up her legs. She didn't think about the pain, only of surviving. She arched her back and swung with Jack again. She kept *hoping* they would make it, but the rope broke another thread. The acid had worked its way through all but the last two threads of hemp.

While Jack and Joan were swinging for their lives, Ralph quickly went to the Jewel and untied him. The Jewel scrambled out of the hemp. He scowled at the mercenary Ralph.

"They are your friends! *Help them!*"

Ralph turned and looked at Jack and Joan. They might even make it without his help if it weren't for the disintegrating rope. Ralph had never been the Good Samaritan type; he looked down into the bottomless pit and then over to the rats as they scurried down the ledge and to the other side of the pit.

Ralph shivered as he looked at Jack—the big rat who'd stolen El Corazon from him.

"Friends! Some friends."

As Ralph steeled his courage and banished thoughts of man-eating rats and infinite black pits, and went to help Jack, the Jewel darted out of the cell and disappeared down the dark tunnel.

Ralph positioned himself on the edge of the pit and dug his heels in. On the very next swing Ralph held his arms out to catch Jack's legs when . . . WHACK! Ralph was hit in the face with one of Jack's boots. Growling and cursing under his breath, Ralph held on to Jack's leg and pulled him over to the side. Ralph's nose stung with sharp pains. He wondered if it was broken. He hoped Colton had insurance. After he grabbed that jewel, he was going to sue Jack for personal injury.

Straining with all his might, Jack got a foothold on the edge of the pit. He let go of Joan's legs with one arm and held onto the edge. Now, with both his arms he pulled himself halfway up the side. He was almost to safety when . . . SNAP! Joan's rope broke.

Like lightning, Jack's arm shot out and he grabbed Joan.

She screamed as she felt her weight pull her down into the pit. It was like being in the elevator at the World Trade Center. As soon as she'd started to fall, she reached out for Jack and found his arm waiting for her. When she grabbed on and he yanked her, she slammed into the side of the pit.

Groaning, Joan dug her toes into the side of the pit and pushed herself up and Jack pulled.

Jack's face was contorted with pain as he pulled her

up. Lying on his belly, he dug his toes into the gravel and rock and inched his way backward as he pulled Joan up. His thigh muscles were taut as he slowly eased her upward. Suddenly, her feet slipped off the edge of the pit and the extra pull on their hands was wrenching them apart.

Joan screamed and tightened her grip. She tried again to "walk" her way up the side of the pit. This time she was successful.

With a final mighty yank, Jack pulled Joan to safety.

Panting and out of breath, they clung to each other. Jack held her face in his hands and peered into her frightened face. She was quivering with fright and relief. She threw her arms around his neck again and held him closer.

They were alive! They'd beaten Omar! She kissed Jack's neck, cheeks, eyes and nose. She wanted to shout with joy, but found she was speechless.

Jack kissed Joan tenderly, and then with more passion than he'd ever felt. How close they had come to dying. He never would have forgiven himself if anything had happened to Joan. He held her closer, feeling her rapidly beating heart against his chest.

Suddenly, a great cheer from the crowd above reached into the bowels of the catacombs and thundered down the tunnels.

Joan looked at Jack. "Omar!" they said in unison.

Jack grabbed Joan's hand and raced out of the cell.

Ralph looked around the empty cell, realizing his pathway to fortune was also gone.

"Hey! Where's the guy!"

Angrily, Ralph stomped his foot and raced after Jack and Joan.

Chapter Twenty-Three

SILENTLY MOVING THROUGH THE CROWD like a slithering asp, Tarak stealthily scanned the faces of the tribesmen for the Jewel. Perhaps the Jewel had escaped and was here in disguise. It was Tarak's last hope. He was sad, for he'd started out with so many hopes. He glanced to the perimeter of the mob, checking the positioning of his brothers. They nodded to him as they saw him look their way. One of the brothers, Sarak, had just exited the catacombs. He was the last to emerge from beneath the earth. He shook his head. Sarak had not found the Jewel, either.

Trumpets blared with a sound so forceful it could shake the heavens. All eyes turned to the stage where Omar's giant insigne began to rise. On a moving platform Omar also rose, his arms outstretched, his eyes reverently toward heaven. The moment for the miracle had arrived.

Omar stepped off the platform and onto the stage. The trumpeters ended their herald and the crowd was hushed.

The spotlights hit a small circle of torches sitting in a holder on stage. Omar raised his arms, spoke a few ancient words, and suddenly, where there had been only air, a ring of fire burst into life.

The crowd was spellbound as the flames shot sparks and heated the cool night air. Omar approached the flames. He knew a million eyes were on him at this moment. Most important, the eyes of the Unseen would crush him. Omar took a step forward and then hesitated. His convictions rattled like loose parts in his head. Suddenly, the mighty Omar, the man who held the lives of millions in his hands, was unsure. All his life he'd known he was special. He'd had dreams of power even as a child. He believed the Unseen had given him so much because his mission was a holy one—didn't he? He'd rid himself of his enemies as he was certain the Unseen had wanted—didn't he? Omar looked at the flames as they came perilously close to licking his robes. He must *believe* to survive. At this moment he held no store in the coating J. T. and Colt had painted his clothing with. This was not a time for trickery. Omar suddenly realized that this was his ultimate test. If he survived, it would be a sign to him from the Unseen that he was the one, true, chosen leader.

J. T. and Colt crouched on the temple wall high above and behind the insigne, looking down at the stage. They scowled at each other. It was apparent Omar had waited too long.

"He's got to go now!" J. T. whispered anxiously.

Racing up the catacomb stairs, Joan, Jack and Ralph emerged from the tombs and raced toward the stage. They hadn't gotten twenty feet when three of Omar's guards stepped into their path. Without missing a beat,

Jack tackled two of them while Ralph grabbed the legs of another.

One of the guards hit his head on a stone and was out cold. As Jack pummeled his opponent with a series of blows to the chest and face, he spied Joan out of the corner of his eyes.

"Run!" he yelled at her.

Joan took off and lost herself in the crowd.

Omar braced himself and closed his eyes as he took another step toward the flames. Losing courage again, Omar looked up to the top of the temple wall above him where J. T. and Colt were perched.

It was at that moment Joan looked at Omar from her vantage point in the crowd. His glance upward was only momentary, but it aroused her curiosity. Omar was not the type to do a fire walk unless he had all his bases covered. She remembered the Americans from the night she'd stalked Omar's palace. It didn't surprise her one bit they were involved in this hoax. She spied a staircase on the side of the stage leading up to the temple wall. Joan bolted for the steps.

Taking the steps by two, Joan silently made her way to the top. J. T. and Colt were so engrossed in Omar's lack of timing in his stunt that they didn't notice her. She glanced behind them and noticed several tall metal cans. She looked down again at the reluctant Omar as he faced the flames.

Those cans could be filled with only one thing. Joan crouched down and, staying close to the backside of the temple wall, made her way over to the metal cans. It wasn't until she picked one up that J. T. noticed her.

"Hey! Stop! That's fuel . . ."

Joan darted away from him and raced to the edge of the wall. Omar was directly underneath her.

Joan pitched the can downward. The can hit with a thud, and in seconds Omar's meager flames exploded. The force of the blast sent Joan stumbling backward. Omar too was blown back. He screamed and raised his arms to shield his face from the heat.

The crowd looked up to see Joan standing on the temple wall. Tarak spied her and knew this was his sign. Omar's stage was a sea of jetting flames. The wood used in its construction provided more fuel.

Frantic, Omar raced to the edge of the stage to avoid the fire. He followed the eyes of the crowd and looked up to see Joan standing above him. That moment Omar saw her only as his albatross, a she-devil sent to torment him. He raised his arm, pointing to her. He cursed her and shouted to the crowd in Arabic that she was the devil's daughter.

Sensing that the moment of salvation was upon him, Tarak let out the ear-piercing dervish cry and threw off his robes. He raised his sword in one hand and his brothers answered cry. They too threw off their robes and began to battle the crowd.

Tarak fought bravely. He could never allow his land to be taken over by Omar and his power-mad fanatics. He had known the freedom of his forefathers and cherished it too much to see it change to a dictatorship where only Omar's laws would be followed.

Omar looked up from the flames to see J. T. and Colt bolting down the stairs. Now he would never have a chance to perform his miracle. His "hour" had been ruined, and all because of Joan Wilder. Omar looked out at the crowd and saw the battle. It was the dervishes again! He did not worry about them, for his warriors would annihilate them. It was a matter of ratios.

Omar started up the stairs toward Joan. This was one murder he would not send his henchmen or guards to perform. Omar wanted Joan to himself.

Joan saw Omar heading toward her. She had no escape. She looked up and saw a set of small grooves in the temple wall that would lead her farther up. Joan inched her way up the wall, digging her toes into the wall and holding onto the next set of indentations.

Just then, Tarak looked up to see Joan's plight. There was no place for her to go once she reached the top. If she even made it that far. Looking around, Tarak grabbed a rope hanging from one of the temple columns. He climbed on to the back of an unsuspecting warrior and swung at Omar. If he could intercept Omar, stave him off, Joan would be free. As he swung across the courtyard, Tarak sounded the dervish cry.

Beneath Tarak, his brothers fought valiantly and took renewed energy from the sound of Tarak's cry.

Finally downing his opponent, Jack raced away from the catacomb guard. He stopped long enough to see Joan climbing the wall. Omar was halfway up the temple stairs. Jack raced toward Omar.

Ralph had bitten his opponent eight times before the guard released him. But he'd successfully landed a right hook square into the guard's face. He'd landed on the ground with an odd-sounding hollow thud. Ralph raced after Jack but couldn't keep up. It wasn't fun being short, especially in athletic pursuits. Ralph tripled his efforts, making his legs whirl like a locomotive's as he raced through the courtyard and to the temple steps. Ralph saw Jack as he spied Joan on the wall and knew immediately where Jack was headed.

Jack raced in between J. T. and Colt as they came running down the stairs. His lungs were burning and his thigh muscles wanted to quit, but still Jack ran on, keeping Joan in his sight.

Ralph had built up a good head of steam by the time he'd reached the steps. When J. T. and Colt bolted toward him, Ralph couldn't stop. With a resounding thud, three collided and went tumbling head over heels down the steps, landing in a heap on the edge of the stage.

The battle between the dervishes and the warriors was drawing to a close. The dervishes were completely surrounded by Omar's followers. They only had seconds until they were captured.

Omar stood on the uppermost steps, cutting off Joan's escape.

Seeing Omar so close and his repulsive black eyes filled with mayhem, Joan lost her footing and slid down the wall to the landing. She stood and screamed as Omar pounced on her.

His hands were around her neck, squeezing—hard.

They struggled and wrestled, and at one point Joan had managed to roll him over so that she was on top. But he held her at arm's length and she couldn't reach his face to scratch his eyes out. Using his greater weight, Omar rolled her over and now had her head hanging over the edge of the landing. Joan could see the treacherous flames shooting up toward her. She could feel their heat on the back of her head.

Omar's black eyes were filled with sadistic lust as he smiled and squeezed her throat even harder. He was worse than a monster, she thought, trying to beat at him—he was the devil. She smacked at his arms, ribs and back, but he didn't flinch. She tried to pull her knee up underneath him and push him away or ram his groin, but he anticipated her move and lay atop her with his full weight. He laughed at her. She spit in his face.

Below Joan one of the young men in the crowd looked up to the flaming stage and shouted.

"*al-Jawahara!*" he screamed loudly.

"The Jewel!" he yelled again in English as he pointed to the stage.

The flames were shooting nearly two stories high now, and in their midst stood the Jewel.

Dressed in blinding white, blue and golden robes, the Jewel walked forward in an ethereal crystal light. It was not the light from Colt's spots, nor the colored lights from the Hollywood lasers. It was an unearthly light that filled the entire temple. The light emanated from the Jewel, giving off rainbow-colored sparks and a nearly tangible energy. The awesome light was more powerful and forceful than the orange and crimson tongues of fire that playfully licked his robes.

The Jewel stretched out his arms as if to embrace all present. His face was solemn but caring. His eyes sparkled with a light equal to that of the fire, but it was compelling in and of itself.

Fearlessly, the Jewel walked through the blasting flames. Slowly, he moved toward the people, showing them he was unharmed. The crowd was awestricken. Everyone present marveled at the miracle they had been chosen to witness.

The Jewel walked unmolested by the earthly flames,

his silver-gold glow still protecting him. He lowered his arms and then raised them again. He smiled gently to the crowd.

Instantly, the men threw down their guns and fell to their knees. Women cried joyously as they clutched their children to their breasts. The day of deliverance had come to the land.

The Jewel spoke not a word, but his thoughts were mysteriously embedded into the hearts of all present. There would be no more wars. Nor would there be fighting, bickering or jealousies among tribes. They would band together and work as one nation to bring about the end of this terrible famine. Just as the Jewel brought them hope, he would bring water and food to the starving. Through his prayers, he had turned the eyes of the world to his land. Now his own people would learn to help themselves. War could never bring about the end to the dying. Only peace could do that.

Omar looked down at his followers as they witnessed the Jewel's miracle. It was the end of his dreams for a new order under his direction. He had no future except to rot in a cell somewhere. Just thinking about incarceration—year upon year with only himself for company—made Omar tremble. He looked down at Joan as she squirmed beneath his hands. Why wasn't she dead yet? Surely he should have crushed her bones by now. Omar clutched her more tightly.

Tarak took out his knife and hurled it at Omar's chest.

"The Jewel has returned!" Tarak yelled as he watched the knife sink into Omar's body.

Omar was staggered by the force of Tarak's knife, and nearly fell off Joan. He burst into demented-sounding laughter. Joan screamed as the lunatic on top of her released her and then reared back on his haunched as he ripped the shirt from his chest.

Omar lived! He was wearing that same steel-mesh vest he'd worn in Monte Carlo. Joan gasped. Just as Omar was suddenly aware of her again, Joan scrambled to the side, trying to get away. She reached over to a still-flaming torch. Omar grabbed her leg. Her reach wasn't long enough.

Far below Joan, Sarak emerged from the crowd leading Ralph, J. T. and Colt. "Here is our Jewel!" Sarak said, and pointed to the Jewel amid the flames onstage.

Ralph followed Sarak's finger to see not the five-pound pearl he'd imagined nor the thirty-karat diamond he'd dreamed of but the familiar Holy Man.

"That's the jewel?"

Ralph dropped to the ground in a dead faint.

Omar lunged at Joan, and she waved the flaming torch in his face. She was terrified as she squared off against him. It was a narrow ledge up here, room for not more than one. She'd been lucky to live through the struggle. She was certain there were bruises on her neck, for it throbbed with pain. She gulped, and found it hard to swallowed as she backed away from Omar on her knees. She jabbed the torch at him, but he laughed. She was only stalling, for she wasn't close enough to him to actually burn him. She inched back, still ramming the torch at Omar. Joan glanced at the burning stage below. It was a long drop to the ground. The flames shot higher until they nearly reached the landing. The heat was intense, but the sweat on Joan's face was not from the fire, but from fright.

Omar leered at her as he growled and moved closer. "I am dead, Miss Wilder. Only an epitaph will be written for Omar ... but I will not go alone!"

Joan scrambled to her feet and stood on unsteady legs. She felt no closer to victory now that she'd gotten out of Omar's clutches than she had when he was choking her. He intended to take her down with him into the flames below. Joan could think of no worse way to die. She would have preferred the bottomless pit to this.

Joan glanced at her torch. The flame was going out. It was her only hope and it was fading. She looked again at the shooting flames below. The irony of her situation almost made her laugh, but she was too terrified.

"Stay back!" she warned Omar, trying not to think about the maniacal gleam in his eyes.

He guffawed. "Who's going to save you now, Joan Wilder?"

Omar's laugh lanced Joan's heart with chills. She didn't want the last sound she ever heard on earth to be his horrid laugh. She jabbed the ebbing torch at him again. She more than hated him. She despised him, and loathed the pestilence he'd brought to this country. If he'd been more intent on saving lives instead of building up his army, there might not be this awful starvation.

Joan's mind was made up. If she had to die, she was taking him with her. She didn't want him to breathe one more second on this earth or inflict one more hardship on his people. His life was a curse. She had to kill him.

Just as Joan was about to spring at Omar for one

last time, she heard Jack's voice in answer to Omar's question.

"The hero will save her, of course!"

Jack hadn't taken his eyes off the duel between Joan and Omar from the moment he'd entered the temple courtyard. All the way up the multitude of temple steps, he kept praying Joan would hang on until he could make it to her. Jack had watched as Tarak had swung across the courtyard on a rope, but his attempt to down Omar had failed. Omar had been too fast, and Tarak hadn't gotten up the proper momentum.

From Jack's vantage point on the outer ledge of the temple wall and just to the right of Joan and Omar, he knew he would not miss. Jack grabbed a long rope that was suspended from one of the columns and pushed himself off the ledge. He clenched his teeth, pulled his knees to his stomach and prepared himself for the impact. He used his shoulders to guide his swing when he veered too much to the left.

Jack cursed Omar's name as the fanatical dictator loomed closer as Jack's swing picked up momentum.

Jack flexed his feet, raising his two-inch heels on his alligator boots to the perfect angle.

BLAM! Jack's boots hit Omar square in the jaw. He screamed, teetered backward on comically shuffling feet before spinning completely around.

Omar pitched forward toward the flames, his eyes saucer-wide as he stared into the fire.

As if anticipating his arrival, the flames reached up to embrace Omar.

Gracefully fluttering like a magnificently robed moth to the flame, Omar tumbled over the wall and into the inferno below.

Joan staggered and slammed her hands over her ears as Omar screamed one last time. Tears were streaming down her cheeks as she shook with relief and fear. Jack swooped her into his strong arms as she burst into hysterical tears. He held her tighter.

Joan sobbed and melted into Jack. It was over. But they were just beginning.

With the end of Omar, the dervishes surrounded their most holy, precious Jewel. The crowd was transformed from a horde of angry, bloodthirsty warriors into a peaceful congregation. The flames swelled one last time and then ebbed and died. The ashes of Omar and his wooden altar mingled on the ground.

But the light around the Jewel remained. With the help of Joan Wilder and Jack Colton, the Jewel brought the light of love to his people.

Chapter Twenty-Four

SPARKLING BLUE-GREEN WATERS LAPPED against the sides of the lazily drifting boats as they sailed in procession down the Nile. The sun rose languorously over the hills, marbleizing the blue skies with streaks of rose, lavender and peach. Animals, both wild and tamed, walked to the edge of the Nile to drink and bathe. They paused, seeing the boats, raised their heads and emitted strange sounds as if paying homage. Brightly colored birds swooped around the snowy sails of the ships. They darted behind the tallest masts as they chirped and sang.

Dressed in flowing ivory African robes trimmed with a sapphire-blue silk border and hemmed in gold, Joan stood next to Jack. It was her wedding day.

Wearing wild river flowers in her hair and carrying a massive bouquet of sweet-smelling vine flowers, Joan thought she'd dreamed of many different settings for a wedding, but her imagination had never concocted anything this exotic. She smiled at Jack and winked. She felt one with the whole world at that moment. She heard the birds singing and the animals chanting. She had been right when she told Jack they had been destined to be together.

Never again would she allow herself to doubt their love. Jack had been sent to her by a power greater than anything on earth. Theirs was no ordinary love. It was sacred and a gift.

Jack held Joan's hand. She was beautiful this morning in a way he'd never seen before. The breeze lifted her hair, creating a golden halo around her face. Her emerald eyes shone with love, but there was something in her eyes . . . a peace, he thought. He hoped it would always be there. He would draw from it, and together they would grow stronger. They had been through a great deal of danger in the year they'd known each other, but none of it—the guns, the plane crashes, the near death drop into a bottomless pit—ever frightened him so much as when Joan had told him she was leaving him.

He winked back at Joan. He'd been a fool not to propose earlier. They could have avoided a lot of heartache if he had. He was glad the Jewel was going to marry them. No priest, no minister, no rabbi he knew of was as holy as this man. This time, Jack thought, he'd left no margin for error. With the Jewel's blessing, there would be no way Joan could get out of this marriage.

The Jewel smiled warmly.

"We begin! . . . Do we have the ring?"

Jack turned to his best man, Ralph. Ralph smiled as he reached into his vest pocket. He gasped and pulled his hand out empty. He patted his other pockets while giving Jack a sheepish grin. Jack was losing patience.

The dervishes all turned and began to stare suspiciously at Ralph.

Ralph chuckled as he looked at the Jewel. Even he was beginning to scowl.

Ralph opened his palm and showed Jack the ring.

"I was just kidding!"

Jack took the ring.

Ralph shrugged his shoulders. "As always, zilch for Ralphie," he mumbled to himself.

Just then Tarak tapped Ralph on the shoulder. Ralph turned and watched as the brothers began flipping something from one to the other. Ralph didn't think this was a good time to start their juggling antics. Still they persisted, until finally Tarak grabbed hold of the object. Smiling, he turned to Ralph and handed him . . . a jewel-encrusted dervish knife.

Ralph looked at it sparkling in the dawn light. There were sapphires, rubies, pearls, diamonds and emeralds. It was a king's ransom sitting in his hands. He looked at Tarak who nodded to him. Ralph couldn't believe it. Someone was giving him, Ralph, a gift . . . with no strings attached. It was a miracle.

"Aw . . . guys," he stammered. He'd never had to thank anyone before. Ralph was speechless. Jack looked once again at his beautiful Joan.

"Let 'er rip," he said to the Jewel.

The Jewel nodded. "On this glorious day we gather to witness your greatest adventure . . ."

Joan looked up into Jack's blue eyes. Her heart swelled with love as she listened to the Jewel's words.

". . . Marriage!"

Epilogue

SITTING IN HER LUMBAR BACK SUPPORTED desk chair, Gloria glanced at her mail. She tossed inquiry letters and two important contracts aside as soon as she spied the exotic-looking stamps on the battered airmail letter. With a silver letter opener, she ripped the envelope open. She smiled as she read Joan's latest letter.

Of course, a lot has happened since then. Ralph went back to New Jersey and pawned his sacred knife. . . .

Gloria read on as Joan described Ralph's new life. Gloria imagined just how he would look, too, standing in the window of his new pizza parlor tossing pizza dough over his head, twirling it like a dervish.

. . . it seems all he ever really wanted was a place of his own. From what we hear, the Jewel is well . . .

Joan's letter described the Jewel's new life as leader.

... Peace has returned and he is busy with matters of state.

Gloria read how the Jewel now had time to spend
with his five tiny grandchildren. They were all learning
to juggle like their dervish fathers. The Jewel wasn't
certain how long a process this would be.

... Oh, Jack and I decided on that apartment on
the Upper West Side ...

Joan stood next to Jack, thinking about the agree-
ment they'd made. Six months in New York. *Newsweek* and *60 Minutes* both wanted her.

Joan looked at Jack as he leaned out of the airplane
and held onto the wing. The wind whipped his hair.
She was glad they'd had a professional fold their par-
achutes. Jack was never one with an eye for details
like that. Jack adjusted his goggles.

Joan leaned out to see tiny farms below them. She
saw cows, fences, trees and a train moving below. On
a dirt road was a battered old Ford truck racing like
the wind. It all looked like an H.O.-scale train set from
here, she thought.

Joan leaned out a bit and pulled her own goggles
down over her eyes. She checked the straps on her
parachute. This was her first jump and she was under-
standably nervous. Jack took her hand and gave her
the "thumbs up" signal.

Joan nodded, but grimaced as they readied to jump.
Holding hands, they pushed off the plane and floated

to earth. It was an incredible feeling, Joan thought as they fell into fluffy clouds.

Like a flash, a picture of their life in New York flitted across her brain as they fluttered from one cloud to another and watched the farm grow larger.

Sooner or later, she would have to decide about *Newsweek* and the rest.

But she didn't have to make that decision until after *Jack's* six months were up . . . providing she didn't tell him how much she liked this!

Catherine Lanigan
writing as

Joan Wilder

Romancing
The
STONE

87262-5/$2.95
**Based on the Screenplay Written by
Diane Thomas**

Lost in the steaming Colombian jungle with brutal killers closing in, she felt like the heroine of one of her romance novels. Except that romance was the last thing on her mind...especially with Jack Colton, the bold American adventurer on whom her life now depended.

But there are certain times, certain places, and nights that may be the last, when a man and a woman can only be meant for each other. And suddenly she knew that he was the right man for her.

Don't Miss the
Exciting Sequel—
Coming soon from
Avon Books and Twentieth-Century Fox

THE JEWEL OF THE NILE

89984-1/$3.50 US/$4.50 Can